CORRUPTION
OF JUSTICE

BOOKS BY BRENDA ENGLISH

SUTTON McPHEE MYSTERY SERIES

Corruption of Faith
Corruption of Power
Corruption of Justice

All available as JABberwocky ebooks!

CORRUPTION OF JUSTICE

BRENDA ENGLISH

JABBERWOCKY LITERARY AGENCY, INC.

Corruption of Justice

Copyright © 1999 by Brenda English

All rights reserved.

This paperback published in 2016 by JABberwocky Literary Agency, Inc.

Published as an ebook in 2013 by JABberwocky Literary Agency, Inc.

Published as a paperback by Berkley Prime Crime in 1999.

Cover design by Jessica Reed.

Interior design by Estelle Leora Malmed.

ISBN 978-1-62567-172-1

To Clay Lowe,
who told me a long time ago that the stories were there,
and to the memory of Don Meiklejohn.

1

FRIDAY

"Please stop apologizing," I said to the good-looking, late-twenty-something cop sitting next to me in the Fairfax County Police cruiser. His name was Dan Magruder. He was tall, blond, blue-eyed, fit, several years my junior, and somewhat mortified at how boring the last seven hours had been.

"Believe me," I went on, trying to reassure him, "after two years of covering you guys, I know it's usually not this quiet." Magruder didn't look comforted.

"I just don't want anyone to think this is some kind of cakewalk job, where all we do is sit around in air-conditioned cars all day, wasting taxpayers' money," he explained.

Especially his boss or the county supervisors.

That was my little voice chiming in, my own personal little Greek chorus that has been pretty vocal most of my life, regularly puncturing my ego's balloon with its pointed observations about my behavior and occasionally throwing in a few about the people around me as well. I have always told myself that, of course, it's just another part of my own brain talking to me. I prefer not to consider any alternative explanations, in spite of the fact that the voice always seems to have a mind and personality (apparently male) of its own. Whatever it is, I put a mental sock in it for the moment.

"Don't worry," I said reassuringly to Magruder. "Sutton McPhee doesn't do boring stories. By the time I'm done writing this one, my readers will be glad to have you out here, whether it's a busy day or a slow one. And besides, everyone knows what August in Washington is like."

August in Washington meant that things were pretty slow all around because Congress was out of session, its members back home in their districts or off on taxpayer-supported "fact-finding" trips to various places around the world, and practically everyone else had left town for the mountains or the beaches. They all were grabbing their last chance at a summer vacation before the approaching September days summoned the legislators and their staffs back to their Capitol Hill offices and recalled the parents of the region's zillions of schoolchildren.

My comment seemed to cheer Magruder up a little, but I had my own unspoken doubts about what, exactly, I was going to say about the unusually quiet Friday shift we had just spent together while Magruder patrolled the district surrounding the Mount Vernon Police Station in Fairfax County's southeast section. I'm one of the police reporters for the Washington *News*, a major metropolitan daily in the nation's capital; my beat is the Fairfax County Police Department in northern Virginia. My plan was for Magruder and the events on his shift to provide the focus for the final installment in a three-part series I was writing about the police on suburban streets, using the Fairfax County Police as my examples. The first of the three stories was scheduled to run in Sunday's paper, just two days from now, and I still had this final one to write. And not much to write about. I make it a habit to ride with the patrol cops around the county several times a year, so I knew Magruder's shift wasn't the norm. But that didn't solve my problem of what to put in the article.

Magruder and I were sitting in the front seat of his cruiser, engine running and the AC working overtime in the sticky August heat. Outside the car, the hot air shimmered above the empty and even hotter parking lot of Mount Vernon High School, which was named after

The Father of Our Country's former plantation only a mile away. Magruder was taking the last hour of his shift to fill out the reams of paperwork that attended even the minor calls to which we had responded.

First, there had been the trailer park resident complaining about the neighbor who regularly took shortcuts through the flower beds in her tiny front yard. Then, we had been pulled away from our Tex-Mex lunches at the Bar-J on Route 1 to search for an elderly physician with Alzheimer's who had wandered away from his Potomac River home in the Riverside subdivision and away from the care of his equally elderly wife. Not long after that, we took a call that turned out to be two thirteen-year-olds who had nothing to do and who were relieving their boredom by using a .38 revolver to shoot rats behind their Route 1 public housing project.

I set my subconscious to stewing over the problem of how to write the Magruder piece, how to turn the day's less-than-exciting dross into gold, while my conscious brain turned to the morning's paper. I had only glanced at it earlier in the day in my haste to get to the Mount Vernon Station and meet Magruder for the beginning of his 7 A.M. patrol shift. But for all their importance, the stories I found in the paper were pretty boring, too.

The front-page lead was about a new outbreak of violence in the Middle East. In other words, just a normal day there.

Below that was a feature piece, which jumped to an inside page, on Henry Bryant, a federal appeals court judge from Tallahassee who had just arrived in town to prepare for his upcoming Supreme Court nomination hearings. Everyone expected him to sail through the process, given his long-standing reputation as a fair, articulate, and learned jurist. I already knew about Bryant and his reputation; I had spent five years as a reporter in Tallahassee before coming to Washington four years ago. I had covered education at the time, however, so Bryant was not someone with whom I had had any contact.

Below the front-page fold was a story on northern Virginia officials calling, for the umpteenth time, for a more rapid closing of Lorton Prison. Lorton was the equivalent of a state prison system for the District, but it had been built in southern Fairfax County, in stages, beginning with the maximum-security facility that opened in the 1920s. Given the regular escapes by prisoners into neighboring subdivisions, as well as the frequent revelations of corruption by prison employees and the not-infrequent outbreaks of inmate violence, the place was a chronic thorn in the side of county and state officials. So Congress had approved a multiyear plan to phase the prison out of existence and to relocate its inmates to federal prisons around the country. To the latest round of complaints about foot dragging on the phase-out, District officials were responding by making excuses or by completely ignoring the complaints, the District's long-standing policy for handling all problems.

Uninspired, I closed the paper and leaned my head against the window, bringing the dilemma of how to make Magruder's shift interesting back to the front of my brain. I was thinking that perhaps I should approach the story from the angle of the potential that today's shift had carried for tragedy, even though nothing tragic had developed. All the calls had ended peacefully.

We had found the doctor a couple of blocks from his house and had returned him to his wife, with a strong suggestion that she consider either getting some live-in help to care for him or putting him in a facility equipped to deal with his problems. The kids with the gun were in a lot of trouble, but they had surrendered the gun and themselves with surprisingly little resistance when two other police cruisers joined us as we arrived at the scene of their target practice. The trailer park spat had concluded with Magruder strongly suggesting that the woman put up a fence and emphatically admonishing the trespassing neighbor not to make Magruder have to come back.

Each of those situations might have ended very differently, however, without the presence of a police officer—and, more importantly, one who knew what he was doing.

While Fairfax County as a whole is one of the wealthiest jurisdictions in the country, the demographics of its Mount Vernon district cover the spectrum, from the largest population of public housing residents and homeless in the county all the way up to multimillion-dollar mansions sprawling along the shoulders of the Potomac River south of Alexandria. And everything in between. There is crushing poverty and oblivious ostentation. Teenage gangs and an area orchestra. Large immigrant populations, both legal and illegal. Sixteen-year-olds driving brand new BMWs and more disadvantaged children than the Head Start programs can handle. The setting often makes for angry resentment in one part of the population and fear and loathing in the other. Combine those ingredients with the easy availability of guns, drugs, and alcohol, and it's a recipe for frequent problems.

I felt it was valid to ask just how volatile the mix could get without cops like Magruder patrolling the streets. Even as young as he was, Magruder seemed to be able to judge each situation independently, not to act in some sort of reflexive, knee-jerk manner that could end up escalating the problem. Good judgment, empathy, and common sense went a long way in not making such situations any worse than they needed to be.

As I pondered the day's calls and struggled to stay awake in the intense afternoon sunlight pouring against my face through the car window, Magruder suddenly shifted to attention in the seat next to me. The dispatcher on his radio was calling out our unit's designation. I jumped as if caught napping, which I almost had been.

With efficient, practiced movements, Magruder spoke into the shoulder mike connected to the radio attached to his belt while also pressing buttons on the on-board computer that took up much of the space between us. I listened to his conversation with the dispatcher and read the words on the computer screen. A Mrs. Ferry on Buckner

Road had called in to complain that a man was exposing himself to her two young children in Grist Mill Park. Grist Mill Park, I knew, was a small community park about a mile and a half away, along Mount Vernon Memorial Highway. I guessed that Buckner was one of the neighborhood streets that surrounded it.

Magruder slapped his paperwork down between our seats in disgust and put the cruiser in drive.

"Well, this ought to be a fitting end to this shift," he said as we rolled up to the stop sign at the parking lot's entrance to Old Mount Vernon Highway and then turned left onto the street, heading south. "Given the number of hookers on Route 1, you'd think these guys could find somebody besides little kids to show themselves to, wouldn't you?"

"Yeah," I answered, "but what would be the kick in that? Hookers don't usually run off screaming."

Magruder shook his head from side to side in an ironic statement of disgusted agreement.

Within a minute, he turned the car to the right onto Mount Vernon Memorial Highway. Another mile down the road, I saw the wooded eastern end of Grist Mill Park on our right, followed quickly by the red roofs and shining white sides of a barn and silo, all that remained of the farm that once had covered the surrounding acres. We passed the park's entrance, where only a blue Volvo sedan sat in the parking lot, and then we angled off to the right onto Old Mill Road at the park's southwest corner. One block down Old Mill, Magruder turned right onto a street that the green-and-white sign said was Buckner. The Ferry house was in the second block of Buckner, and Magruder made a right turn into the driveway of the small 1950s-era brick house from which the call to the central emergency number had come.

In the front yard, under its canopy of massive, forty-five-year-old trees, stood a woman in her mid-thirties, her straight, blunt-cut, shoulder-length blond hair moving around her head as she glanced down in concern at each of the two wide-eyed children who stood within the circle of her arms. The little girl and boy, who looked to be about seven and five, had eyes only for the big navy-and-pewter police cruiser with its neon-bright lettering and insignia and the intimidating rack of red and blue lights on top. As Magruder and I each climbed out of the car, the children's eyes widened even more at the sight of his uniform and the gun hanging from his belt, and in unison they moved closer into the protective shadow of their mother.

"Mrs. Ferry?" Magruder asked as he walked up to the trio.

"The man is still out there," Mrs. Ferry said, nodding her head in acknowledgment of her name and lifting her left hand from her daughter's shoulders to gesture toward the backyard and the park that bordered it. "He's just sitting out there at the playground."

"Okay," Magruder told her, "you folks just hang on here while I go take a look, and I'll be back in a few minutes to talk to you about what happened."

I moved to follow him out to the park, but he halted me with a gesture.

"There's another car on its way, but you might want to stay here until they arrive," he said, somewhat apologetically. "Or at least until I know what I've got out there."

"Okay," I responded, not particularly interested in obeying but understanding that he didn't need the added concern for my safety until he had a handle on how much danger the man in the park might pose. Reluctantly, I slowed my pace but continued to trail him until I got to the edge of the unfenced backyard where the park ended. At least, I thought, I should be able to watch from here without worrying Magruder that I might be in danger.

Mrs. Ferry and her children soon joined me, their curiosity getting the better of their apprehension. I introduced myself and explained why I was with Magruder.

"Oh, please say you won't put our names in the paper about this,"

Mrs. Ferry pleaded, concerned now with the possible public embarrassment my story might pose.

"There's no need to," I reassured her. "We certainly wouldn't use
the children's names, and I don't see any reason to say anything more
than that the incident was in Grist Mill Park and was reported by a
resident of the neighborhood."

She thanked me, very relieved.

In silence, we all watched from the backyard's edge as Magruder,
his right hand on the pistol in his now-unfastened holster, crossed to
the middle of the park, to where a man sat in the dirt, leaning against
one of the posts supporting the massive jumble of bright orange and
yellow playground equipment that dominated the park's landscape.

Even from where we stood, Magruder's wariness was evident in
his body language as he approached the man. But the man remained
where he was on the ground, apparently not moving a muscle or even
noticing the cop walking up to him. From a few feet away, Magruder
spoke to him, his voice carrying to us through the thick, still air, though
the words weren't intelligible. We couldn't hear whether the man
on the ground answered Magruder or not, but in another moment,
Magruder reached down and easily pushed the man into a facedown,
prone position on the ground, then pulled each of the man's arms
up behind him, and slipped on a pair of handcuffs. Magruder had
to struggle to pull the suspect up off the ground and into a standing
position, not because the man resisted but because he apparently was
limp, dead weight.

The man stood uncertainly where Magruder had placed him as
Magruder patted him down, and I heard Mrs. Ferry's sigh of relief at
the same time as my own when we realized that the offender clearly
wasn't going to give Magruder any problems. Mrs. Ferry tightened her
grip on her children in expectation of Magruder walking his prisoner
toward us and the cruiser. Instead of heading back in our direction,
however, Magruder took the man by the arm and started across the

park's southern end toward the parking lot. In puzzlement, I watched as the two made their way to the solitary car still parked there.

A third man, who hadn't been in evidence earlier, now was approaching the lone car from the far end of the parking lot, where the bicycle path that paralleled the main highway ended. The newcomer arrived at the car and reached to open the door just as Magruder and his captive stepped onto the parking lot's paved surface. I saw Magruder raise an arm in a gesture to get the man's attention, and then he went right on up to the car, prisoner and all, and spent a couple of minutes in conversation. Soon, however, he turned and started back across the park in our direction, while the man at the car got inside and drove away.

As Magruder and the exhibitionist drew nearer to us, I noticed the children once again moving closer to their mother, though she had released her hold on them when Magruder had walked to the parking lot. Clearly, the children's encounter with the suspect had frightened them at least somewhat.

"You might want to take them inside until after he's got the guy in the car," I suggested to Mrs. Ferry, nodding my head down toward the two kids.

"I will," she replied, smiling at me in gratitude for the suggestion, and took the children into the house, holding each of them by the hand and speaking to them reassuringly. By the time she returned through the back door, Magruder and his guest had reached the edge of the yard. Mrs. Ferry looked hard at the disheveled, unshaven man, and Magruder passed me with a look that told me this wasn't going to be much of story, either.

Mrs. Ferry and I followed him through the side yard and back out to the front of the house, where we watched as he put the handcuffed man into the rear seat of the cruiser and closed the door. With the man who had frightened her children now securely locked away, I saw Mrs. Ferry visibly relax. Magruder opened the driver's door, reached inside, and came back out with his clipboard, which he brought over to where we stood.

"Now that he's taken care of," Magruder said to Mrs. Ferry, gesturing with his head back toward the cruiser and the man inside, "why don't you fill me in on what happened?"

"The kids decided they wanted to go play in the park," Mrs. Ferry told him, watching carefully as Magruder wrote her name and the address on the top of the incident form. "I always go with them, but I was just finishing up preparing one of the back flower beds to put in some fall plants, so I let them go on ahead without me for once, when I didn't see anyone else out there. I told them I'd be right over in just a couple more minutes."

"Where was our friend?" Magruder asked.

"I don't know," Mrs. Ferry answered, obviously feeling somewhat guilty with the fear that she had put her children at risk. "I think he must have been sitting down on the other side of the playground equipment, where I couldn't see him. All I know is that before I could even finish the flower bed and walk over there, Shay and Matthew came running back across the park, yelling for me at the top of their lungs. It scared me half to death. I started running out to meet them, and they told me that he had unzipped his pants and... and exposed himself to them."

Magruder looked back at the prisoner in the cruiser for a moment, then asked Mrs. Ferry if he could go inside and speak with the children.

"I just need to hear directly from them what happened," he explained, "but I'll try not to scare them or upset them." Mrs. Ferry agreed, and we followed her into the house's small but traditionally and tastefully furnished living room. I sat in one of the two Williamsburg blue upholstered chairs while Magruder sat in the other. The two children perched alertly on the blue-flowered sofa with their mother.

"This is Shay," Mrs. Ferry said, touching the top of her daughter's head, "and this is Matt." She draped her right arm around her son's shoulders.

"Hello," Magruder said solemnly. "I'm Officer Magruder."

Mrs. Ferry looked closely at each of the children in turn.

"I've explained to Officer Magruder what you told me about what happened in the park," she said to them, her voice gentle and reassuring. "He's arrested the man and is going to take him to jail so he can't bother you again, but we need to have you tell Officer Magruder yourselves what happened just so he can make sure he has the information he needs to put the man in jail. All right?"

Shay and her younger brother shook their heads in unison. Matthew popped his thumb firmly into his mouth. Seven-year-old Shay, however, clearly perceived that this situation called for her to be the big sister, as I had no doubt she did often and with relish. She stood up from the couch and said to Magruder, in a firm little voice, "That bad man came over and showed us his penis!" Apparently, with the culprit safely ensconced in the police car, she was now far more indignant than traumatized. Magruder swallowed hard, and I suddenly had to look away toward a pair of large watercolors of the Potomac that hung over the pecan-wood spinet piano sitting at the other end of the room.

"Did he say anything to either of you?" Magruder asked, his voice not betraying the amusement I knew he felt at Shay's little-adult demeanor.

"No-o-o," she answered thoughtfully as I finally got myself under enough control to look back at her.

"Did he touch you or your brother or try to touch either one of you?"

"No-o-o." She still was thinking hard for the nice policeman.

"Did he do anything else at all?"

"Yes!" The shouted answer had found its way past Matthew's thumb. All our heads swiveled in surprise to look at him. "He pee-peed!"

With that pronouncement, Matthew looked back at us as if surprised at himself, then put his thumb back in his mouth.

"He did! He did!" Shay said, not wanting to lose her place in the spotlight. "He went to the bathroom right in front of us!"

Magruder suddenly had to write several things down on his form. I studied the Potomac watercolors in more detail. Finally, Magruder looked back up at Shay.

"Thank you very much," he told her. "You and Matthew both have been very helpful. Now I just need to talk to your mom for a minute outside again, and then we're going to take the man who bothered you away. Okay?"

"Okay," Shay agreed and sat back down on the couch beside her brother.

Magruder stood up, and Mrs. Ferry and I did likewise, following him back outside. Once in the front yard, Magruder told us his reading of the situation.

"This guy," Magruder explained, "is pretty inebriated. He has no ID on him, and just looking at the way he's dressed and everything, I'm guessing he's one of our homeless guys who managed to bum a few dollars off somebody and treated himself to a bottle of something cheap and alcoholic. My gut tells me he barely knew where he was, that he just decided he needed to relieve himself and did it where he happened to be standing. I don't think he really was exposing himself to the children; they just happened to be there, and he's not thinking too clearly. I even went over to ask the guy in the parking lot if he had seen anything, just trying to make sure I wasn't sizing the situation up wrong. But he wasn't around at the time, apparently."

"So what are you going to do?" Mrs. Ferry asked.

"I'm going to lock him up at the station and let him sober up. We've got enough to hold him on for that long. We'll run his fingerprints and whatever name we can manage to get out of him through the computer. If I find he has any sort of record, especially anything involving children, I'll throw the book at him. At any rate, I don't think you need to worry about him again. These guys pretty much confine themselves to Route One, and God knows how he got over here, but I don't think he'll be back anytime soon."

Mrs. Ferry was satisfied with that answer, and we took our leave of her, waving at the two little faces that we could see watching us now through the clear panel of the front storm door. We got into the cruiser to the sounds of drunken snores from the backseat.

"I noticed the backup cruiser never showed up," I said to Magruder as he backed out of the driveway and onto Buckner Road.

"I canceled them," he explained, gesturing to his microphone. "This guy wasn't any trouble."

"I can see why," I commented, glancing into the rear seat. The snoring continued at multidecibel levels throughout the ten-minute drive to the Mount Vernon Station. I used the time to jot a few notes to myself for my article, thinking that, for all its anticlimax, this probably was the closest thing to a lead I was going to get for the story I still had to write.

2

The exhibitionist drunk didn't really merit being the lead in a feature story, but he was all I had. It was eight o'clock on Friday night, a time when most of the weekday reporting staff had finished their weekend pieces and gone home, and the editors are well into the anxieties of their second deadline of the evening. A time when I would have liked to embark on the social life that I wished I had but didn't.

Instead, I was sitting in the metro room at the Washington *News* where, after a valiant struggle, I had managed to come up with a lead about how many times every day police officers have to walk into unknown situations, situations that often turn out to be little more than a nuisance but that carry the potential for something much more dangerous. Situations such as the guy in Grist Mill Park with the drinking and bladder problems, who finally had told the police his name was Clinton Sheets, and who could have been a child molester or even armed. The outline of the rest of the story was forming itself in my mind when my phone rang.

"McPhee," I answered somewhat absentmindedly, my attention still focused on the words on the computer screen.

"Sutton, it's Bill Russell," said the familiar voice on the other end.

"Hey, Bill," I responded, turning both mind and body away from the computer to talk to the man who heads up the Fairfax County Police Department's Public Information Office. "What's up?"

I was hoping it wasn't anything pressing, given the feature I still had to write. I eyed the police scanner on my desk, which carried the Fairfax County Police open frequencies. It had been spouting nothing but the usual Friday night fender benders, shoplifters, and fistfights. But new technology has given police departments more access to closed frequencies as well as the in-car computers, and the most important information these days often gets transmitted out of the hearing of any Tom, Dick, or Mary who has the dough for a scanner. It was why I felt at least somewhat dependent on Bill and worked to stay in his good graces. Nothing required him to call and tell me what was happening, but he often did, partly in the interest of good relations with the press and partly, I suspected, because he had seen me mad once too often.

Bill not only is the chief liaison between the police department and the reporters who cover it and, thus, an important source for me, but he also is someone I've come to admire and to like. He daily walks a fine line between the openness that the press demands and the insistence of the department's investigators that he keep the information in their files out of public view until their cases are made. It's a line that sometimes must look like an obstacle course, made more difficult by the competition pressures among reporters and by the paranoia and distrust that the press engenders in the police ranks.

Bill apparently long ago had learned that the best policy was honesty. If he could answer a question without jeopardizing an investigation, he would. If he couldn't, he said so, no matter how frustrating that answer might be for the reporters and for him. But I had yet to see him have to backtrack on something he had said. In the process of working with him, we all had learned to respect him, knowing he only infrequently indulged in semantics, and never in intentional deception for the sake of deception.

Both police investigators and reporters often were unhappy with his answers to our questions, answers the detectives felt were too informative and that we told Bill were just the opposite. But Bill had learned through years of experience just how much juggling and ego-stroking each case required. And, I was sure, he spent a lot of time behind the scenes educating and placating reporters and police alike so they wouldn't ask the impossible of him.

"Apparently, one of our officers has just been found shot to death," Bill said, the emotion he felt about such an event coming through clearly in his voice.

"Oh, shit!" I said, knowing how personally every police officer on the force felt the killing of a fellow officer. "What happened? Where?"

"Down in the Belle Haven area," Bill answered, his voice still sounding a little shaky. I heard paper rustle. "River View Towers; 1780 Wakefield. It's off the George Washington Parkway, just south of Old Town Alexandria."

"I know it," I told him. "I looked at apartments in that area. Any ID on the officer?"

"Not yet. Officers just arrived on the scene and called in confirmation a few minutes ago. A neighbor called it in. Apparently, the officer lived there. The neighbor said the door to the apartment was open and when he looked in, he could see the body lying facedown, but he recognized the uniform from the shoulder patch."

"I'll see you there," I said, already pressing computer keys to save my story and exit the file. There would be no more work on it tonight, I knew. "Thanks for the call."

Bill said good-bye and hung up, clearly anxious to get to the scene himself.

On my way out, I stopped at Rob Perry's computer at the copy desk. His chair was empty, and so was his metro editor's office a few feet away. Rob keeps a foot in both camps. Although he is editor of the metro section, which means he has an assistant editor on duty at each daytime and evening shift, Rob has never divorced himself from the goings-on at the copy desk. I've always been impressed by his ability to juggle being metro editor while also lending a hand at the copy desk as if he were a subordinate. He oversees the content and layout of the metro pages for each edition, yet he also makes himself available to edit copy, take stories over the phone, and do whatever needs doing to get the pages out by the daily deadlines.

Figuring Rob had only wandered off somewhere for a few minutes, since a deadline was approaching, I jotted my whereabouts down on a yellow Post-it note, along with a suggestion that he hold some space for me in the final edition. I knew better than to leave him in the dark on what had happened. In his role as metro editor, Rob insists on knowing what his reporting staff is up to at all times. It's the only way, he says, that he can fight in the editors' meetings for the space our stories need. Reporters under Rob's supervision usually require only one lesson in what happens to those who let Rob end up looking uninformed. I long since had learned mine.

River View Towers looked as if it were under siege by the time I arrived. An ambulance and numerous police cars—both marked and unmarked cruisers—were parked helter-skelter throughout the parking lot, many with their emergency lights still flashing. And, having driven out from the District on a summertime Friday night (otherwise known as The Traffic Nightmare of the Week), I knew I also was arriving after the reporters from several other area papers as well as from at least some of the radio and television stations. That was clear from the scene at the usually unmanned entrance gate to the twin eight-story brick buildings, where one uniformed officer was checking the IDs of people who lived in the complex before letting them drive into the parking lot and where a second cop was having a heated argument with the driver of a TV station satellite remote truck, who apparently wanted in as well.

I decided it wasn't worth the hassle and turned right onto Potomac Avenue, where I parked my white '76 VW convertible too close to a fire hydrant and prayed to the parking ticket gods for a break. Then

I walked back up to the River View entrance and showed the first policeman my press ID. He waved me through without comment, and I waded my way into the chaos to look for Bill Russell.

I found him standing to one side of the entrance to the west building, surrounded by other reporters, TV cameramen, and a growing knot of tower residents and other onlookers. The members of the Fourth Estate were bombarding him with questions. Bill's answers all sounded like "I don't know yet."

"If you'll all be quiet for a second..." he was saying loudly, just as I walked up to join the group. The knot of reporters shut up long enough to see if he was going to be forthcoming. Bill drew a deep breath.

"Thanks," he said, his voice more conversational now. "I just got here, myself. Before I can tell you anything or answer your questions, I need to go inside and see what the situation is. If you'll just be patient for a few minutes, I'll be back down as quickly as I can with whatever I can tell you. Okay?"

There were a few mutters of agreement from the group and irritated sighs from a couple of TV cameramen as they lifted their cameras down from their shoulders.

"Don't take too long, Bill," I said above the heads in front of me. "I am on a deadline, you know."

"Right," he said, turning his mouth down in a slightly sour expression but not looking in my direction. He didn't have to. I knew he recognized my voice. A moment later, he caught my eye as he went past me without speaking, on his way inside the building, and gave me a quick wink. I hadn't been worried that he was mad. Bill and I were friends when we both were off the clock, but in front of others, we occasionally indulged in some give-and-take for the sake of appearances. It wouldn't do either of us any good to have the rest of the press—or the police department, for that matter—think that I got special treatment. But it was rare that either of us meant any of the gibes we tossed back and forth.

At Bill's departure, most of the other reporters scattered to various parts of the parking lot and driveway, looking to lasso unsuspecting residents and ask them pointless, predictable questions about how a murder in their building made them feel and whether they could feel safe living there now. Having once looked at apartments in River View Towers, however, I took myself off to the east building, where I knew the management office was located, in hopes of finding someone there who might know something helpful.

Thirty minutes later, I returned from my little fishing expedition. I had spoken to Buddy, the assistant day manager, who had come downstairs to watch the office and answer the telephone that was ringing constantly, while the night manager was over in the other building, answering questions for the police.

Buddy, a polo-shirted young man who looked like he might just barely be out of college and whose tan attested to some long weekends at the pool or the beach, had told me that, with the exception of a short spate of car break-ins in the parking lot the year before and an occasional domestic dispute that got out of hand, they had very few problems at the apartment complex, certainly nothing of the magnitude of a murder. And yes, he said, he knew there was at least one policeman living at the towers because he had seen a marked car parked there from time to time, but no, he didn't know the officer's name, and no, it wouldn't be possible for him to go through the rental records to find out.

At least, I thought to myself as I walked back over to the east building, my quotes about the complex's safety record would be more authoritative than the other reporters'. But I really needed the name of the dead officer soon if I was going to have it in time for the paper's final edition. I was mentally scratching my head for a way to find out, when I saw Bill Russell come back out of the east building's glass double front doors. With Detective Noah Lansing close behind him.

Oh Lord, I thought, as my breath caught in my throat and my heart flopped around in a disgustingly erratic fashion. *How,* I asked myself, *does he do that to me?*

It's because of your appalling lack of hormonal control.

For a pain in the head, you're a real pain in the ass, I responded mentally. But my voice had a point.

Ever since the first time I had seen Noah Lansing, just over three months ago, I had found myself hopelessly in lust when I was around him. He had thick, black hair and a tall, slim build that was as much a testament to terrific genes as it was to any workouts. But it was his eyes that always held my attention. They were large and an unusual dark blue that seemed to shine with their own internal light, and they carried an expression of intelligence, experience, and awareness that made me have to remind myself constantly not to stare at him. On top of all that was the intense feeling of recognition that had washed over me the first time I met him.

It was outside the Great Falls home of a Fairfax County supervisor whose wife had just been murdered, and it was Lansing's first case since moving to the area, from his job as a police detective in Virginia Beach, to join the Fairfax County Police Department. I hadn't known Lansing's history then. If I had, I probably would have kept my mouth shut for once, especially considering the effect he had on me.

Later, I learned from Bill Russell that Lansing's wife, Sarah, had been murdered several years earlier by members of a Hampton Roads area drug ring after they learned from a newspaper reporter that Lansing was an undercover cop planted in their midst. Sarah's death had left him a devastated, guilt-ridden widower with a small son.

But I had been busy mouthing off to Bill Russell, in blissful ignorance, when Lansing first turned those blue eyes on me. Later, after Bill told me Lansing's story, I understood that Lansing had been so irritated by my presence—and my sarcastic mouth—because he thought I was just another smart-assed woman newspaper reporter like the one who got his wife killed. At the time, all I knew was that he took an instant dislike to me for some reason, and that I was frozen to the spot with the shock of meeting those eyes. A shock from which I had yet to recover.

It hadn't been a propitious beginning, and Lansing and I subsequently fought our way through that entire investigation. When I managed to connect the death of the supervisor's wife to the earlier murder of Ann Kane, a U.S. Senate aide, Lansing and I finally were forced into declaring a professional cease-fire. We had realized that our cooperation was the only way to ensure that the men responsible for the women's deaths would be exposed, something we both wanted very much to see.

Bill Russell also had taken a stab at peacemaking by telling Lansing my own history, specifically about the murder of my sister Cara two years before, a murder I nearly got killed trying to solve after the Fairfax County Police had found nothing but dead ends. It was something I seldom talked about, not liking the looks of pity that the story usually elicited, but at least it had made Lansing reassess his original opinion of me as a news voyeur who thought the often-violent stories that I covered were amusing. So our relationship was better now, both professionally and personally, and it was the latter that scared the crap out of me.

In fact, it had become increasingly clear, in the weeks since the violent resolution of the investigation into the women's deaths, that a lot of the current tension between us was because Lansing had decided he was interested in me as well. And that presented me with several big problems, not the least of which was the conflict of interest it caused for both our jobs. I had sworn years ago, after a bad experience at my first newspaper job in Albany, Georgia, never again to go out with someone I covered. But I had been out with Lansing on his sailboat three times now, and just a week ago, he had convinced me to have dinner with him. And the kiss Lansing had given me before leaving me at my apartment door also had reminded me of my other big problem, stirring up all my long-standing misgivings about my track record with relationships.

Now there's a sordid story, my nemesis chimed in as I watched Lansing and Bill approach.

I ignored the comment, but I couldn't ignore its accuracy. That track record included a marriage in Tallahassee that had lasted only two years and a short string of love interests, none of whom had ever made it to the take-her-home-to-Mother stage before one or the other of us had bailed out. In the couple of years since the last such relationship, with an attorney named Chris Wiley, I had done some soul searching, and I knew the problem was as much with me as it was with any of the men involved. Eventually, I decided that I have real difficulty with control. I don't like people who try to control me, which explains my divorce and the demise of more than one of the subsequent relationships. And I have a hard time trusting that people won't do exactly that if I let them in.

Now, Noah Lansing was threatening all the shields I had laboriously constructed over the years, and I didn't know which frightened me more: the idea of keeping the shields up or the prospect of finally letting them down. And I thought he must have some misgivings of his own, given the glacial pace—at least by nineties standards—of anything physical between us, our apparently mutual attraction notwithstanding.

•   •   •

Lansing and Bill hadn't even made it all the way to where the press stood before several reporters were calling out their questions again. It occurred to me that most reporters probably start out as those children in elementary school who never learn to take turns. Bill put his hands up in a time-out gesture to shut them up. Lansing was busy scanning the group until his eyes found me standing to one side on his left. His look paused just long enough to let me know he had registered my presence before he turned back to look at Bill.

"Okay, ladies and gentlemen," Bill was saying, even though I had strong doubts that he really believed that about any of us, "for those of you who don't know him, this is Detective Noah Lansing. He'll be the lead investigator on this case, so I'll let him do the talking." He looked at Lansing sympathetically before turning him over to the press.

"If you'll hold your questions for a couple of minutes," Lansing said, "I'll tell you what we know, and then you can ask me about anything that I haven't addressed." When he didn't open the small notebook he was carrying around, I knew he wasn't going to tell us much.

"Sadly, I can tell you that the victim of this apparent homicide was a male officer in the Fairfax County Police Department. While we do know his identity, we can't release it to you until we can contact his family, which we already are working on. The officer appears to have been shot in the upper body. His body was found on the floor inside his apartment when a passing neighbor saw it through the front door, which had been left slightly ajar. You'll notice that I said this apparently is a homicide. Although nothing is official until we complete our work here and the medical examiner can determine cause of death, there were no signs of the wound being self-inflicted. The officer's own gun was still fastened in its holster, apparently unfired, and no other weapons have been found in the apartment. At this time, we have no suspects in the death, no motive, and no witnesses. We are interviewing neighbors in the building in hopes that one of them may have seen something helpful."

He paused, drawing a breath. "All right, let's have your questions."

"How long before you can tell us who he is?" Trudy Gernrich from the Washington *Post* wanted to know. Out of all the other reporters there, Trudy was one of the few I considered serious competition.

Like me, she didn't miss much, and she always knew the important questions to ask when time was short.

"Soon, we hope," Lansing told her. "Just as soon as we can reach his family."

"But you're certain now of who he is?" That was from Barrett Avery, an evening anchorman at Channel 3, who occasionally went out to cover big-breaking stories so he could pretend to have real news reporting credentials and who often had difficulty following the obvious.

"Yes," Lansing said patiently. "He was still in uniform when he was shot, including his badge and name tag. There also was other identification on the body. And the officers who were first on the scene knew the victim personally."

"Does that mean he worked out of the Mount Vernon Station?" I asked Lansing, trying to narrow the possibilities in hopes of finding out who the officer was, just in case they decided to drag their heels on identifying him.

"I'm sorry," Lansing said, looking in my direction, "but I'm not prepared to answer that until next of kin are notified."

It was a no-win situation for him, and his "no comment" answer effectively was a yes, I thought, satisfied at having found out what I wanted to know in spite of his refusal to answer. As soon as Lansing turned away to take someone else's question, I moved a few steps away from the group and retrieved my cell phone from my purse. I wanted to be able to hear the other questions and answers, but I didn't want anyone there to hear the phone call I was about to make.

I double-checked the number in the miniature address book I always carry and dialed the home number for Stan Dozier, another patrol officer stationed at Mount Vernon. I knew Stan preferred the late-night shift and worked it as often as he could because Nancy, his fiancé, was an emergency room nurse at Mount Vernon Hospital, and she worked the late shift on a permanent basis. When Stan was able to work the same hours as Nancy, it meant they could spend more of their free time together.

One of the first feature stories I had done after moving to the police beat was about the unusual number of police who marry or become seriously involved with emergency room staff, firefighters, emergency medical technicians, and other cops, probably because they keep running into each other in the course of their jobs and they all keep the same kind of crazy hours. Nancy and Stan had liked the story, and Stan had been helpful a couple of times since in pointing me toward information I needed for other stories. Tonight, I expected to catch him at home, since his shift didn't start for almost two hours. He answered on the fourth ring, his voice carrying the impatient tone of someone who has been interrupted in the middle of something important.

"Stan, it's Sutton McPhee."

"Hi, Sutton," Stan replied. "Listen, I really don't have time to talk now. They just called me to come in early tonight because they've got so many people over at the shooting at Belle Haven."

"I'm over there now. Who was he, Stan?" I asked, not wanting to hold him up any longer than necessary. "I know he was a Fairfax cop and that he worked out of the Mount Vernon Station, but they're still calling his family, so they haven't told us his name yet. I know they're bound to reach somebody before the night is over, but with my luck, it will be ten minutes too late for me to make the last edition. And my editor will have a stroke."

"This won't come back to me?" Stan asked.

"No way."

"It was a guy named Dan Magruder. I think he was working day shift this week. He had only been at the station a few months. He used to work out of the McLean Station."

My hand tightened convulsively on the phone while I stood there in stunned silence.

"Sutton, you there?" It was Stan, wondering if we were still connected. I managed to find my voice.

"Yeah, Stan, I'm here."

"Did you know him?"

"I just spent the whole day riding with him for a story."

It was Stan's turn to stumble over a response.

"Shit, Sutton," he said finally, "if I'd known that, I probably wouldn't have told you. You okay?"

"Yeah, I'm fine. It just caught me off guard."

"Well, you'd better let the detectives know, if they don't already. I imagine they'll want to talk to you about what you and Dan did today, just in case."

"You're right," I agreed, still trying to absorb what he had told me. "I guess I'd better go do that and let you get to work. Thanks, Stan."

We hung up, and I walked back over to where Lansing and Bill were just making their way back into the building lobby, finally having exhausted the press's supply of questions. The huddle of reporters was breaking up, too, with some wandering off to find some other poor soul to ask silly questions of, and others heading toward their cars or remote trucks to let their news desks know what was going on. I moved toward the lobby door, only to be stopped by another uniformed officer who didn't want to let me in, having just seen me outside at the impromptu press conference.

"Detective Lansing," I called out, leaning past the cop who stood in my way. Lansing and Bill both turned at my voice. "There's something I need to tell you." There must have been something in my expression or the tone of my voice that told them it was important and not just more of the usual Sutton McPhee orneriness. They walked back to where I stood in the doorway.

"What's wrong?" Bill wanted to know. Having known me so much longer, he probably could interpret my body language better than Lansing could.

"I know the dead cop is Dan Magruder," I told them, dropping my voice from the shout that had gotten their attention. Lansing opened his mouth, no doubt to protest that they wouldn't confirm that. I went on before he could speak. "I thought I'd better tell you that I spent the day riding with him today."

Bill looked at me in surprise. I couldn't tell if he was surprised at my apparent talent for finding my way into the middle of their cases or at the fact that I had volunteered the information. Lansing didn't say a word. He just reached out a hand and pulled me in the door, past the officer who was guarding it. He whisked me inside and over to the elevator bank so fast that I didn't think any of the other reporters had time to notice I had gotten in to where they hadn't been allowed to go.

An hour later, I felt as if my brain had been picked clean. We were sitting in the living room of a vacant apartment next door to the sixth-floor unit where Dan Magruder's body still lay. The River View Towers's night manager had opened the unoccupied apartment for the police to use to interview people in the building, out of sight of the body, and had even located half a dozen folding chairs and a couple of card tables. I was sitting at one of the tables, flanked by Bill and Lansing, answering all their questions for at least the third time. I had been completely forthcoming with them for a change, since there was nothing about my story on Magruder that I needed to conceal. One of the other investigators, who would be helping Lansing on the case and whose name I had not registered, sat across from me and listened as well. I was just about to protest the redundancy of their questions when my cell phone rang in my purse. The cops all looked irritated at the interruption, but I answered it anyway.

"Where the hell's my story, McPhee?"

It was Rob Perry. The final deadline was looming over him, which meant the volume knob on his voice was gradually inching its way toward the Yell setting.

"I'll call you right back with it, Rob, I promise," I said, not wanting to get into a long explanation for my tardiness. "I'm talking to the cops right now. It has turned out to be more complicated than we thought."

"Five minutes!" he ordered and hung up. I doubted Rob had ever even heard of Emily Post.

"Are we about done here?" I asked Lansing. "I've still got a story to call in, unless I want to die young. And I've told you everything that Magruder and I did, saw, and said today. There just wasn't anything there that I could imagine someone killing him over."

Lansing and Bill exchanged a look, and then Lansing apparently took pity on me.

"Yeah," he said, standing up stiffly from the table. "We're done, for now."

The rest of us stood as well, just as another plainclothes officer came in to talk to Bill. Not realizing I was a reporter, he told Bill that he had just gotten off the phone with Dan Magruder's parents, who would be driving down immediately from Winchester, Virginia, on the state's western border.

"Is it okay to release his name?" Bill asked, turning to Lansing.

"Yeah, go ahead," Lansing told him, nodding tiredly.

"I'll walk you down, Sutton," Bill offered.

"Okay, but I just have a couple of questions of my own for you guys. Have you found anybody in the building who saw anything?"

"No," Lansing answered. "Just the neighbor who found him. We're guessing that he probably was killed some time soon after he got home from his shift with you, and most people in the building were still at work at that time, so there probably weren't a lot of people coming and going yet. And with Magruder's apartment being at the very end of the hall, it wasn't until the neighbor directly across from him got home that anyone noticed the body. The door was only open a little way."

"Any theories on why?"

"Not yet. Obviously, we'll be going back through the paperwork on the calls he's responded to in the last few weeks and any court cases where he's had to testify. Or it could have been over something personal, so we'll be talking to as many friends and family as we can find. Or it could have been some kind of random thing that had nothing to do with him in particular. We just don't know yet." Lansing reached up with a hand to massage the back of his neck, no doubt thinking of the hundreds of hours of work it might take to find the person who shot Magruder. If they found him.

"Okay," I told him, "thanks." I turned to walk over to where Bill now was waiting for me at the door. Just as I reached him, Lansing spoke again.

"Thanks for telling us what you know. And we may need to talk to you again about it."

"That's fine," I answered. "You know where to find me."

"Yeah," he said, raising an eyebrow, "usually in our way."

I turned back without comment, to follow Bill through the door, and gave Lansing the finger behind my back. I thought I heard him laughing as Bill and I went down the hall to the elevators.

The clot of reporters was somewhat smaller than earlier when Bill and I got back outside to the parking lot. I stayed just long enough to hear him give them Dan Magruder's name, age, and rank and to tell them that there was no other new information at this time. One of the reporters also asked pointedly what I was doing inside the building. Before Bill could answer, I did.

"I had to pee," I said, taking a page from the Grist Mill park drunk. I wasn't about to let the other reporters know about my proximity to Magruder just before he was killed. They could read about it in the *News* tomorrow morning. At my crude response, Bill got the message and closed his mouth. I headed for my car, where I could sit in privacy and jot down a few notes in order to organize my thoughts before I called Rob Perry.

When I dialed his extension, Rob answered his phone by barking his last name into the receiver. I gave him the brief version of what I had and the news I had given the police that had delayed my calling in.

"So what does this do to your series?" Rob wanted to know.

"Makes it more interesting, I hope. I think we should move the Magruder installment up to Sunday's paper as the first piece. I'll come in tomorrow and get it finished. We can do a straightforward news piece on the shooting for tomorrow's paper, and maybe we can mention the upcoming feature in that story or do a sidebar promo on it."

"Yeah," Rob said, thinking with me. "Okay, I like that idea. What approach are you taking with the feature on him?"

"I was doing something on the potential dangers cops have to walk into regularly, even in situations that look relatively benign. Apparently walking through his own front door fell into that category, too."

"Good," Rob said. "You ready to give me your story for deadline?"

Using my brief notes, I composed the story in my head as Rob typed it into the computer system on the other end. Even with the quotes from Buddy, it wasn't terribly long; the police didn't know much.

When I finished, Rob hung up, and I started the Bug to make the drive back across Alexandria to my apartment out on the city's West End. But it wasn't Magruder's murder, as unnerving as that was, that occupied my thoughts on the way there. It was what neither Lansing nor I had mentioned in front of Bill Russell: our plans to go sailing again on Sunday, this time with Lansing's six-year-old son, David. David, whom I hadn't met. David who certainly added one more facet to the complexities of any sort of personal relationship with Noah Lansing.

3

SATURDAY

Saturday, I spent the day with Dan Magruder again. And knowing that he was now dead, that he had been murdered, didn't make writing the feature on him any easier. When it finally was done, I still had to write a sidebar follow-up on his death, in order to provide the context for the feature piece and, I hoped, increase the story's irony and poignancy in the readers' minds.

A call to Bill Russell as soon as I got to the newsroom that morning had provided me with biographical information on Magruder and a promise from Bill that he would ask Dan's parents, who had arrived in Alexandria in the middle of the night, to call me. Bill also updated me on the investigation of the shooting: little progress at this early stage.

When I hung up from my conversation with Bill, I put in a call to Magruder's station commander, James Mannon, who spoke highly of Magruder's performance as an officer and his loyalty to the county police force.

Just before noon, I was polishing quotes from a couple of other Mount Vernon Station officers I had called, when Magruder's parents responded to my message.

"Miss McPhee?" an uncertain male voice asked, when I answered the ringing phone on my desk.

"Yes? This is Sutton McPhee."

"This is Art Magruder, Dan's father. Bill Russell gave us the message that you wanted to talk to us about Dan."

"Oh," I responded, momentarily caught off guard because I had been so involved in the writing. "Mr. Magruder, thank you very much for calling me, and first, let me tell you how sorry I am about Dan."

"That's very kind of you," his father replied. "Actually," he went on, his voice still shaky and soft, "one of the reasons I agreed to call you was because Bill told us you spent the day with Dan yesterday."

"That's right, Mr. Magruder. I did. I was working on a feature story about Dan as part of a series on the Fairfax County Police. It's going to run in tomorrow morning's paper."

"How was Dan when you were with him?"

So I told Dan Magruder's grieving father about his son's last hours, about the people he helped, about his common sense and his professionalism.

"Dan was a good police officer, Mr. Magruder," I assured him. "He had the right instincts for the job, and he did it well."

"It was all he ever wanted to do," the elder Magruder responded, and I listened as he went on to talk about his son. When he finally paused, I asked the question I needed to ask.

"Mr. Magruder, I'm sure Bill Russell told you they don't know yet who killed your son or why. But do you know of anyone who would have had a reason to do such a thing, someone from his past or someone he might have mentioned he was having a problem with?"

For a moment, there was just silence on the other end of the phone.

"Mr. Magruder?"

"That's a question you should ask the police department," Magruder said, his voice cracking but not hiding the anger that dwelt there underneath the grief. "It was the other officers that he had to watch his back around!"

"I'm sorry," I said, "I don't understand what you mean. Was Dan being threatened by someone he worked with?"

The father paused again. "I shouldn't say any more," he finally answered cryptically. "Dan would be upset that I brought it up. Just forget I said anything."

Of course, I couldn't forget it, since he obviously knew something I didn't, but when I continued to press him, he refused to elaborate on what he had meant.

"I'm sorry, Miss McPhee," he said finally, "but I can't talk any longer. The other reason I agreed to call you was because Bill Russell told us about what happened to your sister. He said you would know how hard this is for us, so you'll understand if I have to hang up now."

And he did just that.

At least, I thought, I did manage to get a few usable quotes from him. And I appreciated Bill's ability to persuade the father to call me in the first place. But damn it, I was going to have to get Bill to stop mentioning Cara's murder to other people. It wasn't being reminded of her death that bothered me, although I still had days when the pain of missing her ambushed me all over again. It was the idea of using her death to get sources to feel more comfortable talking to me, to get the information I wanted. It felt sleazy. I didn't do it myself, and I didn't like anyone else doing it, either, no matter how helpful Bill had thought he was being.

I ruminated on the meaning of Mr. Magruder's comment about the police department for the next couple of hours, while I wrote the sidebar on Dan Magruder's death and then went back over it and the feature article a couple of more times, polishing and editing my copy. When I was satisfied, I paged Noah Lansing to make a final check on the investigation. I assumed he probably had been working on it all day, regardless of the fact that it was Saturday, because it was a cop who had been gunned down.

"You're not backing out of tomorrow, are you?" Lansing asked as soon as I answered the phone.

"No, of course not. I'm double-checking on the Magruder killing before turning in my story for Sunday's paper."

"No change there," Lansing said.

If you want him so badly, why do you call him by his last name? How intimate is that?

About as intimate as his calling me McPhee, I thought back. *It just happens.*

It's going to sound strange in bed. Oh Lansing, Lansing!

Would you please stop? I shouted mentally. *And thanks a lot! Now I'll never get that ridiculous image out of my head.*

"You still there?" It was Lansing, wondering where I had gone.

"Yes, I'm here. Just making some notes." I got a firm grip on my brain. "I need you to interpret something for me."

"What?"

"Someone made the comment to me earlier today that I should ask the police department who would have a reason to kill Dan Magruder. You want to tell me what that meant?"

It was Lansing's turn for silence. I decided I must have struck a nerve.

"Who did that come from?" he asked finally.

"You know I can't tell you that. So, what does it mean?"

"I suppose it could mean anything."

He wasn't getting off that easily.

"But it doesn't mean just anything. It means something specific, doesn't it?"

"You know I can't tell you that."

"Okay, touché. Now we're even. So, what can you tell me?"

"That we haven't ruled out any possibilities at this point. We are continuing to investigate all avenues."

"You've been taking lessons from Bill Russell, haven't you?"

Lansing laughed.

"Well, he does know how to handle you," he pointed out.

"You have anything else to tell me at this point? Anything useful?"

"Yes, we'll be expecting you at the boat at ten o'clock tomorrow morning."

"Maybe I'll be there."

"David's really looking forward to meeting you."

I'll just bet he is, I thought as I hung up. What six-year-old wouldn't want to meet the woman trying to horn in on his time with his only parent?

As always, when I finally got home that night, carrying my take-out Chinese dinner, my apartment was just as I had left it.

Husbandless, childless, petless. In other words, lifeless, huh?

Why do I need them, I thought sarcastically as I closed the door behind me and looked around at the place I usually think of as my refuge, *as long as I have you?*

Just doing my job of pointing out what needs pointing out.

Ignoring my tormentor, I walked into my kitchen to the right, to put my dinner down on the counter, and then went out the other side to follow the hall back to my bedroom, the larger of the two in the apartment, where I put away my purse and changed into more comfortable clothes.

I live on the fourteenth floor of a sixteen-story high-rise building that sits two blocks east of I-395 and Duke Street, in the western portion of Alexandria, one of several such high-rises in an area known as Condo Canyon. The area certainly doesn't have the ambience of the other end of the city, historic Old Town Alexandria, established in 1749, but it's hard to beat for its convenience to major traffic arteries and for the incredible view of the area I have from the walls of three-quarter-length windows that stretch the full length of my living room, dining area, and guest bedroom. I always relish the times that I can sit out on my balcony, a glass of iced tea in one hand and book in the other, soaking up the sun and enjoying the breeze that is almost constant at that height.

When I came back from the bedroom in denim shorts and a man's white shirt, the daylight saving sun, still hot and relatively high in the western sky at six P.M., drew me out the balcony door once more. I decided to enjoy the view for a few minutes and sat down on the bright, floral cushion of one of the two white plastic chairs flanking my glass-topped patio table. Instead of seeing what I was looking at, however, my mind quickly went back to thinking about the comment Dan Magruder's father had made. I knew he had something particular in mind when he said it, something involving someone in the Fairfax County Police Department, something that he believed might be connected to his son's death. I turned the possibilities over in my mind, frustrated that I hadn't been able to get anything more concrete out of Noah Lansing.

And, of course, from that thought, it wasn't very far to thinking about Noah Lansing in general, and his little boy in particular. A little boy I would meet tomorrow.

Eventually, I realized that the sun had dropped below the horizon and that I was enveloped in a rapidly shadowing dusk. And that my dinner was now cold as a stone.

This isn't good, I told myself as I got up from the chair in irritation and went back inside to put the egg rolls and sesame chicken into the microwave. I have to keep my wits about me and my mind on my work. I can't let my brain keep drifting off into my personal fantasies about Noah Lansing.

Oh Lansing, Lansing!

Don't be an idiot, I thought, and I wasn't talking to my voice.

4

SUNDAY

I was terrified. I had faced loaded guns before, held by people determined to kill me, but nothing had frozen me to the spot like this. I was standing on one of the docks at the Fort Washington Marina, and staring back at me was a six-year-old version of Noah Lansing. The black hair. The dark blue eyes. Most especially, the serious expression. Which left me wondering what the mind behind those eyes was thinking, what opinions were being formed of me. As I said, like his father.

David Lansing and I contemplated each other across the few feet of space that separated us as Noah introduced us. I swallowed hard and found my tongue.

"Hello, David," I said brilliantly, not knowing whether I should kneel down to become his height or whether he would find that condescending. I bent my knees into a stooped posture that was halfway between the two, then realized how stupid I must look and stood up straight again.

"Hello," he replied simply and held out a hand for me to shake. Which I did. We dropped our hands to our respective sides, and more silence ensued as we took each other's measure. I was afraid mine was coming up noticeably short on whatever yardstick this child was using.

You wimp! Are you really this intimidated by a little kid?

This is no little kid, I thought in reply. *This is a child who doesn't even remember his mother and who probably isn't going to take kindly to some woman with designs on the father who raised him. Those eyes look at least a hundred years old.*

And they did. The body might be just over three feet tall, wearing little navy shorts and a T-shirt with Wallace and Gromit on the front, but there was no childish naïveté in the eyes.

"So, are you two ready to go out?" Lansing Senior asked cheerfully, stepping up to put an arm around each of us.

We both answered affirmatively, with me saying a silent prayer of thanks for his putting an end to the inspection. We walked out onto the finger pier that ran between each of the boats tied up at the marina, and Lansing stepped across to the deck of *Second Wind*, his navy-hulled, thirty-foot sailboat, whose diesel engine already was warming up. He watched eagle-eyed as David took a giant step of his own across the space between pier and deck, and then Lansing held out a hand to help me make my passage across the watery gap, a passage that still was awkward even after three trips on the boat.

Though Lansing had begun to teach me the rudiments of sailing a boat on our last two trips, this time I sat down in the cockpit, content to stay out of the way as he and his son skillfully freed the dock lines that held *Second Wind* to the wooden pilings and maneuvered her away from the pier and out into Piscataway Creek, on our way out to the boating channel in the Potomac River.

I was glad not to have to make conversation yet as I watched the two of them work together, steering the boat with the stainless steel wheel, making last-minute checks of sails and rigging, gauging the direction and strength of the wind in anticipation of what sort of sailing they could expect. When we reached the large green buoy that marked the entrance to the river channel, Lansing killed the engine, turned the wheel over to David to hold the boat steady, and surefootedly moved up onto the top deck to remove the bungee cords that had been holding the mounds of white sails safely on the deck.

Back in the cockpit again, Lansing raised the mainsail, and we were off, moving southeast down the river, pushed along by the current and the midmorning wind. As we sailed, he and David took turns at the wheel. When we tacked, I watched in impressed silence as David handled the lines from the sail, in turn loosening them from and looping them around the metal winches that locked into place to hold the lines secure, his father reaching over to provide only minor assistance. The child was completely comfortable, moving around the boat with ease, responding promptly to his father's instructions. Which was more than could be said for me.

On our last two sails, I had struggled to remember starboard from port. ("What's wrong with good old left and right?" I had asked Lansing. He had laughed, but I hadn't been joking at all.) I still couldn't remember which way to wrap the lines from the sail around the winches. And his insistence on my taking the wheel both times had just about sent me into a panic, especially when I had to move the boat through a change of tack or turn it around, making the sail swing powerfully from one side of the boat to the other.

Perhaps, I thought, I eventually would get comfortable with it all, but I certainly didn't want to flaunt my lack of sailing knowledge or ability in front of this nimble child who clearly had been spending time on this boat since he was a toddler.

A couple of longer tacks found all three of us sitting in the cockpit, looking at each other.

"What grade will you be in when school starts next month?" I asked David, broaching what I hoped was a safe subject, determined that Lansing see I could make conversation with his son.

"First grade." No elaboration.

"Are you looking forward to it?"

"Yes." Although you couldn't have proven it by the still-serious expression.

"Do you have friends from your neighborhood who will be in school with you?"

"Yes."

"Well," I concluded inanely, "that's always good."

I tried to sneak a look at Lansing, where he sat to my left, steering the boat, only to find him watching me with a completely unreadable expression that was matched only by the one on his son's face.

A little while later, David looked at me again and asked, "Are you going to marry my dad?"

Lansing and I both almost choked to death on the spot.

"David!" he said in a chastising voice. "You don't ask a question like that!"

"No, no," I said, motioning Lansing to silence. "It's all right. I understand why he would want to know."

I turned to David, who still watched me solemnly.

"David," I said, hoping I sounded reassuring, "your dad and I haven't known each other nearly long enough to decide something like that. I do like your dad. Very much. He saved my life a couple of months ago, when a bad person tried to hurt me. But I also like him because I like who he is. I think he's a good guy, just like you do. And I enjoy spending time with him."

"Oh," David said, noncommittally. "Okay."

"That's more than she's ever told me," the father commented dryly. I gave him a glare. *God,* I thought, *this is absolutely agonizing. How the hell did I let myself get talked into this, anyway?*

Celibacy looking better and better, is it?

Screw you, I answered silently.

Sorry, can't help you there.

Was that why I was such a sucker, I wondered. Because I was so starved for sex that I would endure anything to get this man into bed? It had been a while, after all. Okay, more than a while.

But I knew that wasn't it. I really enjoyed sex. I wasn't even above having a relationship that was more physical than emotional. As a history of my relationships would make painfully obvious (and might even make one wonder whether I preferred it). But I knew I would never consider putting my career at risk just for sex with a guy who also presented a huge conflict of interest for me. There were too many willing guys out there who didn't. But Noah Lansing was someone I just couldn't seem to take or leave. He had gotten under my skin and into my brain in a way I couldn't remember any other man ever doing, not even Jack Brooks, my ex-husband.

My body felt electrified whenever I was near Lansing, as if every nerve ending suddenly had woken up. His hand on my arm, his arm around my shoulder, were enough to make me want to throw all caution to the winds. And I couldn't even remember the one kiss he had given me without also remembering the feeling of coming home that had overwhelmed me when he had put his arms around me. I didn't know what Lansing was to me or what he would be, but I knew there was nothing casual about it. Except, of course, his son was in the picture. A son I was afraid I was failing to impress in every possible way.

The son in question got up at about that point and asked his father if he could go up to the bow for a little while. We were on our way back up the river and would be reaching the buoy at Piscataway Creek in another twenty or thirty minutes.

"Sure, go ahead," Lansing answered. "Just hook up your safety harness while you're up there. And remember, no dangling your feet over the side."

"I'll remember," David said, standing up eagerly. He and his father clipped a blue nylon line to the floatation jacket David had worn throughout the trip. Then Lansing attached the other end of the tether to a similar line that ran the length of the boat and that was designed to keep David with the boat in case he fell overboard. Once he was in harness, David easily made his way up onto the top deck and sat down in a spot that was back from the edge of the bow but also out of the way of sails, booms, and rigging. He stared ahead as we moved upriver, the wind blowing his hair back from his intent little face.

"I saw your piece on Magruder in the paper this morning," Lansing said once David was settled up front.

"And?"

"And you did a good job. The guys on the street will like it. You obviously have some understanding of what their jobs are about."

"And?"

"And what?"

"And you want to tell me which one of those guys had some beef with Magruder? Which one might have had a reason to shoot him?"

"We're still looking into all that," Lansing said cryptically. "I can't tell you the details of our investigation."

"Does that mean you're still looking generally into who might have held a grudge or that you have someone specific in mind?"

"You know that's what I can't discuss."

"And you know I'll find out anyway."

"Boy, Bill is right about you, isn't he?"

"That depends. What did he say?"

"He said you're so stubborn that you could outlast a redwood if you thought it knew something you wanted to know."

"Some people think that's a good thing," I pointed out. "Like my editors."

"That's only because they don't actually have to spend any time with you. It's the rest of us you're always out here giving a hard time."

"Sticks and stones," I replied, smiling. "You can tell me now or tell me later, but eventually, you know you're going to tell me."

"Never," Lansing responded, grinning at me over the top of the wheel and taking up the challenge. I suspected he was enjoying it.

"We'll see."

Once again, I stayed out of the way as Lansing and David tied up the boat back at the marina. Although I had helped Lansing with the lines and with taking down and stowing sails on previous trips, I knew the two of them could do it faster and with a minimum of hassle if they didn't have to keep tripping over me.

With the boat secured and closed up, the three of us walked back up the pier to the graveled parking lot where my Bug and Lansing's dark green Ford Explorer sat baking in the midday sun. The VW was the more distant of the two, so the father and son walked me over to it.

"Is this your car?" David asked, once we reached the Bug and I started putting the top down.

"For a long time now," I told him. "My parents gave it to me when I finished college."

"It sure is funny looking," David said. "But I like it."

"So do I," I told him, thinking there was at least one thing we agreed on. Although it was used when my parents bought it for me, I had taken to the little Bug, with its white ragtop, instantly and had held on to it, through many a long, hot, Southern summer when I often asked myself why I didn't buy something with air-conditioning, through the recent rebuilding of its engine, and through most of the more than one hundred eighty-five thousand miles on its odometer. I suspected that its connection to my parents, killed in an accident with a semi shortly after I moved to Florida, had almost as much to do with my keeping the car so long as did the fact that it was so simple to repair and maintain.

"I'll take you for a ride in it with the top down sometime, if you like," I told David.

There was no response. Just a thoughtful look on David's face.

"Would you like to come with us to get pizza?" Lansing asked, trying to fill the silence, I guessed. "It's David's favorite lunch."

"Thanks for the invitation, but I really can't," I told him, lying through my teeth. "I've got a lot of things I need to do this afternoon."

Like what? Sitting around, feeling sorry for yourself?

I ignored the voice.

The truth was that I didn't think I could spend another couple of hours gritting my teeth and worrying over what this near-silent little boy at my feet thought of me. I couldn't believe how nerve-racking the morning had been, and I knew I couldn't handle an afternoon of more of the same.

"Sure, we understand, don't we, David?" Lansing answered, smiling down at his son.

David reached up and took my hand.

"Will you come sailing with us again?" he asked. "I like you." Then the kid smiled.

My jaw dropped. I looked up at Lansing in surprise and confusion. He started laughing at me.

"I guess I should have warned you," he explained, obviously delighted at seeing me off balance. "David is one of those kids who gives people a thorough once-over before he says much. But once he decides he likes you, he's your buddy, and then you get to see the real David, who has lots to say."

I turned back to the little boy, whose face was as transformed by his smile as his father's face always was by the larger version.

"Sure," I told him, smiling back now and feeling like an idiot. "I'll go sailing with you again. Any time you like."

Noah Lansing leaned over and kissed me on the check.

"See you soon," he said, brushing away a few stray tendrils of hair that had crept out of the thick braid I usually wear and had blown into my eyes. "Probably when you're butting into one of my cases."

He and David turned and walked back across the parking lot to the Explorer, holding hands and talking about the sail they had just taken. I finished putting the top down on the Bug and had just climbed into the driver's seat when they drove by me, waving.

I put my head back against the seat and tried to figure out what had gone on here.

Getting in deeper and deeper, aren't you?

I started the engine to drown out my other little buddy.

5

MONDAY

Noah Lansing might have vowed not to tell me what it was he knew
about Dan Magruder's murder, but that didn't mean I didn't have
other ways of finding out. I had been covering the Fairfax County
Police Department for two years before Lansing joined it, and my
constant visits to each of the county's police substations meant that I
had a more-than-nodding acquaintance with many of the patrol officers, detectives, and clerical staff who spent their working hours at
one station or the other. I had traded information with several of them,
had done favorable stories about others. One of them was bound to be
in a talkative mood.

I got to the Mount Vernon Station just as Officer Allen Reider was
heading out the back door to his patrol car. Reider, a black veteran of
some ten years on the force, had been one of the highlights of my feature story on the training and education of the county police. He was a
street-smart, no-nonsense cop by day and a law student by night, with
plans to become a prosecuting attorney once he passed the bar exam
in a couple of years. When I greeted him in the parking lot, he told me
he had just finished booking an early-morning shoplifter whom he had
arrested at the 7-Eleven on Richmond Highway, just south of the giant
Mount Vernon Multiplex movie theater complex.

"The idiot did it while I was standing in the store, talking to the
manager," Reider said, laughing and shaking his head in disbelief.
"Another customer noticed him stuffing his pockets full of candy bars
and came over to tell me about it, just as the guy was walking out the
door."

I commiserated with Reider on the intelligence level of the average criminal and was wondering how best to work the conversation around to Dan Magruder when Reider did it for me.

"I really liked the story you did on Dan Magruder," he said. "Too bad he won't ever get to read it."

I agreed. "That's not the way I prefer to get my pieces noticed," I added. "He seemed like a really good guy. I just wish I could get a handle on why someone would want to kill him."

Reider got a funny look on his face. Funny strange, not funny ha-ha. He looked down and studied his shoes.

"You know, don't you?" I asked him, certain that was what the expression I had seen cross his face meant.

"I've heard some things," Reider said, looking up at me again. "Some talk."

"Talk about what?"

"Off the record?"

"Absolutely."

"I overheard a couple of the detectives talking about something that happened when he worked at the McLean Station, that it was the reason he transferred down here."

"What happened?" I wanted to know.

Reider grew hesitant again. I could tell he knew details, and I wanted to know them, too. Just as he opened his mouth to speak—I hoped to tell me what the big secret was—his radio crackled to life. The 911 emergency center, the dispatcher explained, had just received a call about a body found in Grist Mill Park. All available units were told to respond immediately.

"Shit," Reider said, flinging open the car door. "A body on Monday morning!" Obviously, all thought of what he knew about Dan Magruder had just fled his mind.

"Talk to you later," I told him as he started the patrol car. Reider tossed a wave in my direction, and I turned and ran for my own car, to head to the park as well. Sixty seconds later, as I maneuvered the Bug out into the traffic on Sherwood Hall Lane, I called the *News* to ask for a photographer to meet me at the park and told Ray Holt, an assistant metro editor who worked the early shift, where I was headed.

Within ten minutes, I was pulling into the parking lot at Grist Mill Park, the scene of my recent stop just three days before with the now-late Officer Dan Magruder. Allen Reider was getting out of his cruiser in front of me. A second cruiser already was on the scene, and a third, with two people inside, pulled in right behind me, with a full complement of flashing lights and eardrum-destroying sirens.

At 9:15 in the morning, it was a little early for any neighborhood children to be in the park. But there was a small crowd of adults, several of them accompanied by dogs on leashes, and most of them dressed in comfortable clothes that told me they probably had been out for their morning walks, jogs, or bike rides.

I could see one man at the edge of the group, talking to the first officer, whose back was turned to me. The man clearly was excited or upset, punctuating his remarks with wild arm gestures that kept pulling his gray T-shirt up to reveal his potbelly and jerking the leashed cocker spaniel at his feet off balance. Allen Reider quickly joined the officer to whom the man was telling his story and asked a couple of questions. Reider was talking into his shoulder mike just as I walked up, followed closely by the cop from the third cruiser and his passenger, a young man dressed in the dark blue uniform of the police auxiliary. Reider turned in our direction.

"I'm going with Mike to see what this guy found," he said to the cop behind me, whom I didn't know. Mike was Mike Monroe, the first cop on the scene, who now had turned so that I could see his face. I knew him to say hello to, but I had never dealt with him on a story. He was about Dan Magruder's age, and it was clear that he was happy to defer to Allen Reider's additional years of experience in this particular case.

"We need you to keep everyone out of there while we check it out," Reider was saying to the third officer. He gestured to the auxiliary officer. "You go down the bike path a ways and stop anyone else from coming down here or going into the woods. Phil, can you keep all these people here in the parking lot and off the bike path?"

Phil, the cop who had followed me into the park and who I didn't know at all, said he could. His auxiliary partner started down the bicycle path at a quick jog.

"Allen?" I said, hoping to talk my way as far in as possible.

"Sorry, Sutton, that means you, too," he replied, knowing what my question would be before I could get it out. He turned to follow Monroe and the excited witness, both of whom had started down the bicycle path as well.

I watched for a minute as the three, led by the dog, walked 150 feet or so down the bike path and then stepped off into the woods to their left. Around me, the neighbors were silent for the first few seconds and then broke into concerned conversations with each other.

"I'm Sutton McPhee with the Washington *News*," I said, interrupting them in a voice slightly louder than theirs. "Did any of you hear what that man said to the police, what exactly he saw?"

"That's Harry Watson, dear," said an elderly lady who had long since picked her shiny black Scottie up in her arms to calm him down in the excitement. "He lives just over there on Ferry Landing Road."

"He said he found a dead guy in the woods," added a second woman, who was dogless, forty-fiveish, and dressed in white running shoes, black compression shorts, and a white tank top. "His dog dragged him into the trees to where it was."

"Was he certain the guy was dead?"

"Harry would know," a third neighbor responded, this one an elderly man who was holding onto a red bicycle. "He worked on a morgue detail in Vietnam. Said he knows a dead guy when he smells one."

A pretty good bet then, I thought to myself, that the body Harry had found definitely was dead.

I asked a couple more questions, but no one in the group had anything substantive to add. Like the police, they all had arrived on the scene after Harry had discovered the body, so they knew only what they had overheard Harry tell the police.

I was about ready to walk over and start asking questions of Phil, the cop who was keeping us away from the bike path, when I saw Allen Reider step back onto the path from the woods. Monroe and the witness apparently had stayed with the body.

Good, I thought, *maybe I can get some answers out of Allen now.* That hope died a quick death, however, when I turned at the sound of another car pulling up behind us. This one clearly was an unmarked police sedan, if its hulking gray profile and the forest of antennae that sprouted all over it were any indication. Its driver's side door opened to disgorge Detective Jim Peterson.

"Aw, shit," I muttered to myself as I started in Peterson's direction. Clearly, he had caught the call on this and would be the detective in charge of any investigation. Just as he had been when my sister Cara was murdered. I had not been the most cooperative of relatives during that case, having insisted on conducting an investigation of my own when the police failed to come up with any solid leads in Cara's death. Peterson was a good cop and a pretty straight shooter, but before it was all over and the men who killed my sister were in jail, Peterson was threatening to have me fired or arrested or both. True, I had managed to find the killers when he hadn't, but I also had stepped on a lot of toes in the process, mostly his.

Then Rob Perry had added insult to injury by moving me over to the police beat to cover Peterson and the rest of the Fairfax County Police. It had taken me a large part of the two years since then to defuse most of Peterson's anger and frustration with me, of which he got reminded every time we bashed heads over one of his cases. All things considered, he actually treated me pretty civilly, but he never looked particularly thrilled to see me when I turned up at a murder scene to which he had been sent. Like now.

Peterson reached into the front seat of his car and took out a light brown jacket, as if to put it on over the short-sleeved white shirt and tie he wore, then looked around at the midmorning sunlight, thought better of his decision, and put the jacket back inside the car.

"Morning, Sutton," he said as we met halfway across the parking lot. As usual, he was cordial and professional, at least when he wasn't pissed off at me about some specific transgression.

"Detective Peterson," I responded, reaching out to offer my hand for shaking. He took it in his own much larger one and gave it the firm handshake I had come to expect from him. He was another four to six inches taller than my five-foot-eight, and strong. Even with his thinning brown hair and the extra pounds that had crept up with middle age, everything about him still said that he worked out from time to time. And his temperament and contact with reality were as solid as his physical presence.

"I'll save you some time," Peterson said when he released my hand. "I don't know anything more than you do at this point, so I can't answer any questions until after I see what's in there." He gestured toward the woods behind me.

"Okay, fair enough. I'll wait."

"And would you tell them the same thing?" Peterson said, thumbing his hand toward Mount Vernon Memorial Highway as he started around me to go to where Allen Reider was motioning to him from the end of the bike path.

By "them," Peterson apparently meant the TV remote truck, emblazoned with the Channel 3 logo, that was pulling into the parking lot. My mood sank. It was the vanguard for what I knew would be the imminent arrival of the rest of the local press who covered the police. So much for any chance at prying exclusive information out of Peterson when he returned.

• • •

By the time I saw Peterson again, the usual crime scene circus was in full flower. The patrol cops had draped the areas where the bike path entered and exited the woods in yellow crime scene tape, further reinforcing their orders that no one other than the police was to venture into the woods or down the bike path. Several more of my esteemed colleagues from the press had arrived, including Guy Campbell, the photographer the *News* had sent out, as well as the reporters and crews in two more TV remote trucks, a reporter from the all-news radio station, and reporters from the Washington *Post* and a couple of local weekly papers.

Overhead circled a Fairfax County Police helicopter, recognizable by its dark blue and gray paint job, and just off to the east was a television helicopter from Channel 19. Apparently, the police wouldn't let it fly directly over the crime scene. An increasingly large retinue of neighbors joined all of us in the parking lot, prompting Officer Phil to call on his radio for a couple more officers to provide backup. Clearly, he had no intention of being responsible for letting any of us contaminate the crime scene, and I didn't blame him. I had had to answer to an angry Detective Peterson once or twice. It was no fun.

An additional detective, two crime scene specialists, and the shift supervisor from the Mount Vernon Station also had arrived just after the new batch of cops, but they all had quickly disappeared down the bike path to join Peterson and Reider.

I long since had run out of people to question and had retired to my car, to sit in the shade, when there was a stir in the press ranks. Through the windshield, I saw Mike Monroe walk back into the parking lot with Harry, the witness, and his dog. Right behind them was a grim-looking Peterson. I scrambled around to find my notebook and pen, which had fallen out of my lap and onto the car's floor, so I could go over and ply Peterson with questions. When I finally retrieved them and started to get out of the car, however, I saw that Peterson had been cornered by the rest of the press some yards away. Monroe and the witness, on the other hand, were coming my way, apparently headed for the cruiser two parking spots away from me. Some instinct told me to wait.

Monroe opened the passenger door for Harry, who looked grateful for a chance to get off his feet finally, and then walked around to the driver's side, where he opened his own door and sat down inside the car as well. Immediately, he began a conversation over the radio, on what I guessed was one of the private frequencies, and I could hear every word he said to the person on the other end.

"Peterson wants you to get Bill Russell out here," Monroe said into his mike. "Looks like this guy was high-profile. There's ID with the body that says he's some guy named Robert M. Coleman." Monroe spelled out the last name. "The ID says he's the director of The Phoenix Group, some big charity setup over in Tysons."

Well, that was one way to describe The Phoenix Group, I thought, as I grabbed my cell phone and started dialing the newsroom. I could hear Peterson answering questions from the other reporters, but I knew that, whatever he was telling them, this was more important.

"Metro desk, Ray Holt," the voice in my ear said, cutting the third ring off in the middle.

"Ray, it's Sutton," I said, speaking as softly as I could.

"What have you got, Sutton?"

I told him. With my new digital phone, I didn't worry as much about transmitting sensitive information over the airwaves the way I had when everything was analog and an easy mark for eavesdroppers.

"*Oh-hh-hh* boy," Ray responded, his emphasis on the first word telling me he understood the magnitude of the story. Robert Coleman was a long-time fixture in the power circles of both Washington and northern Virginia. The Phoenix Group was an endowed foundation, started two decades ago to comply with the will of Martin Bird, a multimillionaire bakery magnate who had died without any heirs. The Phoenix Group had proven to have very deep pockets indeed, doling out at least four million dollars a year to community programs, medical research, and a variety of other good causes. Coleman had headed it up for the last ten years or so.

"Is Rob in yet?" I asked Ray. With three failed marriages and two grown daughters to his credit, Rob's life these days centered around his job at the *News*. Actually, not just these days; it always had. That's why he had three failed marriages. Though his workday at the morning paper officially began at midafternoon, it wasn't unusual to find him there well before lunch.

"Haven't seen him," Ray said.

"Find him if you can," I told Ray. "He'll want to know about this because it's big enough for page one. And do me a favor?"

"Sure."

"Call down to the library and ask Cooper to pull up whatever he can find on Coleman. I'll need it for background." Cooper Diggs was the head research librarian and a computer Wunderkind. He could locate and coax out information from the electronic forest better than anyone I knew. His expertise had provided me with critical puzzle pieces for more than one of the bigger stories I had covered, and had even provided a key bit of information in solving Cara's murder.

"Will do."

"Thanks, Ray. I'll be back in touch as soon as I know anything more." Which, I thought as I climbed out of the VW and headed toward Peterson's question-and-answer session, I intended to know as soon as I could get my hands on Peterson outside the hearing of the rest of the press.

6

"No," Peterson was saying when I stepped up to the edge of the group of reporters clustered around him, "we can't give you any sort of ID yet or a cause of death. All I can tell you at this point is that the body is male, definitely dead, and appears to have been dead for a while, at least a day, maybe two or three."

That meant, if you knew how to translate it, that the police might know the identity of the corpse, but they weren't telling yet. That they might or might not know how he died, depending on the state of the body. And that the state of the body probably wasn't too great at this point, given the fact that it had been lying out in the open in the woods in August heat and humidity for one or more days. Decomposition can set in pretty quickly in those circumstances, not to mention what insects and animals can do, making any sort of definitive statement about cause of death a proper topic for the medical examiner, who would be able to speak with authority after conducting an autopsy.

"Was it a homicide?" Beth Bleek from the all-news radio station wanted to know.

'Obviously, we have to treat it as a possible homicide until we know differently," Peterson explained, "until the medical examiner can tell us exactly how the person died."

Peterson had dealt with enough reporters at enough homicide scenes that he wasn't about to get trapped into saying anything that he might have to take back later. But I decided to make him sweat a little, not that we all weren't sweaty enough already. The August sun in Virginia can shine with just as much intensity as the one they have in Florida, even at ten o'clock in the morning.

"Was there any sort of ID with the body, anything to tell you who the guy is?" I asked, now knowing full well there was.

Peterson gave me a hard look, but he still wasn't giving away the store.

"There were some personal effects on the body, but you know we can't release anything until we can confirm that those effects were his and until we reach next of kin." I did know that; I was just having a little fun. Because, of course, the other reporters now began clamoring for a name.

Peterson finally managed to extricate himself from our clutches without saying anything more forthcoming and went over to Monroe's police cruiser, where he spoke briefly with Harry, the former Vietnam morgue jockey who had had the bad luck to find the body. Then Peterson told Monroe to take Harry down to the station where, no doubt, Harry could sit in air-conditioned comfort, free of the press, to wait for one of the investigators to come and take a formal statement from him. Monroe agreed, and Peterson took himself back down the bike path. Apparently, the company of a dead guy was preferable to that of the press.

I knew it would be a while yet before the body would be brought out of the woods. The crime scene would have to be thoroughly documented with the body in place before the victim could be moved. Only then would the two guys I saw pulling up in a medical examiner's van be allowed to take the body away.

I went back to the VW to sit out of the sun's glare again and was making notes to myself on what questions I needed to get answered when my cell phone rang. It was Rob Perry, whom Ray Holt apparently had managed to locate.

"You're not gonna like what I have to tell you about your corpse,"

Rob said without preamble when I pressed the Talk button and said "Hello."

"What?"

"If it really is Robert Coleman, it's definitely a page-one story."

"But why wouldn't I like that?'

"Because I just found out that one of Mark Lester's people has been working for several weeks on a big piece about Coleman." Mark Lester is the national editor who oversees the stories that make it onto the paper's front page. He also manages the investigative team that breaks some of the paper's biggest stories.

"Why are they looking into Coleman?" I wanted to know.

"Because, apparently, he was under investigation by the feds. The IRS and the justice department, for starters. Improper use of The Phoenix Group's money, maybe tax evasion. That kind of stuff."

"Nice guy," I said, "but what's the problem with the national side?"

"The reporter on the story is Sy Berkowitz, and he's on his way out there to meet you now."

"Goddamn it!" I yelled. "He's not taking over this story!"

Sy Berkowitz was one of the least-liked reporters at the paper. He had followed Mark Lester down from a paper in Philadelphia three years before, where he also had worked under Lester's tutelage. He had done some okay investigative pieces since coming to Washington. He also was an unpleasant, obnoxious jerk who treated the other reporters like they were morons and who did his dead-level best to horn in when one of us was onto a story big enough to make it to page one.

I never had much cared for Sy, anyway, just on general principles, but he had gotten onto my permanent shit list three months before, when he tried to take away my stories on the murders of Ann Kane, the Senate aide, and Janet Taylor, the wife of Fairfax County Supervisor Hubbard Taylor. Rob Perry repeatedly had fought off Sy and Mark's attempts to steal the story for Sy, and I had had several unpleasant personal exchanges with Sy as well. He was about the last reporter in the world I wanted to have here covering the same story I was.

"Cool your jets, McPhee," Rob said, trying to sound calming. "He's not taking the story away." I sighed in relief.

"But you are going to have to work together on this."

I should have known there was another shoe to drop. "Why?" I asked, knowing the answer but hoping I could change reality somehow.

"You know why as well as I do. Because Coleman was Sy's story already. But you're the Fairfax County Police reporter, and now it's your story, too, at least until somebody gets charged with killing the guy and the case gets moved into the courts. So make the best of it. And behave yourself!"

"Fine," I said, not hesitating to let Rob hear the sulk in my voice at what I took to be his letting me down.

"And if Berkowitz tries to fuck you over," Rob went on, ignoring my pouting, "I want to hear about it. I'll ream him so many new assholes, he'll spend the rest of his life in the can."

I laughed. I should know Rob better than that, I chided myself. He would expect me to act like a professional and to get the best story possible. But he wouldn't expect me to take any crap off Sy Berkowitz, either.

"Okay, Rob," I told him, "I'll try to be a good girl. But if I've got to work with Sy, it had better be share and share alike. I want to know everything he knows."

"I've already told him and Lester both the same thing," Rob said. "In front of Mack Thompson. I think they got the message." Mack Thompson was the managing editor, and it wasn't the first time he had refereed some fight between Rob and Mark over story ownership.

I turned and looked over my shoulder as I heard another car pull into the parking lot. It was Bill Russell, come to keep the press out of the investigators' hair.

"Gotta go, Rob," I said. "I just found another cop to aggravate."

Rob snorted a laugh and hung up.

Bill Russell turned out to be no more forthcoming than Peterson had been, but I hadn't really expected that he would be. After listening briefly to what he had to say, which was a rerun of Peterson's comments, I decided I should try to confirm for myself that the body really was Robert Coleman, but I didn't want to mention Coleman's name in front of other reporters, who at this point still were completely in the dark about the corpse's identity.

"Does the victim fit the description of any missing persons reports that you have?" I asked, figuring that someone as high-profile as Coleman couldn't just drop out of sight without somebody noticing.

"None that come immediately to mind," Bill said, "but there hasn't been time to go through them that thoroughly, of course."

Bill was dissembling. If a missing person report had been filed on Coleman in the last few days, Bill would have known about it immediately. His answer meant that no one had reported Coleman as missing. Could that be because the dead guy wasn't Coleman after all? Perhaps the body had Coleman's ID on him because he had mugged Coleman at some point and then ended up dead in Grist Mill Park, I thought. I left the press huddle and walked back over to my car.

"Bell Atlantic Mobile Information. May I help you?" a woman's voice said when I dialed 411 on my cell phone.

"I need the listing for The Phoenix Group in Tysons Corner," I told her. I expected I would feel pretty stupid if I stirred everyone up over Coleman being dead only to find out after the fact that he was happily at work in his office.

I dialed the number the telephone company computer gave me and asked the switchboard operator at The Phoenix Group for Robert Coleman's office. As I expected, I got a secretary.

"No," said the woman who identified herself as Kate Barnard, "Mr. Coleman isn't in this morning."

"When are you expecting him?" I asked.

"Actually," she said, "he's a little late. But I haven't heard from him, so I'm sure he'll be in at any moment. Is there a message?"

"No, no message." I thanked her and pressed the Clear button. So Coleman hadn't made it in to work yet, nor had he called in to explain why he wasn't there on time. I called information again and got Coleman's home telephone number.

No, said the female voice who answered the phone at Coleman's house and who identified herself as the housekeeper, Mr. Coleman wasn't at home, either. When I pressed her, she told me that she had just come in to work, having had the weekend off, and she hadn't seen Coleman and didn't know where he was.

Reasonably certain now that it probably was Coleman who lay dead and decomposing in the woods, I turned off the phone. Putting it back into my purse, I started grimly across the parking lot to meet Sy Berkowitz, who had driven up as I was talking to Coleman's housekeeper.

"I can't believe they've saddled me with you on this!" Sy said as he climbed out of his tiny red car. I thought to myself, not for the first time, that it was just about the kind of pseudo-sports car I would expect him to drive. While there was nothing wrong with it, per se, a real sports car would leave it in the dust. And I always thought of it as a red bug, which gave me a chuckle, because in the Deep South, red bugs were what we called the almost microscopic biting red mites that live in moss and on blackberry bushes. I found the parasitic comparison highly amusing and appropriate where Sy was concerned. And no offense to the bugs intended, of course.

"Well, somebody has to tell you how to do your job," I replied sarcastically. And then we went at it, though even we had the good sense to do it in lowered voices.

After a couple of minutes, when we each had gotten enough bile out of our systems to be able to get to work, I told Sy he would have to keep his mouth shut about why he was even there.

"The police aren't releasing a name yet," I explained, "and no one else in the press knows that the cops think it's Coleman. There's no point in tipping our hand to any of them."

Still smarting at the insult of having to work with me, Sy wanted to know what the police were saying and how I knew for sure it was Coleman. So I told him about overhearing Reider talking on the radio and how I had checked Coleman's home and office, only to be told no one knew where he was.

"Maybe he offed himself," Sy speculated. "He was in some pretty hot water."

"It's possible," I agreed. "The police aren't saying anything about how he died, if they can even tell yet. Now, I've told you what I know. It's your turn."

Sy glared at me, obviously not liking the bitter taste that our forced cooperation was leaving in his mouth. Still, he knew better than to disobey Mack Thompson's direct order.

"The feds were about to take Coleman to a grand jury," he offered finally. "They've got him on a long list of numerous counts of fraud, embezzlement, income tax evasion, and apparently even some insider trading on the stock market with money that wasn't his. He's apparently had a pretty free hand with the Phoenix money all this time and has been dipping into it regularly to finance his lifestyle."

"What lifestyle was that?"

"A big house over in Great Falls and condos in Aspen and the Bahamas. A string of girlfriends barely old enough to vote. An antique car collection. A stock portfolio that would make your eyes bug out. And rumors of a numbered offshore bank account somewhere."

"I take it he couldn't have managed all that on his salary?"

"No way," Sy laughed. "And apparently he not only was embezzling money directly from the fund, but he also had a nice little scheme going with the heads of two or three of the organizations that The Phoenix Group gave money to. In return for fat grants to their charities every year, they were using some creative accounting to disguise the kickback payments they were making to Coleman. And in another week or so, it was all going to come tumbling down around him and take him and several of his buddies with it."

"How did the feds get onto what he was doing?"

"The story I hear is that they were putting the squeeze to one of his kickback cronies on something else entirely, and the guy offered up Coleman to them in return for them letting him off more lightly."

"Sounds like Coleman had ample reason to kill himself," I agreed.

"Or one of his other charity pals did it for him," Sy added.

By this time, we had started walking over to where Bill Russell and the rest of the press waited patiently for something more to happen. Sy and I still were eyeing each other warily when the medical examiner's crew came out of the woods, put the bagged body on a stretcher, and wheeled it up the bike path in our direction. Even the bagging, however, couldn't completely hide the odor that came along with it. It wasn't a new experience for me, which didn't make it any easier to bear, but at least I was prepared for it, unlike Sy, several of the other reporters, and all the neighbors and other gawkers who still were standing around.

"Jesus Christ!" Sy said, slapping a hand over his nose and mouth and trying not to gag in front of me. A couple of people in the crowd lacked his self-control and took themselves off to the other side of the barn in a hurry.

Within minutes, the two bearers of the body had it enclosed in the van and were driving out of the parking lot. The odor it had brought didn't dissipate quite as quickly.

"You folks might as well go on back to work," Bill Russell told the press finally, when the weaker stomachs in the group seemed under control again. "This is as close as you're going to get to the crime scene until they're completely finished with it, so there's really nothing more to see here. If you want to stay in touch with me, I'll let you know as soon as we have anything new to tell you."

"He's right," I said to Sy. "If you want to go back, I'll hang around here just to be on the safe side."

"You sure they're not going to come out of the woods and say anything else?" he asked, all his suspicions of me coming back into his eyes.

"Trust me," I told him and immediately realized it was a stupid thing to say. Sy Berkowitz trusted no one because he was so untrustworthy himself.

"The detectives won't say anything before they absolutely have to," I explained. Well, that part was true. What also was true but which I felt no compulsion to explain to Sy was that, sometimes, I could make the police have to a little sooner than they had planned.

I called over to Guy Campbell, our photographer, who had taken himself to a small patch of shade at the edge of the trees. "Can you stay to get pictures of the scene once they pack up?" I asked him. There would be little to see at that point. Still, better to have photos of a spot in the woods and not use them than to have some editor ask for them and have to say we hadn't gotten them.

"Yeah, as long as they don't page me from the paper to go to something more pressing," Guy answered.

"Okay," Sy agreed, apparently deciding I was right. "I'll go back and get started on the writing. When you get back, you can fill in anything else you have." And, no doubt, play a definite second fiddle, if he had anything to say about it. But it was an argument we could have when the time came, which wasn't now.

"Sounds good," I said. "I should be there soon." *To stand over your shoulder and watch every word you write,* I added in my head but didn't say out loud. Sy turned and strode off to his little red toy, and I went over to where Bill Russell had sat down on the grass to wait and joined him.

"Who was that?" Bill wanted to know. He didn't miss much. He had seen Sy walk up to me and the two of us talking.

"He's a reporter at the *News.* We're working on a story together, and we needed to compare some notes." Well, it was the truth. I just didn't tell Bill it was this story. He would find out soon enough, like this afternoon or, at the latest, when tomorrow morning's paper came out.

He was giving me the evil eye, that look I get from him when he thinks I know more than I'm telling, when Peterson walked up from the bike path.

"All done?" Bill asked.

"Not yet," Peterson said. "We're going to get some more people in here to give the woods a good going over to make sure we haven't missed anything. But I've got stuff to go check on, so I'm heading out."

"I might as well get back up to Fairfax," Bill said, standing up and brushing the grass and dust off his pants. "My phone probably is already ringing off the hook."

The two of them took their leave from me, and I joined the remaining two reporters in walking over to the parking lot. Instead of driving away, however, I waited in the Bug for a couple of minutes and then dialed the number for Peterson's pager, a number I had gotten when he was investigating my sister's murder and one I had put to good use several times in the two years since. He called me back from his car phone.

"It's Sutton," I said, when he rang me back and identified himself.

"I haven't learned anything new in the two minutes since I last saw you," Peterson said pointedly.

"My question is about what you already know," I replied, refusing to be baited.

"What do you need?" Peterson asked tiredly, apparently expecting to have to rehash everything he already had told the press.

"I need to know if Robert Coleman was murdered or committed suicide."

"Goddamn it!" he interjected angrily. "Who told you it's Coleman?"

"Nobody told me, although you just confirmed it. Let's just say I had my ear to the ground and heard a rumor that it might be him. Now, how did he die, and will you confirm his identity? And am I going to look like an ass if I say in print that it's Coleman?"

Peterson thought about it for a while.

"No," he said finally, apparently deciding it wasn't a battle worth fighting, "you won't look like an ass. If you don't quote me, you can say we've tentatively identified it as Coleman, based on effects found on the body and by matching the driver's license photo with certain physical characteristics. He has a white streak in his hair that's pretty distinctive."

"How did he die?"

"You promise to keep my name out of this story?"

"Yes, you're now an anonymous police source."

"The body's a little rough, but I'm guessing that he was shot in the heart. Probably died in seconds. There was no sign of a gun anywhere, so we're assuming it's a homicide."

I jotted his statements down in my notebook.

"You finished with me, yet?" Peterson wanted to know.

"No, now I have something to give you in return."

"Well, that's a switch," he observed dryly. "What is it?"

"You have to promise this doesn't get out to the rest of the press before tomorrow."

"Fine, fine. Now what?"

"Tomorrow's story will say that a federal grand jury was about to be convened to indict Coleman for a long list of illegal things he apparently has been doing with The Phoenix Group's money. That ought to give you some interesting ideas about homicide suspects. And as soon as they know who the corpse is, the feds probably will be all over your case, too. So get ready."

"Well isn't that just my damned luck?" Peterson said. "As if having you on my back wasn't enough."

"Okay, so we'll talk again soon."

"Sutton?"

"Yes?"

"Thanks for the heads-up."

"I just thought you ought to know."

I turned off the phone and got back out of my car. There was one more thing I had to do before leaving. Officer Allen Reider still had information I needed, and he was coming across the parking lot to his cruiser.

"You have a second?" I asked when I intercepted him just as he reached his car and was brushing from his dark uniform pants all the dust and bits of brush and grass that his treks into the woods had left there.

"Just about," he replied. He looked pretty enervated, probably the result of a combination of the heat and humidity and of having to stand around for a couple of hours with a decomposing body.

"What did Dan Magruder do that got him transferred to the Mount Vernon Station, that you think might have gotten him killed?"

It was clear that Reider had long since put Dan Magruder out of his mind. It took him a few seconds to switch mental gears back to our previous conversation from the morning. At first, I thought he might not tell me, but like Peterson before him, he apparently decided he was too tired to argue with me about what he knew or didn't know.

"He turned in a couple of other officers at the McLean Station for stealing part of the money they recovered in a drug bust."

"What?"

"Magruder was one of the patrol officers who responded when some kind of drug buy between a couple of groups of thugs went bad and ended up with bullets flying," Reider explained. "He knew there was money recovered, so when he saw the incident report that the officers who got there first had filed and then one of the suspects told him the amount had been higher than what was in the report, Magruder went to the station commander and IA with it." IA is internal affairs, the office responsible for investigating cops who decide that one law or another doesn't apply to them.

"He did the right thing," Reider went on, "but it apparently didn't set well with the officers he turned in and their friends. When word leaked out about how IA got onto them, Magruder even got some anonymous death threats. So it was recommended that he request transfer to another part of the county, and Mount Vernon was about as far away as he could get."

"Were the threats serious or just intended to scare him?"

"The guys in IA and his station commander thought they were serious enough to move him down here."

"What happened to the two cops who stole the drug money?" I wanted to know.

"They agreed to return the money to stay out of jail themselves, but they both were fired. They lost all their benefits and pension rights, and they can forget ever working as cops again."

"Where are they now?" I wondered if either had an alibi for the time Magruder was being murdered. I also was wondering how I had managed to miss Magruder's involvement in the story when it had happened. I had done a brief item at the time about the firings, but I had assumed, and no one with the police department had bothered to correct my assumption, that Internal Affairs already had been investigating the two men because of something suspicious in their behavior. Instead, I was now learning, they had been turned in by another officer at the scene: Dan Magruder. I gave myself several mental clouts because I had learned long ago, through pointed lectures from Rob Perry, never to assume I knew anything when checking out a story.

"Beats me," Reider said.

So Magruder might have been killed by another cop. Or an ex-cop, anyway. Would that explain how the killer had gotten into Magruder's apartment without breaking in? Because Magruder had opened the door to someone he knew, even if it was someone who carried a grudge? And a gun?

I ran the possible scenarios around my brain on the drive back up the George Washington Parkway and into Washington. I had to get back and stake my claim to the story on Robert Coleman's murder, but some time during the afternoon, I also was going to have to make time to put in a call to Noah Lansing, in his role as police detective, and give him a grilling about Dan Magruder's past run-in with his fellow officers. No wonder the police department didn't want to talk about who might have had a reason to kill Magruder. The guys at the top of the list were a couple of their own.

7

Sy Berkowitz had an audience, but he wasn't thrilled about it. Mark Lester, Rob Perry, and I all stood and looked over his shoulders as he finished writing his version of what we knew about Robert Coleman. I was biting my bottom lip hard to keep my mouth shut, based on the warning look I had gotten from Rob the one time I started to point out something Sy had left out. I knew Rob's look; it said for me to shut up and let him handle it.

"Okay," Rob said when Sy stopped typing and read over the last couple of paragraphs he had written, "if you're done for the moment, ship a copy over to Sutton's queue and let her take a stab at anything else it may need from the police angle. Then Mark and I will go over that version together to see what we think." He looked up at Mark as if asking for agreement. I saw Mark nod his head affirmatively.

I turned and started back to the stairs to go down to the metro newsroom on the third floor.

"I'll come back up as soon as Sutton's done," I heard Rob tell Lester, and then he was right behind me on my way out the national newsroom door.

"What I saw of his story didn't look too bad," Rob told me as we walked down the stairs. "It didn't sound like he was trying to take all the credit for the story, but you'll have some blanks to fill in and some tweaking to do in places."

"It'll be fine," I agreed. "I can handle the police end of it, and

Cooper gave me copies of the information he had pulled on Coleman when Sy first started looking into him." I wanted to reassure Rob that my ego wouldn't be the stumbling block that Sy's usually was. And as long as I had Rob in my corner to go to bat for me with Mack Thompson, I knew Sy and Mark probably would behave themselves, more or less. They had lost more than one fight with Rob in the past; they were a little more wary of him these days.

Rob was right. Sy's version wasn't too terribly lopsided in his own favor, probably because he had known Rob was watching him write most of it. I added the information that I thought it needed from the police investigation, including Peterson's anonymous information about Coleman dying from a gunshot to the heart, and fiddled around a little with the lead paragraph and a few of the others.

When I was satisfied with it, I put in a call to Bill Russell and a page to Peterson to check on any new developments. But things were about where we all had left them in Grist Mill Park. I saved the final version of the story and transmitted copies to Rob and Mark. Then I called across the newsroom to Rob to let him know the story was in his computer queue. He opened the file, rapidly scanned through the new version, gave me a thumbs up, and got up to trek back upstairs to Mark Lester's office. I picked up the phone and paged Noah Lansing, thumbing through my clip files for a copy of the story on the McLean police firings while I waited for Lansing to call me.

"When can we have dinner again?" Lansing asked when I answered the phone.

"We can discuss it later," I told him. "But right now, I'm calling about the Magruder shooting, and you'll probably be mad at me again by the time we're finished with that."

I heard Lansing sigh.

"You're never going to make this easy, are you?" he asked.

"Probably not," I agreed, remembering how my relationship with the assistant principal in Albany had ended. I was the education reporter at the Albany paper, and things had turned very ugly when I had to interview my lover for an investigative piece on financial irregularities at the school where he worked. I had ended up with no relationship, an angry and bitter ex-boyfriend, and a stern lecture from my city editor about the folly of mixing work with pleasure.

And apparently you still didn't learn anything, did you? a little voice whispered in my ear. I swatted it away with my free hand.

Lansing sighed again. I didn't think I liked whatever that sigh meant.

"What do you want to know?" he asked, back now in his role as police detective.

"I need to know if it was Dan Magruder who got those two cops fired in McLean last year. And if it was, are they still in the area, and do they have alibis for the time when Magruder was shot?"

"If you know that much, then you know that was an Internal Affairs matter, and I can't comment on what happened then. As for now, all I can say is that we are checking out anyone who might have had a reason to try to harm Magruder."

Clearly, I was going to have to play dentist and start pulling teeth.

"All right," I told Lansing, "let's try it this way." I looked at the story clipping in my hand. "Have you questioned Ed Monk and Terry Porter in the death of Dan Magruder?''

"Yes, we've interviewed them, among other people."

"Do they still live in the area?"

"Monk does. Porter lives in Austin, Texas, now."

"Is either of them a suspect in Magruder's murder, or have you ruled either of them out as a suspect?"

"Monk has provided us with reliable witnesses that he was in New Hampshire attending a family wedding during that time. He says he also can give us photos and videotape if necessary."

"What about Porter?"

"All I can say is that Porter has told us he was at home in Austin, having called in sick at his job with a security firm that day."

"So, you're telling me he hasn't given you a convincing alibi yet, no eyewitness to place him at home instead of catching a plane to D.C.?"

"I'm telling you that we're still looking into Porter's whereabouts."

"You're being coy again, Lansing."

"It comes with the job, McPhee," he replied. He sounded frustrated, and I sure as hell was.

"Okay, can we go off the record here for a minute?" I asked, trying to get at what I needed some other way.

"Ask your question, and then I'll decide," Lansing said.

Now it was my turn to sigh loudly.

"If I can also get it from someone else, will you confirm all this off the record for me? That it was Magruder who turned Monk and Porter in. That he received death threats afterward and transferred to the Mount Vernon station at that time. That Porter is still a suspect in the shooting."

"Okay, get it from a second source, but yes to all of it but the last thing. At this point, let's just say we're still talking to Porter, that we haven't ruled him out as a possible suspect."

Well, that was progress, at least.

"Thank you," I told him, trying to sound appreciative. Giving birth probably would have been easier, but at least he had confirmed that I was looking in the right direction.

"Hey, McPhee," someone shouted. I looked up to see Curt Driver, one of the assistant metro editors, holding his telephone receiver and pointing it at me. "Rob says to get off your damned phone and go upstairs."

"I'll be right there," I called back to Curt. Then I told Lansing I had to go.

"Think about dinner," he said.

"Okay," I agreed, finding myself hoping that our situation wasn't completely impossible after all.

Upstairs, Sy was making a last-minute pitch to separate our stories, to have one about the discovery of Coleman's body, under my byline, and a much longer one about the federal investigation under his. Rob Perry wasn't buying it, and for once Mark Lester was agreeing with him.

"I don't want to hear it, Sy," Lester was saying to him. "There's no reason to make it two stories, especially if there's any reason to think it was the investigation that might have gotten Coleman killed."

Rob gave me another stay-quiet look. If Lester was doing our job for us, there was no reason for me to put in my two cents' worth, it said. I obeyed.

"But Mark, how am I supposed to—" Sy started in again.

"Enough," Lester said, cutting him off abruptly. "We're going with what we have."

Sy's face colored, turning a sort of strangled red and purple, but he shut up. Then he announced he needed a cup of coffee and walked out of the newsroom without asking if we'd like some, too.

Better call the Post *and report him to Miss Manners.*

Even she couldn't salvage him, I thought back as I followed Rob back down to the metro floor, using the time to tell him that I also would be giving him a follow-up on the Magruder story as soon as I could make a couple more phone calls.

"It's six o'clock," he said, looking at his watch. "You've got half an hour." Our first deadline was at seven.

I tried calling Todd White, the guy who heads up the Internal Affairs section for the Fairfax County Police, but he was nowhere to be found. So I called Bill Russell again. I knew that he knew the full story on Porter and Monk. Maybe I could pry something out of him.

We did the same little dance that I had gone through with Lansing, but eventually I got him to confirm, also anonymously, what Lansing had told me off the record.

"And although I don't have time to get into a discussion about it at the moment," I told Bill when he finished, "don't think that you're getting off so easy here."

"What are you talking about?" he asked.

"Just because I missed it the first time around doesn't mean I haven't now figured out that you kept the real story about the firings to yourself when they happened," I said. "Now, I look bad. There will be a day of reckoning."

"I don't doubt it for a minute," Bill said, laughing. "I think I should go on vacation just about now."

Okay, I said to myself when I got off the phone with Bill and cleared my computer screen to write the story, *I can't attribute it to anybody by name, but at least he and Lansing both are saying that what Reider told me is right. So now I've got it from three different people. I can call them reliable police sources, at least.*

I decided I would have to be content with that for the time being. I turned to my computer and opened a new file to write the Magruder follow-up for the next morning's paper.

8

TUESDAY

I was deep into that dreamless state of sleep in which even identity is lost when the roar of the explosion ripped into the predawn stillness outside my apartment building. In one instinctive motion of self-preservation, I went from lying on my bed to standing beside it, trembling from the fright my heart had received from the as-yet-unidentified noise. But I still needed a couple of seconds to access the corner of my brain that knew who and where I was.

Finally oriented but with my heart still pounding, I looked around my bedroom to try to locate the source of the horrific sound that had awakened me. The clock beside my bed said 4:12 A.M. Seeing nothing, I went across the hall into the spare bedroom and looked out the window that faced onto the building's parking lot. Below me, a fire burned furiously in the far corner of the lot where I had parked the Beetle the night before. The fear came back in full force and started squeezing everything in my chest.

"Oh God," I breathed out loud. "Oh my God!" The fear told me what it was I was looking at.

I turned and ran back into my bedroom to slip on a pair of loafers. There was no need, and no time, to worry about putting anything over the gray sweat clothes that I used for pajamas. Nor did I take the time to do anything else about the way I looked. With my hair falling loose around my face, I literally ran out of the apartment, pausing only to scoop up my keys from the small ebony Chinese chest that sat just inside my front door.

Other residents already were standing at the elevators ahead of me, a couple in their nightclothes and a third man in a pair of jeans and flip-flops but with no shirt, waiting in agitated conversation for one of the four elevator cars to arrive. Guessing that every floor in the building now had a similar group of passengers pressing the Down buttons, I headed for the fire stairs instead. The fourteen floors of landings and 180-degree turns in the stairs seemed endless as I pounded steadily down, but finally I reached the fire door at the bottom that opened out onto the parking lot itself. I threw open the door, letting in the night air and the sound of sirens on the fire trucks that were already coming this way from the fire station two blocks up Paxton Street.

As the exit door crashed closed behind me, I hurried out to join the other residents who already had managed to make it outside to find out what had happened. They instinctively stopped at a point that was close enough to see but not close enough to worry about being injured. I pushed my way through to the front of the rapidly growing crowd, their questions and exclamations to each other filling the air around me. But I consciously heard none of them.

Some fifty feet away, in the last parking space near the tall, gray-painted metal fence that marked the western edge of the lot, was the already skeletal outline of the Beetle, flames still leaping from its body, smelling of gasoline and burnt synthetic fabric, mixed with whiffs of another, even less pleasant smell, all drifting toward me on a ribbon of smoke. A second car, which had been parked next to the Beetle, had burning seat covers, shattered windows and windshields. The warped and blackened hood of the VW sat on top of the second car's own hood. On the driver's side of that car was an empty parking space. In the adjacent space to that one, an obviously frightened but quick-thinking owner was backing his car—sans windows—out of its space and out of the reach of the fire.

I had thought I knew what I was going to see. What I wasn't

prepared for, however, was the body I saw, lying crumpled at the bottom of the fence against which it had been thrown, its shredded clothes still smoking, one leg folded underneath at an unnatural angle, the other leg nowhere in sight. A man in a navy blue bathrobe, apparently another resident of the building, was rising to a standing position and shaking his head, having knelt down to check the body for a pulse or any other sign of life. Clearly, there was none. As the fire trucks—three of them at least—and two ambulances roared up to the end of the parking lot where we all stood, I turned my back on the scene in front of me and grabbed the side of a nearby car while I threw up the remains of my dinner from the night before.

The sun was fully up and promising a beautiful day ahead. Numbly, I sat in the backseat of an Alexandria police cruiser and looked at the remains of the chaos that had erupted almost three hours before. All the cars near mine—or, I should say, what was left of mine—had been moved, giving me a clear view of the carnage the explosion had wrought. The body—a male, the police had said—was now covered by a tarp. A few feet away, a second tarp covered the missing leg that someone had located. All but one of the fire trucks had left on other calls, the remaining one staying behind to make certain there was no further danger from the fire.

Most of the building's residents had left the parking lot in ones and twos and now were returning the same way to go to their own cars or to the bus stop down the street to leave for work. Police officers posted at each of the building's exits checked the residents' names off master lists provided by the rental office in an effort to identify the body or at least to say who it wasn't.

The crowd now in the parking lot was made up of Alexandria police, both uniformed officers and detectives, as well as a couple of guys who had introduced themselves as investigators from the fire department and several men in street clothes and dark blue jackets that said ATF in capital letters across the back. The latter were from the federal Bureau of Alcohol, Tobacco, and Firearms. An Alexandria detective had explained that, without its own bomb squad, the police department relied on the ATF to handle the forensics—the collection and analysis of physical evidence—any time Alexandria had a case that involved a bomb or some other type of explosive.

There also was the usual contingent of reporters from every news medium, some of whom I recognized, some of whom I didn't. And to none of whom I was talking, except for a very brief conversation with Penny James, the *News* reporter who covered the Alexandria police. She had been dispatched to the scene by Rob Perry when I had called him at home, once I had finished throwing up in the parking lot and before the police had gotten organized enough to find out who owned the demolished car. Even with the shock of seeing the body lying next to my poor car, I still had had the presence of mind not to allow Rob to be uninformed any longer than necessary or to let my own paper get beaten out by the competition.

I had identified myself to the cops as the owner of the VW once I got off the phone with Rob. Which meant that, when Penny got there half an hour later, I had to argue with the police, who already were grilling me, to have a few minutes alone with her. Since then, investigators from each of the law enforcement groups had been back and forth several times to ask me questions. The raised eyebrows when they learned what I do for a living and the looks that passed between the police detectives and the ATF agents just confirmed what I had known instantly in my gut when I looked out my window and saw my car on fire: that it was my car and not the one next to it that had exploded and that it had not exploded on its own. Someone had caused it to blow up, someone who really, really wanted me dead.

The question at the moment was whether it was that someone whose body lay under the tarp, literally a victim of his own device, or whether the body belonged instead to some unwitting passerby who had been caught in the explosion somehow. A stranger whose charred face, which the police had asked me to look at in an unproductive effort at identification, was now a permanent image in my still-reeling brain.

"Ms. McPhee?" I groaned as I opened my eyes and raised my head from the back of the cruiser's seat. One of the police detectives, whose last name I now knew was Moore but whose first name had escaped me, was standing beside my open door. No more questions, I thought. Give me some answers.

"Yes?"

"We don't think there's anything more you can do here," Detective Moore said. "If you have no objection, I'm going to take you down to headquarters to get an official statement from you."

In spite of his polite words and tone of voice, I knew that it was more than a request.

"Fine," I said. "Whatever you need." Putting it off wasn't going to make it any easier or more appealing later.

"We appreciate your cooperation," Moore told me. He closed my door and opened the driver's door. "Hey, Perez! Let's go," he called out to someone across the parking lot, and then sat down in the car and started the engine.

Within a few seconds, a woman in a dark brown suit, who I had noticed in the parking lot but who I hadn't met, walked up to the passenger's side of the car and opened the front door. She slid in, closed the door behind her, and turned to look at me in the backseat.

"Hi," she said as Moore put the car in gear, her smile seemingly genuine and lighting up her dark brown eyes. Her jet black hair was cut short, its glossy strands tucked behind her ears. "I'm Detective Reya Perez."

I acknowledged her introduction with one of my own, but I was too tired to offer much in the way of a smile in return. Her eyes said she understood, and then she turned to look at Moore as he pulled out of the parking lot and took a right onto Holmes Run Parkway.

"I thought we'd go ahead and get her statement down for the record while these guys finish up here," Moore said. "One of the ATF guys is going to meet us there to stay abreast of things as well." Perez nodded in agreement.

The rest of the trip to Mill Road, where the Alexandria Police Department headquarters is located, took place in silence.

"But I can't do my job if I've got a cop tagging along everywhere I go," I protested, looking back and forth from Perez to Moore, who sat across from me at the end of a small conference table.

My statement, such as it was, was now an official part of the case file. I had told Moore and Perez, truthfully, that I wasn't working on anything that should have put me at such tremendous personal risk. True, two of the stories I was following were murders, but I had no personal connection to either of those cases. There was nothing about them that should have represented any sort of danger to me. I also had gone over my activities and schedule from the previous day and had reiterated my inability to identify the body that lay, burned and torn, a few feet from my car. I was waiting to sign the written statement that was being typed somewhere down the hall and of which Gary Phillips, the ATF agent, had gone to wait for copies, when Moore had broached the subject of putting an officer with me for a few days as a safeguard. To say the least, the idea didn't set well with me.

"Well, you can't do your job if whoever wants you dead is more successful next time, either," Moore pointed out in response to my negative reaction. "We don't know whose body that is. If it wasn't the person who rigged your car, then whoever did is still out there somewhere, and he'll try to get at you again." There was some truth to what he said, I had to admit to myself, but that didn't make his plan any more palatable.

"How do you know someone tried to kill me?" I asked. "Maybe something mechanical caused the car to blow up. It's more than twenty years old, you know. Things go wrong. Parts wear out." I didn't believe it for a minute, but if it helped convince Moore that I didn't need a baby-sitter, then I would let him think I did.

"The ATF guys say their initial reaction is that it looks like dynamite," Moore replied patiently. "I assume that '76 VWs didn't come equipped with that as a standard item."

I sighed, knowing I probably was defeated, at least temporarily.

"Maybe the dead guy was the one who planted the bomb," I said hopefully. "He can't very well try to kill me again."

"It's a possibility," Moore agreed. "But what if he had a partner, someone else who isn't dead? And I have to tell you that from the looks of the body, I'd say the dead guy was just a kid. Most likely, he was trying to hot-wire your car or steal something from it, and he set off the dynamite in the process. The building manager says there have been several cars broken into in the last couple of weeks. Chances are this guy was responsible. This morning, he just happened to pick the wrong car."

"You're going to stick me with a bodyguard whether I want one or not, aren't you?"

"We can't force somebody on you, but I can't advise you strongly enough to agree. How about if we take it a day at a time? You agree to let us send someone home with you for now, and tomorrow we'll see where the investigation is."

So I rode back to the apartment building with Officer John Baillin, who was walking closely behind me a few minutes later when I entered the chromed-and-mirrored lobby and saw Noah Lansing sitting there. Seeing me come in, Lansing stood up, concern evident on his face.

"Are you okay?" he asked, coming forward to meet me at the top of the interior steps that led up to the lobby's main level.

"What are you doing here?" I asked back, ignoring his question. He was about the last person I wanted to see at the moment and under the circumstances. And we weren't in Fairfax County.

"A detective Perez called one of our investigators to ask questions about you and what you've been covering," Lansing said, looking a little taken aback at the tone of my voice. "Our guy called Bill Russell, figuring he needed to know about it, and Bill called me. I came over to make sure you were all right."

"Why would Bill call you?" I asked in irritation, which was made more pronounced when it dawned on me what I must look like at the moment, given that I had gone with the Alexandria police without even going back upstairs to change clothes or brush my hair. "It's not your case or even your jurisdiction," I pointed out.

Lansing started to answer, then paused, apparently to consider his words carefully in view of the reception he had just gotten from me.

"I suppose he thought I would be interested anyway in what happened to you," he said.

The thought that Bill Russell already had figured out there was something going on between Lansing and me, and that the two of them thought I needed checking on just pissed me off even more. It would be a gross understatement to say that I don't react graciously when something makes me feel vulnerable or when I think someone else perceives me as being unable to take care of myself. As the initial shock of the morning's events had worn off, I had gradually become angrier and angrier at the unknown person who had tried to kill me, who had made me feel less than competent to watch my own back. Detective Moore's insistence on a protective escort had added fuel to the fire. Lansing had just stoked it several degrees hotter.

"Well, why don't you just tag along with my other knight in shining armor here," I said sarcastically, gesturing toward Officer Baillin. "Apparently, all of you think I'm just some helpless woman who needs a bunch of men around to make sure she's safe."

With that, I stomped off to the elevators and tried to push the Up button out through the other side of the wall. Behind me, I could feel Lansing and Baillin looking from me to each other and wondering what they had done to piss me off. Both joined me in the elevator when the doors slid open, however, and the three of us rode in silence up to the fourteenth floor.

At my door, Baillin insisted I stand in the hall with Lansing while he checked out my apartment to make sure there were no killers lurking around who had been stupid enough to go inside while police had been running around everywhere.

It's only common sense, my niggling little voice pointed out, apparently having decided that Officer Baillin needed defending from me. It did nothing to improve my mood.

"All clear," Baillin said when he reappeared in my living room. Lansing and I stepped inside. Baillin walked past us, into the hallway. "I'll be on duty out here," he explained.

I gave him another angry look and walked over to get one of my dining room chairs, which I carried back out into the hall.

"At least sit down, for God's sake," I told him, putting the chair down at his feet. "And if you need to use the bathroom, you're welcome to use mine!"

Baillin colored slightly at that, but thanked me for the offer.

His manners are sure better than yours, my personal critic observed dryly.

I closed the apartment door to cut off its annoying voice and turned to deal with Lansing.

"If you're just here to tell me I need a bodyguard," I said to him, "you can go back to work! I've already had that lecture several times over from the Alexandria police."

"McPhee," he said, grasping my arms with both hands.

"What?" My mood wasn't getting any better.

"Would you please just shut up for once?"

To ensure that I did, he immediately pulled me to him and kissed me. I wanted to hit him, but since I couldn't easily do that with my arms in captivity, I kissed him back instead.

You are so easy.

And you are so not welcome here, I thought back.

Lansing let go my arms and put his own around me, continuing to kiss me all the while. I found myself responding in kind and holding onto him as if he were a life raft. Finally, he raised his face from mine.

"Well?" he asked, looking at me. "Surely you must have something to say to that."

I shook my head from side to side and then put my face down against his chest, thinking, *Don't let me go yet.* My defenses had momentarily disappeared with his embrace, and I just wanted to sink into him, to spend a few minutes someplace where I didn't have to worry about who wanted me dead.

"I think we ought to sit down," Lansing said into my hair, his voice carrying over the beating of his heart that I could hear clearly in his chest. "You've had a rough morning."

I raised my head and looked at him. "What I'd really like to do is go to sleep," I said, having just realized that it was so.

I had gone to bed at one A.M. and had been awakened three hours later by the explosion. It was now almost noon, and I had been dealing all that time with the shock of what had happened, with the constant questions from the police, and with my own reaction to the attempt on my life. I was no longer numb, but as the reality of the morning's events was seeping into my brain, I realized I was exhausted and becoming more so by the minute. The practical part of my mind knew that there were things I had to do: call Rob Perry again to keep him updated, call my car insurance agent with the bad news, arrange for a rental car so I could get back and forth to work. But the rest of my brain was saying that, except for the call to Rob, it all could wait a couple of hours.

"That's probably a good idea," Lansing said, looking at me

assessingly. His expression said he wasn't pleased with whatever he was seeing in my face. "Would you like me to stay?"

Would he never learn?

"I'm not three years old," I answered, my irritation flaring again. "You don't have to sit by my bed and hold my hand. I just need a nap. And I already have one armed cop sitting outside my door!"

Lansing thought about it for a minute.

"Okay," he agreed finally. "I need to get back to work, anyway. But I'll go only under one condition."

"Which is?"

"At six o'clock, I'll be back here to pick you up. You're coming home with me. I don't want you here alone tonight, guard or no guard."

"What?" It takes a lot to surprise me, but that certainly managed to do it.

"Not just for your safety," he was quick to reassure me, "even considering how little you regard that. I also don't think you ought to be by yourself tonight. Do you really think you're so superhuman that what you've seen and dealt with this morning isn't going to hit you all over again once the shock wears off?"

It was clear that we could argue about this all day without either of us budging an inch, but I was getting more tired by the minute. I really just wanted to find my bed. Alone. I gave in, though not good-naturedly.

"Fine," I said, conceding the battle. "I'll go. But just for tonight and just to get you out of here."

I fully expected to see the smug expression of victory on Lansing's face, but he continued to surprise me.

"Okay," he said simply, his expression neutral. "I'll be here at six. I'll come upstairs to get you."

Once more, he put his arms around me and kissed me. Then he was gone. Still feeling his lips on mine, I stumbled off to the bedroom to call Rob Perry and then to find short-term oblivion.

9

When my alarm clock went off and called me back from frightening dreams of bombs and dead bodies, I washed my face in cold water and then called my insurance agent to tell him my car was scrap metal.

After expressing his initial shock at my news, he congratulated me on having had the foresight to pay the extra premium for comprehensive coverage that would cover even someone having blown up my car. I couldn't steel myself to ask him whether I would ever be able to afford—or even get—such coverage again, from any insurance company, once they learned that people wanted to kill me.

When he had all the information he needed from me, including Detective Moore's name and number so he could get a copy of the police report, he gave me the phone number for the rental car company I needed to use to ensure reimbursement. I called them next.

I was hanging up from the conversation with the rental car company when my doorbell rang. I glanced at the clock by my bed. It was 4:45 in the afternoon. Lansing would be here in slightly more than an hour. My earlier exhaustion had enabled me to drop off into a deep sleep for a couple of hours, though not untroubled by images from the morning's carnage, and I now was feeling a little more clearheaded and alert. I got up from my seat on the bed and went into the living room and foyer to answer the door. It was Vance Ellert, the building's manager.

"Hi, Sutton," he said when I opened the door. He was putting his wallet back into his back trouser pocket, apparently having had to identify himself to Officer Baillin's satisfaction. "May I come in?"

I stepped back into the foyer and held the door open for him.

"Please sit down," I said, closing the door and motioning over to the sofa and club chairs in my living room. I had seen him in the parking lot all through the morning's insanity, his red hair atop his six-foot-six frame easily visible in the crowd, but between his conversations with the investigators and my own, I had spoken to him only once, when he had come over to where I stood near my smoking car to make certain I was okay. Now, Vance thanked me and walked over to take a seat on the sofa. I joined him in a facing chair.

"Other than my having a really bad day, what's up?" I asked. Clearly something was, judging by the anxious expression he wore.

He crossed and uncrossed his long legs, then swallowed hard a couple of times before finding the words he wanted.

"Ah... Sutton," he began. "Ah... this isn't easy to tell you. But because of what happened this morning, the building's owner has decided that your living here presents a danger for the rest of the tenants." He reached up for a sheaf of folded papers protruding from the left breast pocket of his white sport shirt. "This is an eviction notice. You have ten days to move out." He held the papers out to me.

I looked at them for a moment as if they were a snake, then finally put my hand out to take them. Vance wasn't joking, I saw as I opened them and glanced at the first page. They clearly were eviction papers.

"Why?" I asked him, looking back up.

"I tried to talk her out of it," Vance said quickly, wanting me to know that this wasn't his idea. "But she said that if you have a job that makes people want to kill you, she doesn't want you living in her building. She said the bomb this morning could have killed a lot of people and that even one was bad enough. I couldn't change her mind. I'm sorry."

All things considered, I supposed I actually could see her point.

If the car bomb had exploded a couple of hours later, as I started the car to go to work, it would have happened in a parking lot full of other people leaving at the same time. Though he had died for it, the young man who apparently had tried to steal my car at four o'clock in the morning probably had prevented a far worse outcome. I knew that I could challenge the eviction in court and probably delay my ejection from the building by several months, if not completely.

"Why only ten days?" I asked. "I thought the lease required thirty days' notice."

"Ordinarily, yes," Vance explained. "But if you go back and read it, you'll see that, if a tenant represents a safety risk to the other tenants, we don't even have to give you ten days. You actually could have been evicted effective immediately. I managed to convince her to give you time to find a new place."

Oh, what the hell was the point in arguing, I thought.

"It's okay," I told Vance finally. "I appreciate your going to bat for me. Tell your boss I'll be gone within ten days." Although where I would go, I had no idea.

"Thanks for understanding, Sutton," Vance said, standing up from the sofa, the glum look on his face echoed by my own. "And I really am sorry."

Beginning to understand a little of how Job must have felt, I showed Vance out and then walked back over to where he had sat on the sofa. Sitting down myself, I stared for a while out the expanse of windows on my apartment's west wall, my thoughts chaotic and nonproductive. *First my car and a dead guy, and now this*, I thought, feeling depression threatening to settle heavily over me. What on earth could I possibly have done to have brought all this down on my head, I wondered. To whom did I represent such a threat? Was this job really worth putting my life and others' at risk? One young man already was dead because of me. Granted, he might not have been a completely innocent bystander, but he certainly didn't deserve to be blown to bits for trying to steal a car. My funk deepened.

I know how you love self-pity, my self-appointed mentor took that moment to offer, *but hadn't you better postpone it long enough to go pack your bag before Romeo gets here? And let the cops know they can call off your bodyguard for the night?*

"Shit!" I said into the empty room. The little bugger was right. I had forgotten to call Detective Moore and tell him where I would be going so he wouldn't send a relief officer over for Baillin. I dug into the pocket of my sweatpants for the business card Moore had given me that morning—which said his first name was Edward—and dialed the number for his pager.

When Moore called, I explained to him that I wouldn't need a night nurse, because I would be at Lansing's tonight, or a baby-sitter the following day, when I would be at the newspaper, surrounded by dozens of people. Although he wasn't too thrilled about not having me under the watchful eyes of one of his own people, he finally gave his blessing to my plans for the evening. But only because Lansing was an armed police officer, too, he said. Fortunately, Moore didn't express whatever opinion he might have had about my apparently personal relationship with a member of the same police department that I covered as a reporter. As for my refusal of an escort during my working hours, however, he did voice, in the strongest terms, his opinion that I was putting my life at risk needlessly.

"Whoever tried to blow you into little pieces is still walking around out there," he said, forcefully and graphically. "And you have no idea who it is. It could be anyone, including the person who's standing next to you at any time."

But I was adamant, agreeing only that we would talk the next afternoon about whether I would need an officer at my apartment for the following night. We hung up, and I went back to the bedroom to take a quick shower and put on clean clothes and to pack the things I would need for the night and the next day. And to wonder what Lansing and I would have to say to each other during the hours ahead, and how David would react to an overnight guest.

10

"Do you really think this was necessary?" I asked Noah Lansing as we turned into an older neighborhood just east of Fairfax City. Lansing had appeared at my apartment right on schedule at six o'clock and had taken me downstairs and out a service door, where he had parked his Explorer in a fire zone. We had taken I-395 to the Beltway and then followed that to Route 50 West, with Lansing glancing into his rearview mirror every few seconds throughout the entire trip.

"Do you think I would put up with all your abuse if I didn't think so?" he asked by way of reply as he negotiated the curving residential streets along which a variety of two-story brick or brick-and-wood-sided homes sat back among heavy canopies of mature trees.

"Okay," I conceded. "You're right. Someone obviously wanted to kill me. But why take me home with you? Why not let the Alexandria police baby-sit me? Do you really want people to know that we're... that we're..." I stopped, at a loss for a word to describe whatever we were.

Lansing looked at me and smiled. Apparently, he enjoyed seeing me at a loss for words.

"That we're seeing each other? That we're dating? That we're having a personal relationship?" He didn't seem to be stumbling over the idea nearly as much as I was. "No, I'm not worried about that," he said, "which isn't to say I haven't thought about it. But I'm entitled to a personal life outside work. And I also don't intend to let my personal and professional lives get crossed up. When you're a reporter, I'll deal with you as a police detective. Whatever is between us the rest of the time is our business."

I turned my head and looked out my window as Lansing turned the car to the right, down a short street that ended in a cul-de-sac. He made it all sound so simple, so clear-cut, so easy, I thought. I wished I were as sanguine as he apparently was about our being able to keep our personal and professional relationships separated. But I had been over this ground before; he hadn't, as far as I knew. I was painfully aware of just how quickly it could turn into a minefield, blowing a relationship—and careers—sky high without warning.

You mean like someone did to your car?

Though I was sure my shadow thought it was being amusing, I didn't much care for the simile it had chosen to describe where my relationship with Lansing might be headed. I pointedly ignored it.

"Here we are," Lansing announced, maneuvering the Explorer into the driveway in front of a two-story house, one of the smaller ones in the neighborhood. The all-brick exterior had been painted white. Navy blue shutters framed each window. The healthy green lawn that began in the large front yard ran back along each side of the house to merge into the darker green of many large trees growing in the backyard. A very large magnolia of three or four decades' standing was the show-piece of the front yard, it's wide glossy green leaves shading the house's sizable bay window from the afternoon sun. As Lansing turned off the ignition, the front door opened, and David Lansing came barreling out of it and down the front walk, followed by a plump, Hispanic-looking woman who stopped in the doorway.

"Dad's home! Dad's home!" David was shouting as he ran up to the driver's side of the Explorer. Lansing opened the door.

"Hi, Chief," Lansing said in greeting, and his son flung himself up into the cab and into his father's arms. As they hugged, David looked over and saw me.

"Hi," he said to me across his father's chest. "Are you coming to have dinner?" Before I could answer, he looked back at his father. "Is she, Dad? Is Sutton staying for dinner?"

"She is," Lansing said simply.

"Ya-a-a-y," David shouted, showing an exuberance that was very different from anything I had seen a couple of days before at the marina. He clambered down out of his father's arms to stand outside the Explorer again. "Hurry up and get out!" he said, looking over to me excitedly. "I'll show you my room." Then he disappeared around the door.

"There's still time to escape," Lansing told me as he disembarked. But by that time, David already had run around to my side of the Explorer, where he started rapping on the door.

"I think my escape just got cut off," I replied, opening my own door. Except, I wasn't so certain I was talking about the son.

As soon as I set foot in the house, David pulled me upstairs for the promised tour of his room. It was a young boy's room, with sturdy oak furniture and lots of cars and trucks and spaceships on shelves and in brightly colored plastic boxes. And even a couple of well-worn teddy bears stuck in one corner, apparently nostalgic reminders from his babyhood. In another corner was a child-sized desk with a low book-case next to it. And on top of the bookcase was an eight-by-ten color photo of a sweet-faced blond woman, smiling up at the camera from where she sat on a blanket with a picnic basket in her lap.

Sarah, I thought, and my heart felt squeezed by emotions I didn't want to examine too closely at the moment.

"That's my mom," a solemn little voice said at my side. I realized I must have been looking at the picture for more than just a few seconds. "She died when I was real little."

"She was very pretty," I said, smiling down at David, "and I'm sure she loved you very much." He returned the smile and slipped a hand into mine.

"C'mon," he said. "Let's go eat. I'm hungry!"

In the dining room, we were finishing up the last of the baked chicken that Gradella, the housekeeper and baby-sitter who had waited in the doorway as David had rushed out to greet us, had made before leaving for her own home.

"And on TV, I saw they have lots and lots of really big roller coasters," David was explaining to me, his arms reaching out to their limits to show just how big. As he had throughout dinner, he still was giving us all the details of the delights and thrills to be found at King's Dominion, a large amusement park some eighty or ninety miles south of us, just outside Richmond, to which he had been invited for the next day by a neighborhood friend's family. Then his face fell. "But Dad says they won't let me ride on the big ones. I'm not tall enough, and I'll fall out and get hurt."

"They do have some you can ride, though," I told him. "They aren't the biggest ones, but they still looked pretty big to me when I rode them."

"Really?" David wanted to know, his eyes growing large again at the prospect. "And you rode on them? Were you scared?"

"A little," I fibbed for his benefit. "They go pretty fast, too."

"Did you hear that, Dad?" he asked, turning back to his father.

"I heard," Lansing said. "You're going to have more fun than you can handle. But now it's time for you to go get your bath and get ready for bed so you can save up all your energy for tomorrow. When you get your pajamas on and brush your teeth, give me a yell, and I'll come up and read to you for a few minutes."

"Can I come back down and tell Sutton good night?"

"Sure."

With that, David slipped out of his chair and left the dining room. Once he rounded the doorway to the front hall, we could hear him break into a run and pound up the stairs, his footsteps only partially muffled by the carpeting.

"He's very bright, isn't he?" I asked Lansing as he turned back to face me after watching his son leave the room.

"Much brighter than I was at his age," he said, standing up and starting to clear the table. I got up from my chair and began helping him.

"Between television and what they hear from their friends, and now having access to computers, it's frightening sometimes to realize how much they already know by the time they're five or six," Lansing continued, carrying the stack of plates and flatware through the door to the kitchen. I followed him with the glasses and the bread basket.

Lansing rinsed off each item before putting it into the dishwasher, then filled the soap reservoir in the door from a large yellow container that he kept under the sink. He closed the dishwasher door and pressed a few buttons. The dishwasher came on with a sucking, whooshing sound.

With a wet dishcloth, he proceeded to wipe down the counters and stove top. He poured water into the coffeemaker and turned it on. Then he got a dustpan and whisk broom and cleaned up the bread crumbs scattered underneath David's dining room chair. By the time he was finished and we were having coffee at the kitchen table, David, now wearing pale blue summer pajamas, came running back down the stairs. Lansing stood up and tossed the remains of his coffee down the sink, turning on the faucet to rinse it all down.

"Okay, Chief," he said, walking over to sweep his son up in his arms, "tell Sutton good night and let's get you up to bed."

David leaned toward me from his father's embrace, his thin, little-boy arms reaching out. I hesitated for a moment, awkward with surprise, and then, feeling foolish at my hesitation, I got up from my chair as well and walked over to meet him. His arms went around my neck in a tight hug. My right hand found its way to his back, where I held it for the couple of seconds that the hug lasted.

"Night, Sutton," David said, squeezing hard.

"Good night, David. Sleep well."

David released me from the hug, and Lansing started up the stairs, still carrying him.

"I'll be back down in a little bit," Lansing said, looking back down at me over his shoulder, where David was waving at me. "We just have to read a story."

"That's fine," I answered, waving back at David. When they reached the landing at the top of the stairs, I turned and went into the living room to wait for Lansing to come back. Tiredly, I dropped onto a sofa upholstered in dark green and looked around.

What I saw, I suspected, were things chosen in Virginia Beach by a younger, happier Lansing and the woman whose picture sat on David's bookcase, things now transplanted to a house in northern Virginia. A pair of overstuffed chairs, upholstered in tan with a dark green trim, faced each other from either side of the sofa. Across from me was the fireplace, its bricks painted white, its opening now closed off by glass doors and sitting cold and empty in August. Above it hung a large watercolor of dunes and sea oats, up close and from a low angle, with an impression of ocean in the background. In an outside corner of the room, behind me and to my left, a small but elegant secretary of cherrywood sat next to a large green plant that I couldn't identify. In the other outside corner, a matching bookcase with glass-fronted doors held three or four dozen books and what looked like several large seashells of varying descriptions.

She was everywhere I looked. Sarah, whom Noah Lansing had loved very much. And for whose death, I knew, he still felt responsible. How, I wondered, could I ever compete with a dead woman, a woman who never would grow any older in her husband's mind, a woman whose imperfections probably had long since dropped from memory? The woman who gave Lansing a son and then was murdered by the people her husband had been investigating.

You can't. You don't have what it takes to qualify for sainthood.

For once, I couldn't have agreed with my voice more. Trying to measure up to Lansing's dead wife was a goal far beyond my ability to achieve, I suspected. I changed the subject, making myself think of more practical things, such as the fact that I had to find a new place to live and a car.

It was the idea of a new car, though, that brought unexpected tears to my eyes.

Are you really crying over a hunk of metal?

No, I thought back angrily, wiping away the tears, which quickly were followed by more. And I knew I wasn't crying over the car itself, as much as I had loved it and enjoyed it. Instead, I was crying because, for the first time all day, I had let myself think about what the car had represented. It had been one of the last remaining links with my family—my parents and my sister—all of whom now rested in their graves in a small cemetery in southern Georgia. I realized that, as long as I had the Beetle, somehow I still had some part of them. And now it was gone, torn and burned beyond any repairing. And I felt terribly, frighteningly alone.

But Noah Lansing would be coming back downstairs at any moment, I thought, and the last thing I wanted him to see was me crying, looking lonely and afraid—and vulnerable. I got up and walked over to a box of tissues that sat on the corner of the secretary, then wiped my eyes and blew my nose.

There was no time for indulging in useless regrets, I told myself, sitting down on the couch again. I had far more pressing things to worry about at the moment. Like who killed Dan Magruder? And who killed Robert Coleman? And who wanted to kill me? And I knew the answer to the last question would be Rob Perry if I let the ball drop on either of the first two, exploding car or not. I also knew I still had some legwork ahead of me to try to pin down details of Magruder's role in the firing of the two police officers in McLean. And the more I thought about it, the more convinced I became that, unless the police quickly nailed down a suspect among Robert Coleman's fellow financial conspirators, someone also would need to go to Tallahassee and take a much closer look at his years there.

God, I thought, resting my head against the back of the sofa and closing my eyes, there weren't going to be enough hours in the day to get it all done, especially if I had to keep fooling around with a police escort. I remember thinking that I definitely would have to call Detective Moore and firmly decline, once and for all, his offer of a bodyguard, and then I must have fallen asleep, there on Sarah Lansing's sofa. I have a vague recollection of someone, presumably Lansing, putting a pillow under my head and a blanket over me at some point during the night. And kissing my forehead. Beyond that, there was just deep, dreamless, healing sleep.

11

WEDNESDAY

After seeing David off with his friend's family to King's Dominion at eight o'clock, Lansing drove me to my apartment building, where I repacked my bag and reminded myself that I also needed to start apartment hunting soon. Then he gave me a ride to the car rental agency in Arlington.

"Promise me," he said, as I climbed out of the Explorer and lifted out my overnight bag, "that you'll be careful, that you won't take any unnecessary chances."

"I'll be fine," I told him in a tone that I hoped sounded convincing. "I'll be in rush-hour traffic, and then at the paper. There'll be lots of other people around all the time. I'll be okay."

"If you see anything, anything at all suspicious, you'll call Moore or 911 for help?" He didn't sound as if he were very reassured by my attempts at sounding confident.

"Yes, I promise. Now, go to work!"

"Okay," he agreed, "I just don't want anything to happen to you."

I softened a little at that, knowing that the attempt on my life probably brought back painful memories of what had happened to Sarah. If Lansing had any personal interest in me at all, the violent death of someone he cared about probably wasn't an experience he wanted to repeat.

"Thanks for watching out for me last night," I said. That earned me a smile, but it quickly was replaced by another concerned look.

"Will you call me and let me know for sure whether you're going out of town?" he asked. On the drive over to the apartment, I had explained that I was hoping to convince Rob Perry that I should go to Florida for a couple of days. "Actually, I'd feel a whole lot better if you were several hundred miles away until they figure out who rigged your car."

"I'll call you. And I'll be fine. Now, go." I closed the door firmly and turned to walk up the steps of the 1930s-era bungalow that housed the car rental company. Behind me, I heard the Explorer back out of its parking space and then pull out into the street, taking the weight of Lansing's concern for me with it. I went inside to pick up the keys to the rental car, which turned out to be a small white Pontiac.

"Christ, McPhee! You'll do anything to get a story, won't you?" It was Sy Berkowitz, walking into the metro room with Mark Lester.

I was in the middle of reassuring Rob Perry that I was as safe at the paper as anywhere and that my mental state was sufficiently recovered to get back to work. Rob had come in only a few minutes earlier, just as I was hanging up from a call to my source at the northern Virginia medical examiner's office, where Robert Coleman's body had been autopsied. At Sy's interruption, I stopped talking to Rob and turned to give what was intended to be a searing look at Sy.

"Ordinarily, I would respond to that with some witty comment of my own," I told him, "except someone else got killed by a bomb intended for me, and I don't think that's particularly funny."

"Cut it out, Sy," Mark told him. "We've got work to do. We don't have time for you and Sutton to get into one of your little duels."

"When we're finished here," Rob went on, talking to me as if the exchange between Sy and me hadn't occurred, "make sure you find James and let her know anything you know that she doesn't about the police investigation on your car."

"I will," I assured him.

Rob stood up from where he had been sitting on top of the metro copy desk and started toward his office.

"Let's all go in here," he said to the three of us, "so we can talk without being interrupted." We followed him in and found seats in the guest chairs around his desk.

"Now, where are we?" he wanted to know once we all were settled.

"The cause of death is official," I said, looking from Rob to Mark to Sy. "Coleman was shot once in the chest with a .38-caliber handgun. The bullet severed the aorta, then went right on through his chest. He was dead pretty quickly, within seconds if not instantly. The police also recovered a spent slug at the scene, a short distance from the body, that they think is the one that killed him. Of course, at this point, they don't have a murder weapon to try to match it to. And there's still some question as to the time of death, given how far gone the body was. They're waiting for the results of a couple more tests before they know."

"What about suspects?" Mark asked, his head swiveling between Sy and me.

"Everybody and nobody," I told him. "Detective Peterson told me this morning when I called him that they've managed to rule out most of the staff at the foundation. They're still checking on a couple of people there, but neither of those looks like a real possibility. There's an ex-wife who couldn't take the teeny boppers after a while, but she lives in California now and apparently has witnesses that she hasn't left town in weeks. They've also ruled out the three girlfriends who they've identified, although there could be more of them. Who knows?"

Sy snorted a laugh at that, his editorial comment on Coleman's reputation for a weakness for very young, very blond women.

"And the guys Coleman was getting kickbacks from?" That was Rob again.

"The feds aren't being very cooperative in saying who they are, according to Peterson, who doesn't sound real happy to have federal investigators poking around in his homicide case. Apparently, the Justice Department is still hoping to bring indictments against whoever the guys are, even with Coleman dead." I turned to Sy. "If you could give Peterson some help with names, he'd owe us big on this."

"You see any problem with that?" Rob asked Mark, rather than asking Sy, who would have to cooperate if Mark ordered him to.

"If he'll agree to keep the source out of the investigation file so Sy doesn't have the feds coming after him, no there's no problem," Mark said. He looked at Sy. "Go ahead and help him out."

I jotted Peterson's name and pager number down on the top page in the notebook in my lap and tore it out, passing it over to Sy.

"How much checking had you done into Coleman's background before he came to Washington?" I asked Sy as he folded up the sheet of paper and put it in his shirt pocket.

"Not much yet," he told me. "Just cursory stuff. Everything the feds are looking at involves his job with The Phoenix Group here, and that has kept me hopping since I got onto it. I'd figured there'd be time to do the Tallahassee bit in detail once they indicted Coleman."

"One of us needs to go down there," I said, turning to Rob.

"She's right," Mark said, shaking his head in agreement. "It was a long time ago, but it's hard to believe a guy like Coleman was squeaky clean until he got to Washington."

"Still," Sy said, sounding defensive now, "if there had been anything big enough to have gone public in Tallahassee, he probably would never have gotten the Phoenix Group job. That's a pretty sanctimonious board of directors."

Rob looked thoughtful for a minute.

"I think Sutton ought to go," he said, looking at Mark. "She's lived there, she knows the city, she's got some contacts. If Sy's going to be in touch with Peterson anyway, he can handle the police end of things until Sutton gets back."

"Makes sense to me," Mark said.

Rob turned to me.

"Any idea how long it might take?"

"There's no way to know. It could be two days. It could take a week or more. I have no idea what I might find, if anything."

"All right," he said, "stay as long as it takes to either find something on Coleman or decide that there's nothing down there to find. When can you go?"

"How's today?"

"What about the car bombing? Don't the Alexandria cops want you around while they look into that?"

"They know I didn't do it," I told him, "and they probably would be just as happy to have me somewhere a long way away. Then I'm either out of reach of whoever tried to kill me, or if he gets me in Tallahassee, it'll be in somebody else's jurisdiction." Although I hadn't told Detective Moore yet that I might have to leave town, I fully expected that, given my refusal of a police guard, his reaction to the news probably would be exactly what I had just said.

"Okay, make the arrangements," Rob said. "Now, what about your other stories? Like the cop who was murdered?"

"I can stay on top of them over the phone, and I'll call Penny if I need any leg work on anything," I assured him. "I'll take another run at the Internal Affairs office to ask about Magruder before I leave town, but I'm not holding my breath waiting for them to tell me anything. And Noah Lansing, the detective in charge of that case, is still checking out the alibi of one of the former cops Magruder turned in. I'll make sure I call Lansing again before I leave. The big thing on that one is the funeral tomorrow. Do you think Penny could catch it for me? It should be pretty pro forma, and I'll call in anything I get on the investigation to be added to the story."

"I assume you'll be talking to her about your car bombing story before you leave today," Rob said. "Tell her I said to put the funeral on her list for tomorrow, and give her the names of anybody she needs to make sure to talk to."

"So have we covered all the bases?" Mark wanted to know. "Sutton, you'll keep Sy and Rob updated on the Florida angle by phone, and one or both of them will keep me in the loop?"

We all nodded or spoke up in agreement, looking around at each other. As we got up and filed out of Rob's office, Sy gave me a smile that stopped at his mouth. It was obvious that working with me still left a bitter taste, but the idea of my leaving town probably cheered him up somewhat. Especially if he thought I was being sent on a wild-goose chase while he stayed where the real story was. I, on the other hand, wasn't so sure that was the case at all. Like Mark Lester, I didn't think Coleman had turned venal only after reaching Washington. I suspected that his shenanigans at The Phoenix Group probably had been perfected only after considerable practice, practice that might well have begun in Tallahassee. And at the very least, if there was nothing to find down there, then we could rule it out and turn our energies in more productive directions.

12

Tallahassee is one of my favorite places: the prosperous, eclectic state capital, an amalgam of the cultural influence that comes with two universities, of the intrigue and activism that are intrinsic in a political atmosphere, and of the history of its very Southern roots. Which didn't mean that coming back was a completely positive experience. Tallahassee also had been the site of my disastrously brief attempt at marriage to Jack Brooks.

As the jet had dropped down toward the runway, I had felt my heartbeat speed up from more than just the adrenaline surge that a plane landing always induces. Jack, a city planner when I was married to him, was now, according to reports from friends still in the area, a private consultant. But he had remained in Tallahassee, and it was almost as if I could feel his presence even though I knew he probably was at work in his downtown office, several miles away.

Gonna stop in and surprise him with a visit?

What the hell do you care? I thought back. *You never had anything good to say about him, anyway.*

A little defensive about the ex-husband, are we?

I didn't reply. What was the point? I was still defensive about the way our marriage turned out. I still hadn't decided whether it was his fault or mine, whether the things he said about my lack of a heart were true, or whether I really was incapable of a real relationship with a man, or at least one that lasted. Since no one was meeting me, I had waited for the other passengers to clear the aisles before retrieving my one bag out of the overhead bin. I got it down now, hoping to shut out the voice in my head, and made my way out of the plane.

In my second rental car of the day, this one a Ford Taurus for which I had picked up the keys at the rental desk inside the Tallahassee Regional Airport, I took a sharp right from Lake Bradford Road onto Gaines Street and followed Gaines east into downtown. The sedan's air-conditioning, a luxury I was unused to in my poor Beetle, was working at a dull roar in the northern Florida heat and humidity. The car's tires swished through the remains of a late-afternoon thunderstorm, probably the same one that had necessitated the pilot's change of direction as we had approached the airport.

All around me were the landmarks I remembered from a different chapter of my life, some four calendar years but a million emotional years ago. At Duval Street, I turned left, noting the Collins Building across the intersection to my right, a sign that I was entering the area dominated by the governmental offices of Florida's capital city.

I negotiated the one-way traffic heading north on Duval Street, now bumper-to-bumper in the late-afternoon exodus of the federal, state, city, and county employees whose offices clustered in a square mile of downtown real estate. Stopping and starting, I passed the Florida Supreme Court building on my left, directly opposite the rear entrance to the newer of the two state capitols, and I couldn't help smiling. As that new capitol had neared completion in the mid-'70s, the hoopla over its design by a noted architect and over its long-awaited construction had given way to gales of derisive laughter. Residents and visitors alike quickly discovered that, with its slim center tower and its two domed wings for the state senators and representatives, the new capitol had looked, from the westbound lanes of the Apalachee Parkway, like nothing so much as a giant phallus and testicles, reaching into the sky in priapic self-parody. It was a story I had heard repeatedly in my stint in Tallahassee almost two decades later, and the sight of the building never ceased to bring a grin to my face at the accuracy of the lewd nicknames that had appended themselves to the structure.

When I finally reached the northern edge of the downtown governmental and historic district, I turned left onto the westbound lanes of Park Avenue. In reality, Park Avenue actually is a pair of one-way streets that run for seven blocks through one of the city's loveliest and oldest tree-lined districts, from the Old City Cemetery on the west to Meridian Street on the east. At the west end of the block along which I drove was the Leon Collins/Leon County Public Library, to which I had decided to head first. I could have gone to the Tallahassee *Democrat* on Magnolia Drive and used their newspaper library. After all, I had worked there for five years, and several of my then-colleagues still did. But if the *Democrat* was following the Coleman murder and any local angles, I didn't want to let anyone there know that they had competition. And if the news staff somehow had not picked up on the story yet, I certainly didn't want to be the one to point it out to them.

I parked the car and stepped out into the August oven, in which the streets and parking lot now literally steamed with the additional humidity added by the thunderstorm. Too brief to cool things down by any noticeable amount, the rain had lasted just long enough to pour more moisture into the already palpable air. Still, it was a familiar climate, one in which I had spent the first three decades of my life, in southern Georgia and northern Florida, and it brought back a flood of memories, both welcome and painful. Not the least of which, of course, involved Jack.

Don't start thinking about all that again, I chastised myself. *You've got more important things to do at the moment.* And that certainly was true. As I went through the glass front doors and into the cool, fluorescent interior of the library, I reflected that Jack was ancient history, no matter how painful it might still be. I could think about him after I had learned what there was to learn about Robert Coleman.

What there was to learn, at least about Coleman's years in Tallahassee and at least from the newspaper, apparently wasn't much. I found only a handful of articles in which his name appeared, all but one of them local business-page stories about Three Rivers Development.

Three Rivers, according to the stories I read, was a real estate development company that had thrived during the early and mid-'70s, and that had been owned by a former real estate agent named Arthur Williams. The company had been very much the golden-haired child of the Tallahassee/Leon County business community as Three Rivers bought up and developed real estate throughout the area, also taking in large amounts of investor money in the process. Robert Coleman had been the vice-president and Williams's top deputy in Three Rivers until 1977, when Coleman left to join The Phoenix Group.

To all appearances, the never-married Williams had lived the life of a successful developer, residing in baronial splendor in a near-mansion on the grounds of a golf course in one of his developments, where he regularly entertained the city and state's movers and shakers. Then, in 1978, Williams's housekeeper had arrived one morning to find that, at some point during the previous evening, he had gone into his study, put a loaded revolver into his mouth, and killed himself. Within days, Three Rivers had collapsed as investors learned it had been a veritable financial house of cards, almost a pyramid scheme in its last two years, in which Williams had gotten in over his head and had been using the money of new investors to keep up the facade that things were going well.

Although Robert Coleman had been out of the Three Rivers picture for a year at that point, the final mention I found of him was in an article about Williams's suicide and the shock waves that the company's collapse had sent throughout the area's business and social communities. The article quoted a Tallahassee-based spokesperson for Coleman as saying that Coleman had severed all financial ties with the company when he left the area, that he had admired

Williams greatly, had considered him a mentor, and was saddened by Williams's death. And that Coleman had no knowledge of any financial irregularities in the operation of Three Rivers up until the time of his departure.

Eventually, I managed to locate several follow-up pieces to the Three Rivers debacle. They described in detail the ways in which Williams had played fast and loose with investors' money until a couple of his developments failed and brought everything else down with them. But there was no further mention of Coleman, who either had covered his tracks well or really had not known what Williams had been up to. Given what I knew of Coleman's activities in Washington, I found the latter difficult to believe.

As the photocopy of the last of the articles slid out of the side of the microfilm reader, I flipped the switch to turn off the machine, leaned back in my chair, and closed my eyes to concentrate on what I had just read. Mentally, I sorted back through the details of each of the articles, looking for anything that might tell me there was something other than a dead end here. No pun intended. My skeptical, suspicious nature said that Coleman knew exactly what Williams had been doing at Three Rivers, that he probably had learned his lessons well at Williams's knee, lessons that he had put to good use among the higher rollers and bigger stakes of Washington, D.C. But I also knew that Three Rivers probably had been audited and investigated three ways to Sunday after Williams's suicide. If no one back then had been able to tie Coleman to the financial disaster that Three Rivers became, how could I hope to do it now, all these years later? Still, I knew I wasn't ready to stop looking.

Sighing, I opened my eyes and leaned forward to look back through the photocopied articles one more time. Halfway through the small pile, I uncovered Williams's obituary, which I had only scanned previously. Now, in desperation, I read it in detail as it compressed the forty-four years of Williams's life into three paragraphs and then gave the reader information on survivors and when and where funeral services would be held. None of that took much space either, since there was only one survivor listed, a Mrs. Marshall L. (Gladys Monroe) Williams of Panama City, Arthur William's mother.

If Mrs. Williams had been twenty or so when her son was born, which I thought was a reasonable guess for a woman of her generation, she would now be in her eighties. What were the chances, I wondered, that she might still be alive, and that she would, or even could, tell me anything useful about Robert Coleman? Not great, I thought, but what else did I have at the moment?

I gathered up the photocopies I had made, folded them in half, and put them into my shoulder bag. In the process, I glanced at my watch and saw that it was 6:30. Given that I had had nothing to eat since breakfast and that I had not yet checked into a place to spend the night, I decided it was high time to do both.

Pleasantly stuffed from my dinner at the northern location of Lucy Ho's Restaurant on Halstead Boulevard, where one could enjoy the world's best egg rolls as far as I was concerned, I sat down on the double bed in the room I had checked into at the Days Inn North and reached for the phone.

I could have stayed in more elegant surroundings at any one of several other hotels, of course. But the Days Inn certainly provided the basics, which was all I really needed at this point, and it offered two advantages that the downtown hotels didn't. The first was that I was far less likely here to accidentally run into anyone I knew from my years in Tallahassee. The second was that the Days Inn's proximity to the North Monroe Street intersection with I-10 meant I could avoid the bulk of the next morning's rush-hour traffic if the phone calls I was about to make resulted in my needing to drive to Panama City.

When the information operator answered my call, I asked her for the Panama City area and then for any listings for either Gladys M. or Mrs. Richard L. Williams. Without a street address to narrow down the list, she eventually gave me four listings for the various name combinations, the second of which was for a G. M. Williams. It was that one that I dialed first, thinking that Mrs. Williams might very well have used only her initials in order to disguise her gender, a tactic often used by women who live alone or who want to avoid being identified as female for one reason or another.

On the fourth ring, a clearly elderly woman's voice answered.

"I'm trying to reach Mrs. Gladys Monroe Williams," I said.

"This is Gladys Williams. Who is this?" Judging by the quiver in the voice and the apparent shortness of breath with which she spoke, I guessed that this Mrs. Williams was at least as old as I had estimated, if not older.

"My name is Sutton McPhee," I told her. "I'm looking for Gladys Williams who was the mother of Arthur Williams in Tallahassee."

"I'm that Gladys Williams," she said, "but my son has been dead since 1978."

"I know, and I'm sorry that your son died. Mrs. Williams, I'm a newspaper reporter from Washington, D.C. I'm in Tallahassee investigating a man named Robert Coleman, who was murdered in the Washington area a few days ago and who used to work for your son at the Three Rivers Development Company. I was wondering if you knew Robert Coleman and, if you did, whether I might come to Panama City and talk to you about him."

I paused, waiting for her to respond, but except for her troubled breathing, there was silence on the other end.

"Mrs. Williams?"

"Robert was murdered, you say?" she asked finally, just when I had concluded she was going to hang up on me.

"That's right. Someone shot him in a park in Virginia. He was being investigated for illegal use of money at the foundation he ran, and I'm trying to find out as much as I can about his years in Tallahassee. I know that he went to Washington about a year before your son's death and before the problems at Three Rivers came out. But I can't help but think Coleman might have played some sort of role in those problems."

Again, Gladys Williams waited for several seconds before replying.

"What was your name again?" she asked.

"Sutton McPhee."

"All right," she said when she finally spoke again. "You can come talk to me if you like. I live at the Spring Hill Retirement Center now, but I have my own apartment, and we can talk privately. How is two o'clock? We're all finished with lunch by then."

"Two o'clock is fine," I said. It meant I could make an unhurried trip to Panama City, some 120 miles away, and find some lunch for myself before meeting with her.

Mrs. Williams gave me the address of the retirement center but no directions.

"I'm not good with directions anymore since I no longer drive," she explained, when I asked for them. "But pick up a Panama City map as soon as you get to the area, and you'll find it without too much trouble."

I thanked her genuinely for agreeing to see me. Even after this many years, her son's suicide and the scandal surrounding it still had to be painful subjects for her. And I had no way of knowing what her health was like these days or what kind of strain talking about her son's death might place on it.

We hung up and, with my plans for the next day now made, I went into the bathroom to wash away what was left of the day's makeup and brush my teeth. When I walked back into the bedroom, I glanced at the TV set that I had yet to turn on and considered the possibility that I should watch CNN long enough to catch up on the news of the day. But a look at the bed pushed the idea from my mind. It had been a very long last two days, and I just wanted to crawl under the covers and get a decent night's sleep.

Once I was there, however, I realized how much tension I still carried in every limb and muscle of my body. I called on what I had learned in more than seven years of yoga classes, taking in and letting out several cleansing breaths, then consciously relaxing the tension, one set of muscles at a time, from my feet and toes, up to my scalp. At about the level of my shoulders, my chronic nuisance decided to put in an appearance.

So, are you gonna call Jack while you're here?

Not that again, I thought. I hadn't spoken to Jack in almost six years, not since the brief but unpleasant afternoon in the Leon County Courthouse when our marriage of two years officially was dissolved on the grounds of irreconcilable differences. Irreconcilable because Jack had announced, six months into the marriage, that he wanted me to quit my job, the only job I had ever wanted to do.

We had argued about it for a year. Then Jack had told me, in one of our final shouting matches, that he always had hated what I did for a living, but that he had tolerated it while we were only dating because then it had had little effect on his life and because he had thought he could convince me to change jobs once we were married. I had remained unconvinced. Instead, I had accused him of hypocrisy and deceit in not telling me how he felt before the wedding. At that point in the breakdown of our marriage, all gloves had been off, and we both had said more than a few ugly, hurtful things to each other, things for which neither of us had ever apologized. And that state of affairs had left me with a nagging conscience at the way I had let things end and remain all this time, at my lack of any effort toward some sort of civil closure. But was I ready yet to try to make any sort of amends? And had I let far too much time go by already? And why did I care whether Jack and I had parted civilly or otherwise? He had been incredibly dishonest with me from the beginning. Did I really owe him even civility?

That part of my life is dead and gone, I told my voice.

Yeah, that's why you're so happy about the idea of getting involved with Lansing. Because Jack is such a faded memory.

I don't know, I thought back as I dropped off into the sleep I had sought. *I just don't know.*

13
THURSDAY

Fortified by an uncharacteristically sizable breakfast of waffles and bacon, I took my time on the trip over to Panama City from Tallahassee, driving along I-10 at the speed limit. It was pleasant to once again drive through the gently rolling hills of northern Florida, hills that mark the southern end of the fall line that runs across Georgia, the Carolinas, and Virginia, separating the piedmont from the hills. A sort of last hurrah, if you will, of the Appalachian mountain chain. It's a topography that is very different from the flat, sun-seared landscape in the southern half of the state. I realized, too, how much I missed the spreading-limbed live oak trees that are so-called because they are green all year, even though they are deciduous. As the miles rolled across my odometer, I also registered the familiar Florida Panhandle names that drifted past me on large, green interstate highway signs: Quincy, Gretna, Chattahoochee, Marianna. Small towns, but each with a considerable store of history that went back, in many cases, to well before the recent unpleasantness between the states. I had been to them all more than once in my time in Florida.

West of Marianna, I turned south on U.S. 231 to Panama City, stopping at a gas station and convenience store combination several miles outside of town to get a soda and a Panama City map. The store was completely out of those particular maps, of course. Frustrated, I decided to go on into Panama City, figuring I could always call Spring Hill for directions and that I might as well get at least a glimpse of the beach and have a light lunch while I was there, before my two o'clock meeting.

The beach thing turned out to be a mistake. Rather than relaxing me, all my walk along the white sands of the Saint Andrews Recreation Area did was to bring back memories of more than one trip there with Jack.

God, I thought, as I stood barefooted at the edge of the glitteringly clear green water, letting the gentle wash of low tide slop over my feet, *is he going to haunt me for the rest of my life? He's ancient history. Why can't I get my mind off him?*

Maybe because of what's going on with Lansing? I'd say Lansing's got you good and scared.

I could have argued the point, I suppose, but what if the little bastard was right? Was I afraid of what was happening with Noah Lansing because of what had happened with Jack? If we got seriously involved, would Lansing turn into someone else and demand I quit my job because of the conflicts it created for both of us? I knew that the answer to any such demands from him or from any other man would be the same answer I had given Jack. But did I really want to go through all that again?

"Damn it," I said aloud, to no one in general. I aimed a kick at a wave that was a little higher than the previous ones. It collapsed and sprayed me with droplets of salt water, which I hoped wouldn't leave too many noticeable spots on the jungle-flowered summer dress I had put on that morning. Disgusted with myself, I made the long walk back to the parking lot, where I used tissues from my bag to brush the sand off my feet and legs, and then put my sandals back on.

Maybe, I thought, some fresh seafood would get my mind off places I really didn't want to visit right now. With plenty of time still to kill, I drove back over to U.S. 98 West and found my way to the Saltwater Grill, a local seafood house that was regularly written up in papers around the country and whose owner and chef, Billy Redd, found time from cooking his award-winning cuisine to indulge a hobby in ice carving. Half an hour later, I was indulging myself in a serving of Sesame Crusted Yellowfin Tuna and rice pilaf, having already downed a salad.

What was that about a light lunch?

I was taught never to speak with my mouth full, I thought back, savoring the honey and cream sauce that topped the tuna filet. *Maybe you should learn some manners, too.*

What? And spoil all my fun?

Several swallows of iced tea drowned the voice out for the moment, and within another half hour, I was back in the car and calling the Spring Hill Retirement Center to get directions. Following the receptionist's instructions, I drove back through town and out the north side, on U.S. 231 again, turning west just outside the city limits. The directions then took me down quieter and quieter streets until Spring Hill Center Drive deposited me in front of the retirement center.

The sign at the gated entrance said the Spring Hill Retirement Center had opened only the previous year. Its rambling brick wings had been set down, obviously with some thought to atmosphere, in the middle of several acres of live oaks. The developer and builder clearly had gone to great pains to preserve as many of the trees as possible and to quickly hide any signs of recent construction, and the results gave the center the lush, shaded appearance of longevity and stability, rather than the scraped-earth, raw-wound look of most new construction.

I parked the car in a space marked Visitors Only and followed the sidewalk up to a long, dark blue canopy, which jutted out from the building's glassed, double front doors and reached the sidewalk's edge at a small circular drive intended for picking up and dropping off residents. On the other side of the doors, I stepped into the cool, dry, interior air and went up to the oak reception desk that dominated the left side of the large living-room-furnished lobby.

"My name is Sutton McPhee," I said to the young woman who sat at the desk, a telephone console at her right hand, next to a name plate that read Peggy Banks. "I'm here to see Mrs. Gladys Williams."

Peggy Banks smiled up at me with dark brown eyes, several shades darker than her skin.

"I'll let her know you're here," she said, reaching down to press several telephone buttons. Within seconds, someone answered on the other end.

"Mrs. Williams, this is Peggy," she said into the receiver. "You have a visitor. A Ms. McPhee?"

Peggy listened for a few seconds more and then said, "I'll send her back," before hanging up the phone and looking back up at me.

"Just follow this hall behind me," she said, gesturing and looking over her right shoulder. "At the end, turn right, and it will be three doors down on your left. It's apartment A-6."

I thanked her and walked around her desk to take the hallway she indicated. As my feet sank into the well-cushioned gunmetal blue carpeting and I passed several pieces of pleasant watercolor art on the walls, I could see that, whatever had happened to Three Rivers Development, either Arthur Williams or someone in the family still had provided well for his mother.

At apartment A-6, I raised my hand to knock on the door, but it opened before I could make contact. In front of me stood a short, elegantly dressed, elderly woman, her vibrant blue eyes contrasting pleasingly with her snow white hair and beige linen dress and contradicting the deterioration of her stooped and aging body.

"Come in," she said, holding the door all the way open to make room for me to enter, then closing it behind me when I did.

"I'm Sutton McPhee, Mrs. Williams. Thank you for seeing me." I held out my hand, and she took it, her grasp light and tentative, whether from age or etiquette lessons learned in a time when women didn't shake hands, I couldn't tell.

"Please come sit down," Mrs. Williams said, and she began to make her way slowly to where a tightly upholstered, cream-colored love seat and two oak rocking chairs faced each other in front of French doors that opened onto a small concrete patio. Through the doors, I could see the other wings of the building, jutting out around a spacious green lawn. There were a variety of benches and chairs scattered around the lawn, with a white gazebo in the center as a focal point. Several of the other residents were outside, a couple by themselves, a man with a woman who probably was his daughter, and a several more who had pulled their chairs together into a group where they were talking, gesturing, and laughing.

At the love seat, I stood and waited for Mrs. Williams to finish making her own way over. When she stopped in front of the first rocker, which was turned at an angle to look out the French doors, I stepped over to hold it steady while she lowered herself into it.

"Thank you," she said, and I told her she was welcome as I finally sat down on the love seat.

"I appreciate your agreeing to see me," I said. "Even though it's been a long time since your son's death, I don't imagine that it's an easy subject to discuss."

Mrs. Williams studied me silently for a moment, her blue eyes dissecting and analyzing the person in front of her. I suspected that, even at her age, she didn't miss much where other people were concerned.

"The most painful part was having to live with what my son had become," she said bitterly. "No matter how much I would like to make excuses for him, I can't change the things he did before he died. And he ruined the lives of a number of other people besides himself—as well as his own and mine." It was a pretty damning indictment from someone's mother, I thought, listening to the anger still evident in her voice.

"But he provided somehow for you?" I asked, looking around me. Spring Hill clearly wasn't geared to the Medicare crowd. It was costing someone a pretty penny for Gladys Williams to live out her last years here.

"No, dear, that was my father's doing," she said, her voice becoming softer again. "Papa was a very successful pharmacist here in Panama City, and when he died, he left money in a trust for me, thank heavens. Arthur went through everything that Marshall, his own father, left both of us. After Arthur killed himself and the company fell apart, I had to move out of my house in Tallahassee, of course. Arthur, you see, had mortgaged my house to the hilt without my knowledge, had forged my signature to the papers. So I came back here to Panama City, where I still had many friends."

No wonder she was still bitter, I thought.

"How well did you know Robert Coleman?" I asked, getting to the reason I was here.

"Not well," she answered, and I'm sure my face fell. Had I driven all the way over here for nothing? I wondered.

She wasn't done, however.

"But I knew enough to know that he was just as responsible as Arthur was for what happened with the company," she said, and my suspicious nature took heart again.

"In what way?" I asked. "I know that Coleman left town a year before your son's death, and that he supposedly cut all his connections with the company."

"I don't know exactly when it was," Mrs. Williams said, "but some time not long before Robert left Tallahassee, Arthur came to me. He was very worried, and since he never married, I suppose I was the only person he could unburden himself to safely."

"What did he tell you?"

"He told me that there were some big financial problems with the company, that he and Robert had been spending money they didn't have to keep all their projects going, and that some of the things they had done weren't legal. He said that someone in the state attorney's office had been investigating Robert and that Arthur was afraid they were going to come after him and the whole company next."

"Did he tell you what kind of things they had been doing?"

"No, I'm sure he thought it was too complicated for me to understand. And I didn't ask."

Mrs. Williams paused, clearly somewhat short of breath. I sat silently, waiting for her to gather her energies again.

"I was very worried about him because I didn't want to see my only child ruined and in prison, no matter what he had done. But a few weeks later, he came back and told me to forget about our conversation, that there no longer was anything to worry about."

"But what about the investigation?" I asked.

"That was my first question to him. He said Robert had taken care of the problem and that they could stop worrying about it. Not long after that, Robert left town, and I hoped and prayed that everything would be all right with him gone. I was still looking for a way to excuse whatever Arthur might have done, hoping that it was mostly Robert and that the problems had left with him. But I was wrong."

"After your son died, the investigators went through the company pretty thoroughly, but they never connected anything to Coleman. Did you tell anyone what your son had said to you?"

"No," she said, "and now I'm ashamed that I didn't. But I didn't know anything specific, and Arthur made me promise, when he thought everything was all right again, that I would never breathe a word of it to anyone. He said I could be held responsible for knowing even what little he had told me, so even after he killed himself, I kept quiet. I couldn't change what had happened, couldn't help any of the people he harmed. All I could do was to try to keep his memory from being any more tarnished than it already was."

"Who was handling the original investigation of Coleman that your son told you about?" It was clear that Coleman had pulled a major rabbit out of his hat if he had managed to stall an investigation by the state attorney's office. I wanted to know what kind of rabbit it had been.

"I don't know," Mrs. Williams answered. "I just don't remember if Arthur ever said. I was thinking back on it this morning, and I know that it was during the time that Ford Truesdale was the state attorney for that area. But I don't know if Ford handled it personally or whether it was someone else in the office."

"Well then, I'll ask Truesdale." Surely, I thought, he would remember who was looking into Coleman's activities at Three Rivers and why the investigation had been halted.

"Oh no, dear," Mrs. Williams said sadly. "Ford Truesdale is dead. I believe he died only a few weeks before Arthur killed himself. Of a stroke."

Damn it, I thought, was I just going to keep running into nothing but corpses on this story? Although realistically, I supposed I had to expect that people who had been middle-aged at the time might be dead or dying twenty years later. Still, it was incredibly frustrating to see one line of inquiry after another irrevocably closed to me.

"But you might ask Lawson Thomas," Mrs. Williams continued. "He worked for Ford at one point, although he's a state senator now. Perhaps he would remember, if he was there during that time."

"I will ask him," I said, but I wasn't optimistic. With the way things had gone so far, there was no guarantee that Lawson Thomas had even been on the state attorney's staff at the time. He probably hadn't known Robert Coleman from Adam. Frustrated, I questioned Mrs. Williams a little longer, but what she had told me already apparently was as much as she knew.

Finally, I gave her my card and asked her to call me if she remembered anything else that might be helpful. Then I took my leave of her, thanking her again for what she had been able to tell me and for agreeing to talk to me.

"There may not be any point to it all, now that Robert is dead as well," Mrs. Williams said as she saw me to her door. "Perhaps we should just let the dead rest."

"No," I disagreed, "it's possible that your son wasn't the biggest bad guy in what happened at Three Rivers after all. Or at least not the only one. And I think there's always a point to finding out the truth."

"You may be right, dear," Mrs. Williams said. She didn't sound convinced.

14

The question, of course, was whether I would be able to find out the truth about Robert Coleman and his activities at Three Rivers. I wasn't holding my breath in anticipation as I used my cell phone to call Tallahassee information and asked for the state senate office number of Lawson Thomas.

Although I had never spoken to him, I remembered Lawson Thomas from my years in Tallahassee, when he had been a junior member of the Florida Senate Education Committee and I had been covering the schools and universities in the area. He had struck me then as an intelligent, straightforward guy who genuinely wanted to do what he could to improve education in a state in which retirees already were well on their way to outnumbering children, retirees who saw no reason why they should pay higher taxes to support an education system from which they felt they derived no immediate benefit. I hoped that twenty years of pummeling in the rambunctious tumbler of Florida politics hadn't made Thomas as smooth, unctuous, and hard to pin down as many of the other politicians there with whom I had dealt.

I dialed the number the operator gave me and worked my way through a couple of staff members until I reached one who could tell me that Senator Thomas was in the office, but that he was in a meeting at the moment.

"I apologize in advance for being persistent," I told the secretary, to whom I already had identified myself as a reporter from Washington,

"but I'm only in town for one more night, and I really need a few minutes with him. I need to ask him about a case he might have known
about when he worked in the state attorney's office. I'm driving back
right now from Panama City, and I should get back to town around
five. Could you do me a huge favor and please ask him if I could
impose on him for just a few minutes then?"

Either I sounded so desperate that the secretary took pity on me or,
more likely, she had dealt with enough reporters to know that the fastest
way to get rid of me was to give me what I wanted. Or at least a little bit
of it. She told me to hold.

"If you can be here by five," she said when she came back on the
line, "Senator Thomas can give you fifteen minutes. But he has a dinner appointment, so if you're not here by then, he'll have to leave anyway."

"I understand," I told her. "I'll be there. And thank you very much
for checking with him."

I turned off the cell phone and nosed the speedometer on the rental
car up to seventy, hoping the Florida Highway Patrol would give me a
five-mile-an-hour benefit of the doubt. There was no way I was going
to be late for my appointment with Thomas. I was beginning to feel
like Hansel and Gretel trying to follow a disappearing trail. At the
moment, Lawson Thomas was the only bread crumb I could find.

"I'm Sutton McPhee, Senator Thomas. Thank you for seeing me."

"Pleased to meet you, Ms. McPhee," Thomas said, shaking my out-
stretched hand. "Have a seat." He sat back down in the black leather
executive's chair behind a large mahogany desk and looked toward the
office door where his secretary, a pleasant-faced brunette of about my
own age, still hovered.

"It's okay, Jane," he said, smiling. "We'll be fine. You go on and get
out of here. Go home for a change."

"If you're sure..." Jane said, still hesitating.

"I'm sure."

"All right then, I'll see you tomorrow." Jane turned and went back to her reception area desk. A few seconds later, she went out the office's main door, purse in hand.

"Now," Thomas said, once we were alone, "what is it I can do for you? And do I know you from somewhere? Your name sounded familiar."

"I used to be a reporter at the *Democrat*," I told him, surprised that he had remembered even my name. "I covered education."

"Oh, that's it," Thomas said, nodding his head in agreement as my name clicked into place for him. "I remember reading your stories, now. So you went on to bigger and better things in Washington?"

"That's certainly how people inside the Beltway would see it," I answered.

Thomas chuckled, revealing a host of laugh lines around his brown eyes that did nice things to his approaching-fifty face.

"They do tend to take a fairly provincial view of things," he said, evidently having had some experience with folks in Washington—and with their amnesia for what is important to people outside the Beltway—a time or two himself.

"Jane said you were interested in something about a case from when I was with the state attorney's office," Thomas said, bringing the conversation back to the point.

"That's right," I told him. "These days, I cover the Fairfax County Police in northern Virginia, instead of education, and I'm here about the murder of a man named Robert Coleman. He was involved in the Three Rivers Development company here back in the seventies with Arthur Williams, and he was murdered a few days ago in a park outside Washington. For the last ten years, he was the head of The Phoenix Group, a very large charitable foundation, and our paper was about to break a story that he was under investigation by several federal agencies for some illegal activities with the foundation's money. I'm looking into his years here in Tallahassee to see if he might have been involved in similar activities here, and your name came up in connection with something."

"My name?"

"Only indirectly," I said quickly, realizing I probably had just given him a fright. "I was told by someone with reason to know that, before he left Tallahassee and Three Rivers, Coleman was being investigated by the state attorney's office here. I understand that Mr. Truesdale has been dead for many years, so I can't ask him. But I was told that you might have worked in the office during that time and might remember whose case it was."

Thomas looked thoughtful for a moment. I couldn't tell whether he was accessing his memory or trying to get a handle on me.

"I was working there at the time," he said finally. "It's funny. We all handled a lot of cases, and after all this time, many of them tend to run together in my mind, even some of the cases that I personally prosecuted. But, even though it never went anywhere, I remember the Coleman investigation because of the big argument."

"What argument was that?"

"Between Ford and the assistant state attorney who was handling the case."

"Who was that?"

"Oh, that was Henry Bryant."

It took me a second, the way recognition often does when you run into someone you know in an unexpected setting.

"Henry Bryant, as in Judge Henry Bryant, nominee for the U.S. Supreme Court?"

"That's right," Thomas said, smiling at my surprise. "And he'll be a great Supreme Court Justice."

I had known Henry Bryant was from Tallahassee, but the stories I had read had skimmed over his prejudge years. Although some of them undoubtedly had mentioned his time in the state attorney's office, it hadn't registered with me. I had been more interested in the praises being sung by almost everyone. Henry Bryant was nonpartisan, smart, respected, a judge who held to a centrist position strongly anchored in the law. He also had a large sympathy factor operating as a result of having lost his wife to cancer when she was only thirty years old, leaving him to raise their two young children alone. Bryant had never remarried, and one story I had read had quoted him as saying he had never found a woman he loved as much as he had his late wife.

"I still remember the day Henry went in to have a meeting with Ford about the Coleman investigation," Lawson Thomas went on, interrupting my mental rehashing of the Bryant stories. "He was in there for no more than half an hour, but when he came back out, he looked pretty upset. He didn't say anything then, but we had planned to have lunch that day, and at lunch Henry told me in confidence that Ford had refused to go any further with the investigation. He said Ford told him the evidence just wasn't there and that it wasn't worth wasting any more staff time on. Henry was pretty unhappy with the decision, and I was concerned about him, given what he was already going through. That was during the time his wife was dying, you understand, and he had enough problems on his hands without taking grief at work, too."

"So what did he do about it?"

"Nothing, as far as I know. It wasn't long after that, no more than a few weeks, that the governor appointed Henry to fill a vacant county judgeship. And I think Coleman left Tallahassee for Washington not long afterward, too. The investigation was never reassigned, and as far as I know, that was the end of it."

"Did you ever ask Truesdale about why he told Bryant to drop the investigation?"

"No," Thomas said, smiling. "Ford Truesdale wasn't a man whose decisions you questioned. When he gave an order, it was final, and he didn't tolerate second-guessing. I guess no one was surprised when he died from a stroke; he had very high blood pressure and the temper to go with it. And since the Coleman investigation wasn't even my case, there was no way I would have broached the subject with him."

"But didn't you wonder about it later when Arthur Williams killed himself and Three Rivers collapsed?"

"A little," Thomas agreed. "But by then I had decided to run for the Florida House of Representatives, where I spent a couple of terms before coming to the senate, and so I had left the state attorney's office, too. I had a lot of other things on my mind. And of course, since it wasn't my case, I knew none of the details. But if there had been anything more definite to tie Coleman to anything, I assume it would have turned up again later, in the investigation after the company collapsed. I just figured Ford had been right and there really wasn't enough of anything there to proceed against Coleman."

"So maybe I should talk to Judge Bryant?"

"Certainly he would know more about what went on than I do," Thomas said. "But keep in mind that, even now, he really can't talk about details of any investigation, especially one that was closed without any charges being brought."

"I know," I said. And I did know that those were the rules. Which any number of people bent whenever it suited their own purposes. The question was whether Bryant was as straight-arrow as his reputation. If he was, then I most likely would find myself staring at one more in a series of brick walls. I was about ready to start banging my head against them in frustration.

Clearly, Lawson Thomas had told me as much as he knew. There was no point in browbeating him. I thanked him for his time, let him go to his dinner appointment, and I drove back out to my room at the Days Inn.

15

I really wasn't hungry yet, considering the size of the lunch I had eaten in Panama City, so I washed my face and hands to get the day's grime off them, flopped down on the bed to see what CNN had to say for itself until it was time for the local TV news, and decided I had better put in some calls to Washington. There were several people, I knew, who were wondering what I was up to.

The first person I called was Detective Moore, who wasn't in, of course. So I left a message for him that I wouldn't need another guard yet because I was still out of town and that I would check in with him again tomorrow.

Rob Perry was in his usual predeadline terse mood when I called his metro desk extension, but he stopped reading copy long enough to talk to me.

"Well, just keep digging," he said, when I finished filling him in on what I had been up to all day long. "Maybe Judge Bryant will have something useful to tell you. You do know he's up here at the moment?"

"So I've read. Before I hang up, I'll have you transfer me upstairs to Janice Lane to see if she can tell me how to get hold of him." Janice was the reporter who covered the U.S. Supreme Court and who had been writing the stories about Bryant's nomination and upcoming appointment hearings on the Hill. "What's Sy got going on?"

"He's got another piece going in tomorrow on the Coleman

investigation at this end. The Phoenix Group is in absolute chaos at the moment, as you can imagine, and directors are running for cover every which way, saying they had no idea what he was up to. The police have nothing new on who might have bumped Coleman off, or if they do, they're not telling Sy. Which wouldn't be too surprising. Have you talked to them today?"

"Not yet. I've been a little tied up, but I was going to track down Peterson next and grill him. If I can get anything out of him, I'll call you back. If not, just have Sy throw in a few sentences to the effect that the police are still checking alibis but haven't yet identified any suspects in the case. And what about the Magruder shooting? Did Penny get to the funeral? I still have to talk to Lansing about that one."

"Yeah, I've got the funeral piece in the system, all ready to go, and it's pretty tear-jerking, from the copy I saw. You know what police funerals are like, anyway. Lots of formality, and rows and rows of uniformed cops from all over the country, looking big and strong while tears run down their faces. And media everywhere, of course. But Penny managed to corner the police chief at the service and got a couple of quotes from him as well as several other cops from the Mount Vernon Station and some from Magruder's parents lamenting the fact that they'll never be grandparents, since Magruder was an only child. I think James also talked to Lansing, too, but he was pretty close-mouthed."

"I'll wear him down," I assured Rob. He laughed, having been subjected more than once himself to my stubborn persistence when there was something I wanted from him.

Rob and I agreed to talk again by lunch the next day, and he transferred my call up to Janice Lane who, fortunately for me, was still trying to get out of the office. When I explained to her why I was calling, Janice told me that Judge Bryant was staying at the Mayflower, a classic Washington hotel, completely and elegantly renovated in the last few years and not far from the White House and Capitol Hill. I jotted down the switchboard number she gave me for the Mayflower and hung up to make my calls to Peterson and Lansing.

Detective Peterson was still at work when I called him, buried, no doubt, in the mountains of paperwork that a homicide investigation generates.

"Not much new to tell you," Peterson said, when I identified myself and said I was checking on the Coleman case. "The last time we can confirm that anyone saw Coleman alive was at lunchtime on Friday. He left the office and told his secretary he had some personal business to take care of."

"Did he say what kind of business or who it was with?" I asked.

"Nope. She said she didn't ask questions because he often left early for the weekend on 'personal' business. She just figured he was going to meet a woman. Which he may have been, although we haven't found anybody yet who will admit to being with him then."

"And that was the last time anybody saw or talked to him?"

"Or saw his car, either. We're still looking for it, too. Hold on." I heard Peterson rustling through some papers and then he came back on the line. "Dark blue 1998 Volvo sedan. Virginia vanity license plate P-H-N-X G-R-P. In fact, I was about to call the TV stations to put it out on the air."

"Somebody's bound to notice that license plate," I said, jotting down the car's description.

"Well, we're hoping so, if the car is in a place where other people will see it. But if somebody grabbed him to steal his car, it could be anywhere by now, including chopped into parts or dumped at the bottom of a river. Or even on a ship in the Baltimore Harbor, getting ready to head for the Middle East."

"What about additional autopsy results?" I wanted to know. "Have they pinned down the time of death any closer than a day or three before the body was found?"

"The medical examiner says sometime between noon and midnight on Friday."

"Can you say yet whether he was killed in the park or the body was just dumped there?"

"We're pretty sure he was killed there. The amount of blood we found around the body says he died where the neighbor and his dog found him."

Clearly, I was going to have to call Rob Perry back with all this information and dictate a sidebar to go with Sy's story.

"I appreciate everything you've told me," I said to Peterson. "But can I ask you one more thing?"

"You can ask."

"Why didn't you tell Sy Berkowitz all this when he talked to you?"

For a few seconds, Peterson didn't say anything.

"Because you're only a pain in the ass," he answered finally. "But he's a complete flamer."

Flamer, I knew, was a favorite police euphemism for flaming asshole.

"Well, thanks," I answered, as dryly as he had. "I think."

When we hung up, I took a few minutes to sketch out the bones of the sidebar and then called Rob Perry. The part he liked best of all, however, was Peterson's descriptions of Sy and me.

"So you're going to make me talk business first?" Noah Lansing wanted to know. I had called him at home, and as soon as he answered the phone, he started grilling me about my safety. I had ignored his questions and plowed ahead with one of my own about the Magruder investigation.

"Obviously, I'm alive," I responded. "We can get into details later."

"I think we may have a witness who saw the guy," Noah Lansing said.

"Which guy?"

"The guy who shot Magruder."

"The witness is coming forward only now? Where's this person been for the last six days?"

"He was out of town until now. I just got home from interviewing him. He lives on Magruder's floor, but he left town Friday and just got back last night. He didn't know about Magruder until he started going through the weekend's papers. He called me this afternoon."

"So, what did he see?"

"Maybe nothing. Or maybe the shooter."

"Explain, please."

"This guy says he was leaving the building to go to National Airport about the time we think Magruder was killed."

"And?"

"He passed a guy getting off the elevator just as he was getting on. He said the guy was wearing some kind of police uniform. But he doesn't remember enough about it for us to know what kind."

"Could it have been one of yours?"

"We don't know. He couldn't even remember what color it was, just that it made him think *police uniform*. He said it might even have been a security guard's uniform, but nobody in the building works for a security company as far as we can tell, and the apartment complex doesn't use uniformed security."

"So you're saying there may be something to this idea that Magruder was killed in retaliation for what he did at the McLean Station?"

"No, I'm not saying that. I'm saying we're looking into all possibilities, including the possibility that he opened the door to somebody he thought was another law enforcement officer."

"What about Terry Porter's alibi in Texas? He probably still has a uniform or two hanging around."

"We're still talking to him, trying to find somebody who can place him in Texas on Friday afternoon."

"But you haven't ruled him out?"

"Not yet. But, off the record?"

"Okay."

"Don't get too carried away with that idea. Yes, Magruder got death threats, but we don't know who made those threats or whether they were serious, and I don't believe Magruder would have opened his door and let either Porter or Monk inside. He knew them both personally and knew they would have it in for him in a big way. He wasn't stupid."

"Maybe one of them hired it done."

"It's a possibility, but we've got nothing in that direction, either."

"Okay, I'll just go with the witness turning up for now."

"Can you also say that we're looking for anyone else who might have noticed someone, other than Magruder, in a uniform in the building or the parking lot around that time? The Fraternal Order of Police has come up with a twenty-five-thousand-dollar reward for anybody who can lead us to the killer, so maybe that will jog some memories."

"Sure," I said. "I can put that in."

"Now, can we go back to my original topic?"

"I'm fine," I told him, trying to wipe my impatience with his concern out of my voice. "No one is following me. No one has bothered me. I was very careful when I left the paper. I don't know how whoever blew up my car would even know where I am at the moment."

"When do you think you'll be back in D.C.?"

"Tomorrow. I think I've done everything I can here at the moment. And there's someone I need to talk to who turns out to be in Washington instead of here. So I'll probably come back whenever I can get a flight out tomorrow."

"Will you call me when you get back and let's talk about where you're going to stay until they catch this guy?"

"For that matter, I still have to figure out where I'm going to live."

"What do you mean?"

I realized I hadn't told Lansing yet about the little visit from the manager of my apartment building and the eviction notice he had served on me, perhaps because I had been trying so hard to put it out of my own mind.

"So," I said, after explaining what I meant, "before the end of the next week, I have to find a new apartment and move, on top of everything else. Although I have no idea when I'll find the time to go apartment hunting between now and then.

"That sucks," Lansing said. "Why don't you fight it? It's not like you to take defeat lying down."

Except when it comes to Lansing, of course, when lying down would be your preference.

You really have a dirty mind, I thought.

"Because," I told Lansing, "I have too many other things to do in the next few days. And besides, it probably would only be delaying the inevitable."

"You'll call me when you get back to D.C?"

"I'll call. I'll call. But right now I've got to call my editor in order to get the Magruder stuff into tomorrow's paper."

"I'll be waiting to hear from you."

I told Lansing good night and hung up.

You're scared to death of him, aren't you?

No, I thought back, *I'm not scared of him. He's only a cop, not my editor.*

Yeah, but it's not the cop part that scares you.

I didn't like the frequency with which I seemed unable to come up with an appropriately biting response anymore. So I picked up the phone and dialed Rob Perry for the third time that evening.

The male voice who answered the phone in Judge Henry Bryant's Washington hotel room, when I finally called there, grilled me on who I was and why I was calling.

"And who is this?" I asked, not liking the tone of voice I was listening to.

"This is Dell Curl. I'm Judge Bryant's assistant. And you're not the reporter we've been talking to at the Washington *News*."

"That's right, but we often have more than one reporter working on stories. I need to speak with Judge Bryant to get some information about some of his cases from when he was in Tallahassee. I was hoping he might have some time to see me for a few minutes tomorrow afternoon or evening." I saw no reason to give this Curl guy any details on what case it was I was interested in.

"Hold on. I'll check," Curl said.

I waited, and then waited some more, and finally Curl came back to the phone.

"Judge Bryant says he can give you a few minutes of his time tomorrow afternoon at six. You can meet us in the hotel bar at that time."

"Thank you," I said with as much grace as I could muster. It was clear they didn't want me in the hotel room where they might become a captive audience. In the bar, they could leave my company any time. "And please tell Judge Bryant I appreciate his finding some time for me."

Curl hung up without responding.

Boy, I thought, putting my own receiver down hard, I couldn't blame Henry Bryant for having someone to screen his calls, especially now that he was up for the Supreme Court, but that didn't mean I had to like it when I was the one being kept at arm's length.

I reached into the drawer of the nightstand between the two double beds and took out the area telephone directory, through which I thumbed until I found the reservations and information number for the airline.

What about Jack?

"What about Jack?" I asked back, falling into my not infrequent but clearly worrisome habit of answering aloud when I was alone.

Well, what about closure? When are you going to see him if you leave in the morning?

"Maybe closure isn't all it's cracked up to be."

And maybe you're just chickenshit.

"Fine. Have it your way. I just decided I have enough problems right now without reopening old wounds." To cut off further conversation, especially when the name-calling was hitting uncomfortably close to home, I picked up the telephone and called the reservations number. The ticket agent who answered got me onto an 8 A.M. return flight to Washington.

As I put the phone book away, I looked at the digital clock on the nightstand and saw that it was after nine P.M. Considering the size of the lunch I had eaten in Panama City, and considering the time now, I decided it wasn't worth leaving the motel to find dinner someplace. Instead, I dug a handful of coins out of my shoulder bag and went out to the vending machines I had seen at the end of the corridor, next to the stairs.

Back in the room with a diet soda and two packs of cheese-and-peanut butter crackers, I watched a couple of half-hour sitcoms and the first part of a hospital drama and then got ready to turn in early again. Considering how many different things I had on my mind, I wouldn't have been surprised to find myself lying awake, stewing over it all. But the Florida heat must have been more tiring than I realized, because I fell asleep almost as soon as I lay down.

It wasn't until much later, 2:17 A.M. in fact, that I came wide awake in the bed. Apparently, it had taken that long for my subconscious to clear away all the other things my conscious brain had been dealing with and to point out to me what it was Detective Peterson had said. He had told me that Robert Coleman had been shot to death in Grist Mill Park sometime Friday afternoon and that his dark blue Volvo sedan was missing. Like the dark blue Volvo sedan I had seen at the park on that same Friday afternoon when

I went there with Dan Magruder. The dark blue Volvo sedan to which Magruder had taken the drunk he had in custody in order to question the driver of the car.

After that little epiphany, it was almost dawn before I finally fell asleep again.

16

FRIDAY

I caught a cab to the *News* building once I landed at Washington National. It was 11:30 A.M. by the metro room clock, and Rob Perry wasn't in yet. I sat down at my desk in the relative quiet of the morning newsroom and rewound in my head the tape that I had been playing over and over, first in the middle of last night when I woke up and, later, all through my flight back to Washington. Every time I ran through it, I still came to the same conclusion.

I picked up the phone and called Detective Moore in Alexandria. He might have information that would tell me whether what I thought I knew was wrong.

"I'm glad you called," Moore said when I identified myself. "Where are you now?"

"I'm back in D.C., at the newspaper."

"Are you watching your back?"

"As well as I know how. So far, I haven't seen anything that looks like a familiar face or car, anyone who might be following me. I think I managed to fly to Tallahassee without anyone seeing me go, and I haven't been back to my apartment since I got back. So I'm hoping that, if somebody is trying to tail me, they have no idea where I am at the moment."

"Are you going home tonight?"

Good question. It was something Lansing also had wanted to talk about, which told me he wanted me to come back to his place so he could keep a personal eye on me. Was I sure I really wanted to make that a habit?

"I don't know yet," I told Moore. "If I do, I'll call you again."

"I just don't think you should take any chances until we catch this guy," Moore said.

"I appreciate your concern," I answered, and I did. I just didn't have any intention of letting it get in the way of my job, a job that was looking much more complicated at this moment. "The other reason I called was to find out if there's anything new on that front. Do you have anything yet on who it might be? I'm not working the story myself, but I obviously have a personal interest in knowing what's happening."

"Not a lot yet. We've been going down the list of people you've done stories about in the last year or so, trying to find out where they are. So far, nothing promising. The ATF guys are still running tests and going through the evidence they collected. They say it looks like a simple dynamite package set up to blow when you turned on your car. Just about anybody who really wanted to could get their hands on the stuff to make one. Building the thing wouldn't have required a lot of technical knowledge, and with a VW Beetle convertible, it wouldn't have taken a lot of explosive to turn it into rubble."

"What about the guy who was killed?" I still hadn't been able to get the image of his burned and torn body out of my head. "Any idea who he was yet? Maybe somebody hired him to do it, and he botched it."

"It's possible, but I don't think so. A couple of our gang detail guys say they think he may have been a kid who went by the street name of Espada. It means sword in Spanish. He seems to have dropped off the face of the earth since the weekend, and stealing collector-type cars like yours was one of his specialties, according to his buddies."

"Have you talked to his family?"

"We don't know who they are. He just showed up on the street one day and told people what to call him. His friends say he never talked about who he was or where he was from. My guess is he was a runaway. We've run his fingerprints through the computer, but we didn't get a hit. And we've sent the physical description out around the country, but the odds of finding out who he was aren't high. It's possible he's never even been reported missing from wherever he came from."

"Jesus." Somewhere, I thought, there was a family who either might never know what happened to their son or didn't care. I wasn't sure which I thought was worse.

"Yeah," Moore said. Clearly, he understood what was going through my head.

"So, is it okay for me to pass all this along to Penny James?" While it was true that I wasn't covering the story, neither was I going to take any chances of letting the *News* get beaten on a story in which I personally was involved.

"I already did. She called me this morning from home, just before you did."

I thanked Moore for the information and his efforts, without telling him what I now suspected, and hung up. I had hoped he would have a new theory on what had made my car explode, one that didn't involve someone with a grudge against me, but nothing had changed. He and the ATF investigators clearly were convinced it was a deliberate act on someone's part, an act that had killed the wrong person. After talking with Moore, I also was pretty sure now that I knew *why* someone had tried to blow me to bits. I just didn't know who. But even the why meant I needed to check in with Detective Peterson and Noah Lansing.

"We just found Coleman's car," Peterson said without preamble when he came on the line after being summoned to the phone by another detective. "I was about to go down there, so I don't have time to chat."

"Where is it?"

"In a shopping center parking lot in Woodbridge. Somebody who works at one of the stores noticed it after seeing a TV news broadcast about the license plate. The Prince William County police have it roped off for us, but I've got to get down there while our guys process the scene for evidence and then get it hauled back up here to impound so we can go over it thoroughly."

"Before you run off, there's something I need to talk to you about."

"Not now, Sutton. I don't have the time." He hung up before I could say another word. In frustration, I slammed down the telephone receiver, and then saw the voice mail message light come on. I called down to the photo department to let them know about Coleman's car, and then I dialed into the voice mail system and heard Noah Lansing's voice. I had just missed his call. Fortunately, he was still at his desk when I called him back.

"Are you here or in Florida?" he wanted to know as soon as he answered the phone.

"I'm here, at the paper, and I'm fine."

"You ready to talk about where you're staying tonight?"

"Not yet. There's something else I need to talk to you about first that's a lot more important. I don't want to get into it over the phone, so I'm coming out there. But while I'm on my way, there's something important that I need you to check on."

"What?" Lansing sounded thoroughly suspicious now.

"You need to find out where a guy named Clinton Sheets is."

"That's the drunk that Dan Magruder arrested when you were with him last week," Lansing said after a couple of seconds' thought. Obviously, the name was familiar to Lansing from going over Magruder's response reports.

"Yes, and I think his life may be in danger. Can you find out if he's still in jail or whether they've let him go yet?"

"What do you mean, his life is in danger? McPhee, what the hell are you talking about? What are you up to?"

"I'll explain it when I get out there. Could you please just wait for me and find out where Sheets is?"

"All right," Lansing agreed, sounding not at all mollified. "But you be careful driving out here. And this had better be good."

"I don't think *good* is quite the word I'm looking for," I said. "I think *frightening* is more like it. I'll see you in a little while."

Lansing hung up, and I dialed into Rob Perry's voice mail to tell him I was back in town but out in Fairfax talking to the police, and that I would call him if I had anything in the way of stories.

"Where's Sheets?" I asked as soon as I walked into the door of Lansing's Massey Building office, into which he had moved only four weeks earlier, from temporary quarters at the Great Falls Substation.

"He's still cooling his heels in the jail," Lansing said, his eyebrows raised at my abruptness. "And Clinton Sheets is an alias. Once they ran his fingerprints through the computer, they got hits on two other names, Robert Clinton and Tommy Bob Clinton. Apparently, the second one is his real name. Anyway, he's got a long list of offenses from Pennsylvania for public drunkenness and a couple for resisting arrest. We also turned up a warrant on him for failing to appear after the last time he was arrested up there, so the judge decided we could hang on to him, even with Magruder dead, until the folks in Pennsylvania can come and get him."

"Good," I said as I sat down in one of Lansing's black vinyl guest chairs. "At least I can stop worrying about him, then."

"You ready to tell me what this is about?" Lansing asked, giving me a look I had seen more than once while he was working the Kane and Taylor murders, the case on which I had met him. It was the look that said he thought I might have overstepped my bounds and that it had better not create problems for him.

"I'll tell you, if you'll answer one question for me without bull-shitting me."

"What?"

"I want to know exactly where things are with your investigation of Terry Porter. Could he have shot Magruder or not?"

Lansing grimaced slightly, as if something was causing him a pain in some part of his body. Probably some nether region that was sensitive to reporters, I guessed.

"Yesterday, we didn't know one way or the other," he said finally. "Today, I'd have to say probably not."

"Mind telling me why you don't think so?"

"Oh, hell, why the hell not? You'll find out, anyway. Because we finally got his telephone records. He eventually said that he remembered getting a couple of telephone sales calls that afternoon, but he couldn't remember who from. According to the phone records, someone at his apartment did answer the telephone twice during the afternoon Magruder was killed. Porter lives alone, so it looks like he probably was there, after all."

"Thank you," I said. "That makes me think that I may just be right about what I'm thinking."

"I'm almost afraid to ask this, but what are you thinking?"

"I think I know who shot Dan Magruder," I told him, deciding there was no point in easing my way into it gradually. "Or actually, I don't know precisely who, but I think I know why he was shot."

"Oh? And why was that?" The intensity of the natural light behind Lansing's blue eyes ratcheted up several notches, either because he thought I was on to something in which he had a vital interest or because he thought I'd completely flipped out. I couldn't tell which, but I liked his eyes on me, anyway.

"I think it was the same guy who killed Robert Coleman," I went on, "and I think I may have seen him."

"What?" The word more or less exploded out of his mouth, leaving him gaping at me in surprise.

"Before you get all bent out of shape, let me take you through it, and you tell me if it makes sense."

"Oh, you're definitely going to take me through it, all right," Lansing said, now clearly leaning toward the flipped-out theory. He settled back in his chair as if preparing to listen to a tall tale. "Go right ahead."

"It was the car that clicked for me," I said.

"What car?"

"Don't ask questions yet. Just listen, and let me go through the whole thing."

Lansing looked as if he had all sorts of things he wanted to say, but he didn't respond.

"Okay," I said, trying to organize what I knew in the most logical order, "I told you about riding around with Magruder all day last Friday, and that the last call we made was over to Grist Mill Park to pick up Sheets or Clinton or whatever the hell his name is, for taking a leak in front of the little kids. I assume you went back and read Magruder's report on it, right?"

"Right."

"Did he mention witnesses?"

"Only the kids. He said he wasn't able to locate any others."

"He didn't find anybody else who saw it happen, but he did talk to somebody who was there at the time. There was one car in the parking lot, and the driver was just coming back up the bike path to the car when Magruder got Clinton in handcuffs. Magruder took a few minutes to walk Clinton over to the car and talk to the driver. He told me later that he was hoping the guy at the car might have seen something, but the guy said he hadn't been around at the time. So Magruder came back across the park to the Ferry house, and the guy in the car left."

"And your point is?"

"This was Friday afternoon. At Grist Mill Park. The medical examiner says Coleman died there sometime between noon and midnight Friday. Peterson is down in Woodbridge right now, impounding Coleman's dark blue Volvo sedan, which someone found in a parking lot down there. The car I saw in Grist Mill Park, the one that Magruder went over to, was a late-model, dark blue Volvo sedan. I was too far away to see license plates."

Before I had finished, I saw the deductive train getting on track for Lansing, saw the knowledge of what I was about to say register in his expression. He sat forward, suddenly intent on what I was telling him.

"You saw this car and the guy who was driving it?"

"Yes, although I saw it from across the park. But Dan Magruder went over and talked to the guy. And he had Clinton with him."

"So you think it was Coleman's car, and the guy Magruder talked to was either Coleman or the guy who had just killed him?"

"I do, although I personally think it was the killer. Keep in mind here that I was watching from quite a ways away and that I wasn't paying particular attention to the guy in the car. But from the pictures I've seen so far of Coleman, I don't think it was him. I just have the impression that the guy I saw was probably thinner, maybe taller, than Coleman looks to have been. And he appeared to have lighter-colored hair. I know Coleman's hair was dark except for that white streak."

"And then you think the guy tracked Magruder down and killed him because Magruder had seen him in the park at the time Coleman was murdered? Had seen him close enough to identify him?"

"Right. I mean, think about it from his perspective. Magruder got a real good look at him and the car he was driving. Not only could Magruder ID him by sight and place him in the park at the approximate time of the murder, but for all the guy knew, Magruder had made a note of the license plates on the car. By the way, did he?"

"I can check the report again, but I don't remember any mention of it," Lansing said regretfully. "So, how did he find Magruder again?"

"It wouldn't have been hard. Magruder had his name tag on. He may even have introduced himself by name. If the guy called the Mount Vernon Station, they probably would have told him when Magruder got off work. Or, for all I know, the guy went a block or two down the street and waited to follow us back to the station and then followed Magruder home. He couldn't have gotten into the elevator with Magruder to see what apartment he lived in, or Magruder might have recognized him. But a few bucks slipped to someone in the management office or even to a maintenance person who might have seen Magruder in uniform could have solved that problem.

"And you were afraid that whoever killed Magruder would go after Clinton if Clinton had been released?"

"Yes. I put the Sheets name in my story, after all. He was drunk as a skunk that day, but who knows what he might or might not remember. If I were the killer, I probably wouldn't take a chance on his memory. And how hard would it be to find out if he were still in jail or back out on the street?"

"Not very. Just a phone call. What about the woman who called the park thing in, and her kids? Why hasn't he gone after them?"

"If he even saw them from across the park, in the shade of the trees, he probably figured they were too far away to see anything. And besides, going after a housewife and her two little kids probably would bring down a lot more heat than killing off a reporter."

Lansing laughed at that comment.

"I'm not getting suckered into that one," he said. "So anyway, you're saying that the last part of this would be your car? You think this guy may be the one who rigged it with the bomb?"

"It would be too coincidental if it wasn't him, don't you think?"

"Maybe," Lansing said, then gave me a wicked smile. "Although I'm sure there's more than one person out there who's found you so infuriating that they've thought about doing you in. He probably would have to get in line."

"I thought you weren't getting suckered in."

"Sometimes the temptation is just stronger than the willpower. But back on the subject, if this guy you saw in the Volvo killed Coleman on Friday and was so concerned about witnesses that he shot Magruder that same afternoon, why did he wait until Monday night to go after you?"

"That had me stumped for a while, too. But I finally realized that he didn't know about me until not long before that. If he saw me at all, it would have been from all the way across the park. I was standing in Mrs. Ferry's backyard, in the shade, with her and her kids. If he could even see us, he probably thought I was a neighbor. Or if he followed the cruiser, he might have thought I was the person who called the cops out after the drunk in the first place. It wasn't until the Sunday paper came out that he would have known who I was, that he would have realized a reporter had seen him, as well as a cop. While a housewife and kids might not be a threat, he probably figured a reporter was as bad as a cop. A reporter is someone who pays attention, or someone to whom Magruder might have said something that I could use to identify the guy in the park.

"At any rate," I went on, "my guess is that it took him until Monday to get what he needed to rig the car. And if he's a cop or a former cop of some kind, he would have known how to find out easily what kind of car I drove and where I live. I'm in the phone book. So all he had to do was wait for me to come home Monday night. It was just his bad luck that that kid tried to steal my car before I came back out the next morning to go to work."

And the kid's bad luck, too, of course.

Not now, I thought back. *I'm trying to think straight here.*

Well, let's not get in the way of an occurrence as rare as that!

"So why didn't he just shoot you, the way he did Magruder?" Lansing asked, interrupting my little friend. "When murderers find a method that works, they usually like to stick with it. Why a car bomb?"

"Who knows? But maybe he didn't want our deaths connected, didn't want too many arrows pointing in one direction. Maybe he thought blowing me up would put police off his trail. Or maybe he was being more careful about witnesses this time, and by the time he saw the paper, it was just too difficult to get close enough to shoot me. I was at home from Sunday afternoon when I left you and David until Monday morning when I went to work. My apartment building is much bigger than Magruder's, which means there are usually more people around, and it wasn't a weekday, when most people would have been at work. In other words, too many witnesses to provide descriptions or come around a corner unexpectedly. Without being able to connect it to the Magruder and Coleman shootings, the police would think exactly what they are thinking, that it was somebody who was really pissed off at a story I did about them. And with two different police agencies involved, he has lessened the chances even more that someone would make the connection."

Lansing was looking at me hard again in silence, his mind obviously running through all the permutations of the theory I had presented to him. Then he reached over and picked up his telephone to dial a number. Within a minute, someone answered on the other end.

"It's Lansing," he said, still looking at me across the receiver. "You still in Woodbridge?" Apparently, he had called Jim Peterson on Peterson's car phone. There was a pause as Lansing listened to whatever Peterson was saying. "How soon will you be done there?" Another pause. "As soon as you can get back up to Fairfax, come find me. I've got McPhee in my office, and she's got a story I think you had better hear."

More listening. A grin. "No, I don't think she's gone off half-cocked this time. I think she may be on to something, and it involves the case you're on down there." Pause. "Okay, I'll be here, and I'll make sure she hangs around until you get back." He hung up.

"That was Peterson," he said.

"So I gathered," I replied. "I think it was the half-cocked part that gave it away."

"Will you please come back to my house tonight so I don't have to worry about you?" Lansing asked, as we waited for Peterson.

"I really don't know if that's such a good idea," I told him. "For all sorts of reasons."

"Such as?"

"Come on, I'm sure you can figure them out for yourself."

"Probably, but take me through them anyway, so I can talk you out of them."

I sighed. "Okay, first of all, professional conflicts. I'm a reporter. You're a police detective. I have to cover the cases you're investigating. How am I supposed to be objective if I'm staying at your house? My boss is going to find out sooner or later, because eventually, I'll tell him even if no one else does. And how do you get your bosses to believe you didn't spill the beans to me when I find out something about one of your cases that I wasn't supposed to know?"

"Personal integrity. In both cases. Next."

"You've got a six-year-old son. What's he supposed to think about some woman spending the night there?"

"How about the truth? That there's a temporary problem with your apartment, and you're a friend who needs a place to stay for a few days. He thought that explanation sounded perfectly sensible when I gave it to him Tuesday night."

"Aren't you worried at all that I might represent a risk to you and David? What if the person who wants me dead finds out that I'm staying there?"

A look of pain crossed Lansing's face.

"No more of a risk than my job has always represented to him," he said simply. But I knew the pain I had seen was the memory of Sarah, the wife who had died because of his job.

"Then what about David getting attached to me and then you decide this really isn't such a hot idea after all? Is that good for him?"

"I think," Lansing said, "what you're really worried about is *my* getting attached to you and vice versa. I think that scares the bejesus out of you."

"I don't know what you're talking about," I replied. "Why would I be afraid of that?"

"That's a question *you're* going to have to answer."

Well, he's got you there, hasn't he?

He had, of course. I knew, when I was honest with myself, that that was exactly the problem. I wanted Lansing and was terrified of him at the same time.

"Besides," I said, trying to change the subject, "what if it takes weeks or months to catch this guy? How long can I stay with you before you get tired of it, or before we..." I stopped awkwardly, realizing it was the same subject after all.

"Before we what?" Lansing asked, giving me a wicked smile. He knew exactly what I had almost said, but he wanted to torture me, anyway.

I was saved from having to answer by the appearance of a woman in Lansing's office doorway.

"I've got the sketch for you," she said, handing him a sheet of paper. She looked to be in her early thirties, petite, light brown hair pulled back in a ponytail. A rather plain face on which sat a freckled nose and a pair of intelligent hazel eyes that more than made up for the plainness.

"Sharon, hi," Lansing said, smiling at her. "Let's see what you've got."

The woman smiled at me in acknowledgment as she walked behind Lansing to look over his shoulder while he put the paper down on the desk in front of him. I could see that it held a face. Lansing looked at it thoughtfully.

I stood up and reached out my hand to the woman.

"I'm Sutton McPhee," I said, shaking the hand she held out in response. "I'm with the Washington *News*."

Lansing looked up in embarrassment.

"I'm sorry," he said before Sharon could speak. "Sutton, this is Sharon Pate. She's a new sketch artist for the department. We've had her on the computer all morning, working with the neighbor who saw a man in uniform on Magruder's floor. Here, you should take a look at it, too." He turned the sheet around to face in my direction. "See if it looks anything like the guy you saw in the park."

I studied the long, thin face that looked back at me from the paper.

"I just don't know," I said finally, looking up at Lansing in apology. "It could be him. But I just wasn't close enough to see this kind of detail. I'm sorry."

"I don't know how good a likeness it really is, either," Sharon said, looking from me to Lansing. "The neighbor only saw this person for a second, of course, and we didn't get to pick his brain until several days later, so his memories of the person he saw are all very vague at this point."

"It's okay," Lansing said to her reassuringly. "We weren't expecting a whole lot from him, based on what he already had told us, but maybe it's better than nothing." He looked at me. "We'll get you a copy of this to take with you. Spend some time with it and see if anything comes back to you."

He looked up at Sharon again and handed the sketch back to her.

"Tell Frank to go ahead with distribution on this if the witness is satisfied with it."

"I will," Sharon said, taking the sketch. "It was nice to meet you," she told me as she went to the door.

"You, too."

When she was gone, Lansing and I looked at each other again.

"So you'll come back to the house tonight?"

"Do I have any choice?" I asked in exasperation.

"None."

"Then I guess I'll be there." Trepidation and all.

Lansing looked pleased with himself.

"Having you around is enough to make me believe in this Karma thing," Jim Peterson said as he lowered himself into the other guest chair in Lansing's office.

"Excuse me? I don't understand what you mean," I responded, looking at him in confusion. His comment was a non sequitur, seemingly unrelated to anything Lansing and I had been discussing when Peterson walked in or to anything to do with Peterson's case.

"I keep wondering just how many lifetimes of misbehaving I'm trying to work off here," Peterson explained drolly. "And how many more it will take."

Lansing started laughing. Peterson kept up his severe look, but I thought his eyes didn't look quite as serious as the rest of his face, so I decided not to take the bait and risk getting into a real argument with him. There was too much to tell him at the moment.

"I think Robert Coleman and Dan Magruder were killed by the same person," I told Peterson, indulging in a non sequitur of my own.

He gave me much the same look that Lansing had when I had trotted my theory out for him, even though Lansing had alerted him to expect something unexpected.

I took him back through the same scenario I had run through with Lansing earlier. Peterson listened in silence as I tried to anticipate and answer all his questions before he asked them. When I was done, he looked at Lansing with an expression that asked what Lansing thought of this whole idea.

"I don't quite know what to make of it," Lansing told him, answering Peterson's unspoken question. "I just got the sketch of the man who was seen going toward Magruder's apartment, and I've had Sutton take a look at it, but she couldn't say whether it's the same guy they saw in the park or not."

Before Peterson could respond, Lansing's telephone rang.

"But I do think there's some sense to what she says," Lansing finished saying to Peterson as he lifted the receiver, into which he then said, "Hello." He listened silently for a brief moment, said, "Thanks a lot," and hung up, looking from Peterson to me and back to Peterson.

"That was the ballistics section out at the crime lab," Lansing explained. "I called them as soon as Sutton laid all this on me and asked them to do an emergency comparison on the slug we found near Coleman with the one they took out of Magruder." He paused and looked from Peterson to me and back to Peterson. "We've got a match."

Silence reigned as we all took it in. I suspected each of us was a little stunned, though for different reasons. I was silenced by the impact of having my theory suddenly transformed into a threatening reality, in which my life was still at risk. Peterson and Lansing both were probably looking at all the new dimensions their individual cases had just taken on, in light of the previously unsuspected but now suddenly confirmed connection between them. And I was sure they must have been equally surprised by the fact that the theory, which clearly now was much more than that, had come from me.

Once he regained his tongue, Peterson managed to think up some new questions for me. He apparently still wasn't quite convinced that, whatever connection existed between the murders of Robert Coleman and Dan Magruder, it had anything at all to do with the attempt on my life.

"How do we know the dead guy at your car wasn't the one with the bomb, that it didn't just blow up prematurely?" Peterson wanted to know.

I told him what Detective Moore had said about the kid and Moore's belief that the kid just made a fatal error in choosing my car, that the bomb clearly had been intended to kill me.

"And what about the IA stuff you were looking into on Magruder?" Peterson asked, turning to Lansing.

Lansing explained about Terry Porter's telephone records.

"It's not necessarily an iron-clad alibi," Lansing conceded, "but my gut tells me he really was at home in Texas during the time."

"I suppose the next question," he went on, "is where do we go from here?"

"You sure you want to discuss this in front of a reporter?" Peterson asked.

I heard my cell phone start to ring in my purse. I stood up and started out into the hall.

"Why don't you boys make your plans while I go answer this," I said on my way out the door.

17

"This is Lawson Thomas," a male voice said through the cell phone once I wrestled it out of my purse and answered it in the hallway.

"Senator Thomas," I said, "what a surprise." I was pretty sure when I had met with him in Tallahassee that Thomas had made a genuine effort to tell me everything he remembered—even as little as it was—about the now twenty-year-old investigation of Robert Coleman. Although I had left my card with him, with my standard instructions to call if he remembered something else, I hadn't really expected to hear anything more from him.

"I'm as surprised as you are," Thomas said. "But something a little odd has come up that may or may not mean anything. I suppose the only reason I'm calling you about it is that it bothers me, knowing that Robert Coleman has been murdered."

"So what happened?" I asked, tuning out Lansing's and Peterson's voices in the office behind me, to which I still had been trying to listen with one ear.

"I have to admit that your visit yesterday, especially in light of Coleman getting killed, got me to remembering and got my curiosity up," Thomas said. "To the point that I called over to the state attorney's office, in fact, and talked to the woman who was my secretary when I worked there. She's still a secretary there, although she has to be getting pretty close to retirement by now. I called and asked her to locate the Coleman file. I told her I needed her to refresh my memory about a couple of things."

"So you thought the file might have information in it that would have a bearing on who killed Coleman?"

"Not really," Thomas said. "As I say, knowing he had been murdered just made me curious again about why Ford closed the earlier investigation. I suppose I really just called over there to satisfy myself. Which is why I would prefer it if you would keep my name out of any stories you write about all this. It isn't completely ethical for me to start going through old files there, when I no longer work there and years after I've left. Especially files for cases that weren't mine in the first place. And I wouldn't want to get Martha in trouble, either."

Martha, apparently, was his former secretary.

"I think I can promise that neither of your names will come up in any of my stories," I told him.

"Thanks," Thomas said, "I appreciate that. Anyway, Martha called me back just now and said the file seems to be missing."

"Missing?" I echoed stupidly.

"She couldn't find it anywhere. It wasn't in the inactive files, where it should be, or anyplace else in the office that she could find. There was no record of anyone having checked it out of the files for any reason, and no indication of how long it's been gone."

"Could Coleman or someone helping him have taken it?" I asked.

"He could never have gotten it personally," Thomas explained. "It would have required help from someone in the office, which would really surprise me. Martha says no one there would have given it to him, especially since it involved an investigation of him."

"Any idea when it was taken out last officially? And by whom?"

"Henry signed it out of the inactive files and then back in again just before he left the department to take the judgeship. That wouldn't have been unusual, though. It would have gone into the inactive files as soon as Ford Truesdale closed the investigation. But Henry probably would have needed to tie up some loose ends, even after the investigation was closed. But he signed it back in when he was finished, so it should still be there."

I asked Thomas a couple more questions, but he had no more helpful answers.

"It just seemed very odd to me that the file wouldn't be there," Thomas concluded, "and I thought that might be something you would want to know."

"Oh, very definitely," I agreed. "I can't tell you, off the top of my head, what I think the file's disappearance means. But I have to admit that that kind of coincidence always makes me very suspicious. Do you mind if I call you again if I think of any other questions for you?"

"Not at all," Thomas said, "as long as I can keep my name out of it."

I reassured him on that score again. I thanked Thomas for letting me know what he had learned and repeated the request to call me again if he found out anything else. I hung up, frustrated at the image of another brick wall rising up in front of me. Clearly, I was going to have to do some hard thinking if I was going to find a way around this one, but first I had to find out what Lansing and Peterson were cooking up.

"So what's the verdict?" I asked, walking back into the office doorway.

They exchanged looks again.

"We've decided we need to touch base with Detective Moore and start comparing notes," Lansing said, "in case you're right about your car bombing being connected to our cases."

I groaned. When Moore heard this story, he would be even more determined to put me under armed guard twenty-four hours a day.

"All right," I said, "I've got to get back to the paper on something else, but I'll be back in touch with both of you and with Moore."

"Will you let us send somebody with you?" Lansing asked, not sounding hopeful of the answer.

"Thanks, but no thanks. I'll call you from the paper," I said, then turned and started down the hall.

"Be careful," I heard him call out.

I did make an extra effort to keep an eye on the traffic around me as I drove back into the District. Nobody seemed particularly interested in me, evidenced by the fact that every other car on the road passed me as I kept pretty close to the speed limit. I figured that, in a place where everyone drives ten or fifteen miles over the posted speed limit, it was a good way to quickly spot anyone tailing me.

In between glances out my window and into my rearview and side mirrors, I thought about Lawson Thomas's call. Who would have wanted to make Coleman's investigation file disappear from the state attorney's office? I wondered. Well, Robert Coleman, for starters, obviously. But who would have taken the risk of stealing it for him? The only person I could think of who might fit that description was Ford Truesdale, the late state attorney, who, according to what Henry Bryant had told Thomas, had quashed the investigation for unknown reasons. But if it was Truesdale, there probably was no way now, with both him and Coleman dead, to find out what he might have done with the file or what was in it. And when was the file taken? Last week? Twenty years ago?

Damn it all, I thought in frustration, *so now what do I do?* Finally, I decided to do what I usually do when I've run out of tracks to follow: Go back to the beginning and cast a wider net. As it happened, I also had expert help in that area in the person of Cooper Diggs, whom I planned to visit as soon as I got back to the paper.

Cooper Diggs is a surprising anomaly. He is the handsome, intelligent, eldest offspring of a very prominent family from the Charleston,

South Carolina, area. Cooper refused to follow several generations of forebears into either law or medicine and then dropped out of college and turned his almost magical abilities with computers into a job as director of the research library at the *News*. He told me once, brushing back the blond hair that regularly falls down into his eyes, how he had spent the first two decades of his life in Charleston living in a world of secrets that were rarely acknowledged but that affected the lives of everyone he knew, himself included. And how he hated it. Now, he revels in making a living unearthing people's secrets, using his computers to search databases all over the world for the information trails most of us don't even realize we are leaving.

Cooper also is a first-rate hacker, with an ability to get into places he isn't supposed to be, to take the information and run, often without detection. He's been told by the folks at the *News*, in no uncertain terms, that under no circumstances is he to indulge in such activities at the office. But they have no control over what he does from home. Nor does Cooper offer his extracurricular services to the rank-and-file reporting staff. Although he spends his days helping them with research, his efforts usually stop at the line our bosses have drawn. But away from the office, he has crossed that line, more than once, at my request. Cooper apparently considers me a special case, and I value his friendship and his talents immensely, which I show by keeping to myself just how I obtain certain bits of information.

When I got to the library, Cooper was happily ensconced in his electronic domain, with his fax machine buzzing loudly as it printed out pages, the photocopy machine clicking and flashing, and the screens of both the computers he uses aglow with lists of information.

"Hey, Sutton," Cooper said in greeting when I walked up. "It's good to see you!" He stood up from his desk chair and reached out to shake my hand. Our friendship was just that, a friendship, so I had been expecting the handshake. "Especially in one piece," he added.

"No shit," I agreed, sitting down in the extra chair at the end of his desk.

"The police have any idea yet who tried to kill you?" It was the question of the day as far as I was concerned.

"Not really, although I'm beginning to think I may have some idea why. And that's what I need your help with."

Cooper's eyes lit up, and his smile got even bigger. We'd had some interesting moments together, Cooper and I, on several of the stories I had followed in the last two years since I started covering the Fairfax County Police, and I could tell he was anticipating that I might be bringing him something else that was going to be at least as interesting. It was to me, at any rate, probably because it was me someone was trying to kill.

"So let's hear it," Cooper said, clearly salivating in anticipation, although in his elegant, Southern gentlemanly way, of course.

"To keep it simple for right now," I began, "let's just say that there may be a connection with an old story from Tallahassee that goes back to well before my time there. It involves a number of people, and I'd like you to look into their backgrounds and give me anything you can find on them, no matter how unimportant it might seem to be. I'm still missing a critical piece of the puzzle here, and I'm hoping you can turn up something that will help me figure out what it is."

Cooper reached over for a pen and a pad of notepaper.

"Let's have the names," he said, preparing to jot them down.

"Robert Coleman." I said, and Cooper looked up at me in surprise.

"Wow," he commented, writing down Coleman's name.

"I've got the stuff you pulled for Sy, but I know you can find more on him, stuff that wouldn't necessarily show up in old news stories."

Cooper grinned at me again. "Okay, who else?" he asked.

I decided to throw everyone into the mix.

"Ford Truesdale, now deceased. Formerly a state attorney in Tallahassee. Arthur Williams, also deceased. Owner and head of a

Tallahassee development company called Three Rivers. Coleman once was his business partner. For fun, do a rundown on a Florida state senator named Lawson Thomas. Oh, and you might as well do Henry Bryant, too."

"As in Supreme Court Henry Bryant?" Cooper was getting more interested by the minute. I could see he was going to have a field day with this.

"Right. I can't imagine we'll find anything there, considering he's already been investigated for the nomination. But he was the assistant state attorney who handled an aborted investigation of Coleman at one point years ago. Truesdale was Bryant's boss, and he apparently ordered Bryant to put the investigation on ice. I need to know why, but the late Mr. Truesdale obviously can't tell me."

"What about Bryant? He's in town, you know."

"I'm talking to him in just a little while," I said. "But I've been told by someone else who was there at the time that it was Truesdale who quashed the case, so check on him real closely."

"I'll start on it here," Cooper said, tearing the sheet with the names off the top of the pad and sticking it to his computer screen. "And I'll finish it up at home."

It was my turn to grin at him. We both knew what that meant, that no electronic stone would be left unturned, our bosses not withstanding.

"I owe you another one, Cooper," I said, standing up. I had to get up to the newsroom and touch base with Rob Perry and then produce any copy he might want for tomorrow's paper before heading over to the Mayflower Hotel to see Henry Bryant.

"You know I'll collect," Cooper said. And I would reward him happily. While I understand the basics of computers and computer research, I have neither the time nor the inclination to reach Cooper's level of expertise. So I've returned his favors by buying him more than one expensive dinner in my years at the *News*.

"It will be worth every penny and more," I replied.

. . .

As soon as I reached my desk in the metro section, my phone rang. It was Bill Russell.

"Well you have been busy, haven't you?" Bill asked when I answered.

"I'm sure I don't know what you're referring to," I replied archly. Bill laughed.

"I just got off a conference call with Lansing, Peterson, and Detective Moore in Alexandria," he told me. "It was quite entertaining. But now seriously, Sutton, I wish you'd let them send an officer over to go around with you. I understand why you don't want it. But this isn't a game you're playing here. And I think whoever tried to kill you is going to try again and probably do a better job next time."

"I assume this means you agree with my idea that whoever shot Coleman and Magruder also rigged my car," I responded, ignoring the subject of a watchdog.

"I think the odds are good that it's the same guy," Bill said. "The problem, though, is that you don't know who the guy is, and neither do we. He could be in the car behind you in traffic, and how would you know until it's too late?" Clearly, Bill wasn't willing to let the subject of my safety drop yet.

"Bill," I said, "I appreciate your concern. I really do. But you also know I just can't do my job that way."

"Well," he answered, "if that's your final word on the subject. But I do have another question for you."

"Oh? And why do I have the feeling that this other question is the real reason you called?"

"I need to know," he continued smoothly, ignoring my sarcastic response, "how much time you can give us on this business about the matching bullets before you have to put it in the paper. We need time to get our act together with Alexandria."

"Gee, Bill, you must have drawn the short straw."

"Excuse me?"

"Well, it's obvious, since you got stuck being the one who had to call me and ask me to hold off on a story. I can't imagine you volunteered for it. So what's it worth to you?" I had a reason of my own for wanting to sit on the story, but I wasn't going to ruin the fun I was having torturing Bill by telling him that.

"You're a hard woman, Sutton," Bill said, sounding reconciled to not getting off easily. "How much of my blood is this going to cost me?"

"I don't want your blood, Bill," I answered sweetly. "I can hold off on the story for a day or two on one condition."

"Which is?"

"That you promise me it absolutely, positively isn't going to find its way to the competition in the meantime. Not from your shop, and not from the Alexandria P.D., either. I'm holding you personally responsible for keeping their mouths shut as well."

"Jesus," he said, groaning, "why am I still in this job? All right, it's a deal."

"No ifs, ands, or buts?"

"No ifs, ands, or buts."

"And Bill?"

"What?"

"If you screw it up, your butts will be the least of it."

Bill was laughing when he hung up, but he also knew I meant it.

"I assume the fact that you're alone means you've completely gotten rid of your police escort?" Rob asked when he came into the newsroom and walked over to my desk. While he understood my qualms about having a cop at my side and agreed with them, he also had encouraged me to consider it anyway, since he didn't want anything to happen to me. At least not before I got my stories done.

"They couldn't find anybody who would agree to take the assignment," I said, not wanting to have to have another discussion about it.

Rob laughed. "That's probably truer than you know," he responded. He gestured at the story on my computer screen. "I read Sy's latest piece on the feds' Coleman investigation, for tomorrow's paper. You got anything from the police angle to go with it?"

"I'm sure you heard they found his car this morning, down in Woodbridge," I said as Rob pulled up a chair from the vacant desk next to mine. "I'll do a brief on that. There's not much else to say until the evidence guys go over it or unless they manage to find a witness who saw the person who left the car there. Which they haven't yet."

"Okay, I'll let Mark know there'll be a sidebar on it to go with Sy's piece," Rob said. "Now, what about your other stuff? Anything new on the Magruder shooting?"

I told him about the telephone records Lansing had gotten.

"Although they won't officially cross him off the list yet," I added, "we can say that Terry Porter probably isn't much of a suspect anymore. It's probably worth six or eight graphs."

"All right, we'll find a place for it on the metro front," Rob said. "Anything else?"

"Well," I answered, "there is one other thing I've found out, but we can't go with it yet."

"Oh? What?"

"Dan Magruder and Robert Coleman were shot with the same gun."

Just for a second, Rob looked at me, openmouthed.

"The hell you say!" he got out finally. "The same guy killed them both?"

"It looks that way."

Then he began to glare at me.

"Let's step into my office for a minute," he said and turned to cross the thirty feet between my desk and his office. Clearly, he expected me to follow without protest. Which I did.

"You mind telling me," Rob said when he closed the office door behind me, "why we can't do a story on it now? Obviously, you got this from the police, based on ballistics comparing the bullets."

So I told him the rest. My theory of why Dan Magruder really was killed and why my car had been rigged with a bomb. And that Lansing and Peterson had been convinced enough when the ballistics evidence supported my hypothesis that they now were talking to Detective Moore about the car bombing.

"Christ almighty!" Rob said when I finished. As he considered all the implications, he sat down on the edge of his desk and took off his already-loosened tie. I had noticed a long time ago that the more Rob had to think about something, the more constricting he found the suit and tie he wore to the office every day. By each evening's final deadline, he would long since have gotten rid of his jacket, loosened and eventually removed his tie, unbuttoned his collar and cuffs, and rolled his sleeves up a turn or two. Ken Hale, a fellow reporter who covers the Fairfax County government, and I have a running bet on how long it will take for Rob to completely forget where he is some night and drop his trousers as well.

"You sure we can afford to hold all this?" Rob asked finally.

"We've got at least a day, probably two, before the police are going to say anything about this to anyone else from the press," I told him. "They need time to bring in Detective Moore and figure out how to work these cases together. Since it's almost the weekend, that probably means we'll really have until at least Monday before we have to go with something on it to stay ahead of the competition."

"I don't know, McPhee," Rob said, clearly not comfortable with sitting on such a story. "The connection to your car bombing is hypothesis as this point, so yeah, I can see why we might wait on that. But the match between the two bullets is fact."

"The cops don't want the rest of the press getting onto this yet any more than I do," I said, "not until they've gotten their act together with Alexandria. And I need a couple of days to run down some information from Tallahassee that I'm hoping will help me make some of the missing connections to the bombing. If I can get even part of what I'm after, we can go with a real story early next week that would be more than supposition."

Rob leaned back in his chair and looked at me over the top of his reading glasses. I knew that look. It meant I was being weighed and measured, metaphorically speaking.

"Okay," Rob said finally, apparently deciding that perhaps I could be trusted to know what I was doing for the moment. "You've got until Monday. But that doesn't mean I can keep this from Mark and Sy. We're the ones who yelled about sharing information, after all. And they're going to go through the roof when they hear we want to sit on this over the weekend. But I'm telling you right now, if the story turns up someplace else between now and Monday, it's going to be both our heads on a platter. And you know how happy I'll be about that, don't you?"

Oh, I knew all right. If that happened, I knew Rob would find a way to reattach his own head long enough to chop mine up into little pieces. But it was a chance I was going to have to take if I was going to get at the real story behind the Coleman and Magruder deaths.

"Thanks, Rob," I said, meaning it. "Will you handle telling Sy and Mark so I can get these two briefs done? I've got to be at an interview at six."

"You think they pay me enough for that?" Rob asked as he stood up from the desk and reached to open his office door for me.

"Of course not," I responded. "I know you'll do it out of love." Then I went out the door toward my own desk before he could think of a response.

18

A quick scan of the bar at the Mayflower Hotel showed me Judge Henry Bryant, nominee to the United States Supreme Court, sitting at a table toward the rear, facing to my left and talking with a second man who was looking in my direction as I approached them.

"Judge Bryant?" I asked as I reached where they sat. Both Bryant and his companion stood up. "I'm Sutton McPhee," I said, offering my hand to be shaken.

"Pleasure to meet you, Ms. McPhee," Bryant said, as he nodded his head of prematurely silver hair in my direction and took my hand, giving it a gentle shake. "And this," he continued, gesturing to the man at his right, "is Dell Curl, my personal assistant, to whom you spoke on the phone."

Dell Curl, who said nothing but also shook my hand, was a tall, almost gaunt man, with light brown hair that was cut in a military-looking crew cut, and sallow skin that was at odds with the rest of his coloring. His hazel eyes looked at me unwaveringly, obviously assessing me in a way that I thought had nothing to do with his hormones. The tan jacket he wore over dark brown slacks was taut across his shoulders, leaving me with the impression that he worked out regularly and probably was in very good shape for a man who otherwise looked to be in his midforties. He also towered over Bryant, who was probably within an inch of six feet tall, by a good four inches or more. I had to wonder if Curl's "assistant" duties didn't come under the category of bodyguard and decided it was a sad commentary on the times when a judge has to worry about needing that kind of protection.

"Please have a seat," Bryant said, pulling out the chair in front of me. I took it and then waved away the waiter who had hurried over to ask what I would like to drink.

"So what is it you think I can do for you, Ms. McPhee?" Bryant asked, getting immediately to the point. He apparently didn't want to take any chances on missing whatever appointment he was going to once we finished talking. "I've spoken regularly with Ms. Lane, your colleague, and she seems to have done a very thorough job of covering all the bases."

"Actually, Judge Bryant, I need to ask you about another matter entirely, not anything to do with your Supreme Court nomination."

Bryant gave me a puzzled look.

"What matter would that be?" he asked.

"I'm one of the reporters working on the stories about the murder of Robert Coleman," I said. "I've been checking into his background prior to his coming to Washington, and I understand you actually handled an investigation of him when he was with Three Rivers Development in Tallahassee and you were with the state attorney's office."

"Ah, yes, Robert Coleman," Bryant said, sitting back in his chair now that he knew the agenda for our conversation. "Well, that certainly goes back a ways. So what was it you wanted to know?"

"I understand that the investigation was halted and that Coleman was never prosecuted for anything. Can you tell me about that?"

Bryant templed his hands together, apparently searching his memories.

"I can't go into details, you understand," Bryant said, "but actually, I never got very far into the investigation, not far enough to bring charges, when it was stopped. There's no way to know if I would have found enough to file charges eventually."

"Why was the investigation halted?" I asked.

"Not at my request, I assure you," Bryant said. "It was halted by Ford Truesdale, the state attorney for that area and my boss. I went in one day to give him my first report on the investigation, and he told me he was shutting it down for lack of evidence."

"But you say you were only in the initial stages," I pointed out. "How could he know yet just how much evidence there would be?"

"Exactly what I said to Ford," Bryant agreed. "But he clearly already had his mind made up. He told me to close the case, close the file, and get on with something else. I had never seen him before the way he was that day. He wouldn't discuss it any further, wouldn't tell me why, no matter how I argued with him. And he was very angry at me for questioning his decision."

It certainly sounded like the man Lawson Thomas had described to me as well, I thought. Bryant would have been sticking his neck out to have done any more.

"How did the investigation get started in the first place?" I asked.

"Someone from the community had come to us with a complaint about losing his money after investing it in one of Three Rivers's projects. If memory serves, he had been convinced to invest by Coleman and then, when he changed his mind, he couldn't get either his money or a straight answer out of Coleman."

"How did Coleman avoid getting sucked into the later investigation that went on after Art Williams's suicide?"

"I would have to guess that he made sure, when he left Tallahassee for Washington, that there was no sort of paper trail that could link him to anything that had gone on," Bryant said, "but that's strictly a guess. I was sitting on the county court bench by that time, so I don't know any details of what was found when the company failed. In fact, I left the state attorney's office for the judgeship shortly after Ford closed the Coleman case. And I believe that Ford already had died by the time Three Rivers collapsed. So I don't know what kind of investigation was conducted then."

"I've been told that the case file for your investigation of Coleman is now missing," I said. "Did you by any chance take it with you when you left the state attorney's office?"

"Why, no," Bryant said, his eyebrows knitting together in surprise at that news. "Although we often took material home when we were working a case, once an investigation was closed, everything had to go back into the files. Much of it is confidential information, especially in a case that never was prosecuted. And I had no use for it anymore."

"And you still have no idea, even after all this time, why Truesdale stopped the investigation of Coleman?"

"Nothing concrete I can point to," Bryant said. "And with all of them—Coleman, Art Williams, and Ford—all dead now, I can't see that my speculating publicly would benefit anyone."

I was stumped. Again. And I didn't like it worth a damn. But before I could collect my thoughts enough to try to find another avenue for questions, Bryant and Curl stood up in unison, as if some silent signal had passed between them.

"It's been a pleasure talking with you, Ms. McPhee," Bryant said, looking down at me with a smile. "I'm sorry I've been no help to you at all, but that's really everything I can tell you on the subject, and I'm afraid we do have another appointment to get to. So we're going to have to take our leave now."

I stood up as well and took one of my business cards out of my purse.

"If you think of anything else that might be helpful, anything to do with your Coleman investigation, would you call me?" I asked, giving Bryant the card.

"Certainly," he said, taking it from my hand. "I'll be happy to, but don't expect too much."

Dell Curl put a twenty dollar bill on the table to cover their bar tab, nodded in my direction, and followed Bryant out of the bar and out the hotel's front door.

In the cab on the way back to the parking garage down the block from the *News* building, I used my cell phone to check my voice mail. There was a brief message from Noah Lansing.

"I'll be home by six-thirty," I heard him say. "I'll be looking for you there. And if you'd like me to come pick you up someplace, just call."

Right, I thought. *Like I'm going to get into the habit of asking Lansing to cart me around because somebody has a grudge against me.*

That would be a full-time job, wouldn't it?

Too bad you don't have one, I thought in answer, as I instructed the cabdriver to go right on into the parking garage. *Then you wouldn't have time to nag me twenty-four hours a day.*

At the parking space where I had left the rental car, I gave the driver enough money to cover the fare, his tip, and the parking garage fee, and asked him to wait for a minute while I got into the Pontiac and started it, which he did.

I drove behind him to the exit booth, where he stopped to pay the basic fee for his drive through the parking garage, and then I pulled up, rolled down my window, and put my gate card into the electronic reader. The yellow metal arm went up in front of me, allowing me to leave the parking garage, but at the street I stopped again, not only to look for oncoming traffic, but also because I realized that I still hadn't decided what to do. Do I turn left, I asked myself, and head across the Fourteenth Street bridge to I-395 and my Alexandria apartment? Or do I turn right and take the Memorial Bridge in the direction of Fairfax? Was I ready to face a night alone in my apartment, knowing that someone who disliked me a lot knew exactly where I lived? Was that preferable to another night in the intimacy of Noah Lansing's home?

A car horn blew loudly behind me and, before I could make a conscious choice, I found myself turning right, as if the decision had been made for me. As I crossed the Memorial Bridge a few minutes later, I was still wondering if I hadn't chosen the more frightening alternative.

19

As I pulled into Lansing's driveway behind the Explorer, the front door opened and David came out, running across the yard in my general direction. Behind him, his father stopped in the doorway, where he smiled just as broadly as his son. The usual flutterings started in my chest again at the sight of Lansing, and David's obvious enthusiasm at my arrival just added to the feeling that all my avenues of escape rapidly were being cut off.

Christ, I thought, as I opened the car door and got out, *what am I doing here? This is scaring me out of my wits.*

Before I could even begin to answer my own question, however, David reached me and threw his arms around my legs.

"Sutton, Sutton," he said, looking up at me and trying to jump up and down at the same time. "Are you spending the night again?"

"I think I must be," I said, looking up and across to where Lansing was walking toward us. The heartbeat picked up another notch.

"David," Lansing said sternly, his voice belied by his smile, "turn Sutton loose before you knock her down!"

"Okay, okay," David said, letting me go so quickly that I took a stumbling step anyway.

"Sorry about that," Lansing said, reaching me and putting out a hand to grasp my arm. "He gets a little carried away sometimes."

"He's only six," I said. "At least he has an excuse."

That earned me a quizzical look from Lansing at the same time that my cell phone rang in my purse, which still was lying on the front seat of the car. I reached in to get the purse, and Lansing took the car keys out of my left hand.

"I'll get your bag," he said, walking toward the rear of the car.

"Thanks," I answered and fished the phone out to find out who needed me now. It was Sy Berkowitz.

"McPhee, what the hell is this bullshit about not running with the ballistics story?" he yelled at me when I said "Hello."

"Hold on," I responded, and put my hand over the mouthpiece to tell Lansing I would be inside in just a minute. As soon as he and David went through the front door, I turned back to the telephone.

"Fuck off, Sy," I said, just as vociferously if not as loudly. "You know why. I'm sure Rob explained it to you, even in the simple terms you require."

"That's crap, McPhee, pure, unadulterated bullshit! You got the information straight from the police, so you know it's good. Now, let's run with it!"

"It's only one piece of the story, Sy. The rest has to do with somebody trying to kill me, and we don't have that piece yet. So shut the hell up and do what you're told. At least Mark seems to know what he's doing here. Listen to him!"

"Yeah, well, maybe next time whoever is after you will get it right, and I can do *that* story without you getting in my way all the time!" He hung up in my ear, loudly, leaving me listening to a dial tone. I turned the phone off and dropped it back into my purse, then walked slowly up to Lansing's front door, trying to get all the names I needed to call Sy said under my breath before going inside.

20

Lansing and David were coming back down the stairs, apparently from having deposited my bag in one of the upstairs rooms, when I came through the front door.

"Come join us in the kitchen," Lansing said, as David went down the last two stairs ahead of him in hops. "Gradella has gone for the weekend, so David and I are cooking tonight."

"We're making spaghetti!" David said, coming up to grab my hand and tug me along after his father.

"It's one of David's basic food groups, along with pizza," Lansing told me over his shoulder. "But we make a pretty mean spaghetti, don't we, Chief?" he asked looking back at his son.

"It's real good," David assured me. "You'll like it a whole bunch."

"I'm sure I will," I agreed as we walked through the hall doorway that led into the kitchen. I was promptly relegated to a chair at the kitchen table, given a glass of iced tea, and ordered to do nothing except enjoy myself while Lansing and David cooked.

They were a fascinating study in contrasts, I had to admit, watching them together. David was all energy and excitement, with his enthusiasm far outrunning his physical coordination, which I guessed was the case with most boys his age. Lansing was all patience. I had yet to hear him, in any of the time I had spent in their company, raise his voice to David more than one increment. Yet, that seemed to be all it took to get David's attention when he was getting a little too carried away with something.

I wondered how much of what I was seeing was the result of losing Sarah. While it must have been incredibly stressful for Lansing to have been left alone with a baby, I could see how it might, at the same time, have given him an extra appreciation of David's importance in his life. And while David probably had been too young to remember his mother's death, I also guessed that her absence had to have made his surviving parent that much more important to him, important enough to want to please that parent as much as possible.

As I sipped my tea and watched the two of them working together, we talked about inconsequential things from our day. David, who was perched up on a bar stool from which he could stir the pot of spaghetti that soon was boiling on the stove, had spent much of the afternoon at a neighbor's swimming pool, playing with the neighbor's two sons.

Lansing told us about a traffic accident he had happened to witness in Tysons Corner, involving a truck full of chickens and a station wagon full of people dressed in clown suits on their way to some kind of neighborhood fair. No one was hurt, he told us right away, so we were free to laugh until we cried at the images of clowns chasing terrified chickens all up and down Route 7.

It was apparent to me that Lansing probably told David little of what his job really was like. The details would have been far too gruesome for a six-year-old. I followed Lansing's lead in choosing conversational subject matter and asked David if he had ever flown on an airplane. When he said he hadn't and wanted to know whether I had, I told him about my flight back from Florida earlier in the day.

Before long, the spaghetti was ready, as were the salads and garlic bread Lansing had been making while David had supervised the spaghetti. I helped them carry the food into the dining room, where the table already was set for the three of us, and we sat down to eat.

It was later, as I helped Lansing clean up the dishes and put away the leftovers, while David was upstairs getting ready for bed, that Lansing first broached the subject that hung in the air between us.

"You want to talk about why you have that trapped animal look in your eyes?" he asked, drying the large stainless steel pot in which the spaghetti had cooked and which was too big to fit into the dishwasher.

I looked at him in surprise, not having anticipated what he had been about to say. He returned my look, the drying cloth pausing in its swipes around the bottom of the pot. There was no escaping those eyes, no hiding behind glib talk or euphemism. I could see he wanted an honest answer, which, I thought to myself, was the kind I generally gave.

And the kind that usually gets you into big trouble, my ever-present little friend chose that moment to remind me.

"Because," I answered Lansing, leaning against the counter behind me for support, "I think I'm finding all this a little intimidating."

"And all this is?"

"This," I answered, gesturing largely at the room and house around me. "The whole thing. The house. The yard. David. You. The whole domestic family thing."

Lansing looked offended.

"Wait," I said quickly, "that came out all wrong. It's all wonderful, I'm sure. I'm just not sure I know why you've brought me into it." I felt as if I were seriously foundering in trying to describe what it was I was feeling, and that made just one more situation in which I wasn't used to finding myself.

Lansing put the pot down on the countertop, folded the drying towel in half, and draped it across an edge of the sink before turning back in my direction.

"Don't you know?" he asked quietly. "Don't you?"

I was saved from drowning in his eyes by David, who chose that moment to appear around the kitchen door in his pajamas.

"I'm ready," he said to his father, who looked at me a second longer before his eyes released me.

"On my way, Chief," he said, turning and walking across to sweep his son up into his arms. David laughed, and they both turned back to look in my direction.

"If you want coffee," Lansing told me, "everything you need is in the top cabinet right behind you. I'm going up to read to David before he goes to sleep, but I'll be back down soon, and we can finish our conversation. And no falling asleep on the sofa this time."

"Okay," I answered. "Good night, David. Thanks for the spaghetti."

David grinned and waved at me over his father's shoulder.

"Night, Sutton," he replied, and the two of them went out into the hall to head upstairs. Instead of making coffee, I picked up the drying towel Lansing had been using and took the blue enameled colander out of the drying rack. I began drying it, but I soon was lost in the tangle of thoughts and feelings that the look in Lansing's eyes had brought rushing up for me.

I was brought out of whatever trance my chaotic emotions had transported me to by Lansing's reappearance in front of me. He looked from my face down to the colander and drying cloth, both of which I still held but which, apparently, I long since had stopped noticing. Lansing reached down and took them from my hands, putting them down on the counter next to the spaghetti pot.

"Is he asleep already?" I asked, deciding as soon as I said it that it was a stupidly obvious question.

"Already?" Lansing responded in surprise. "I've been up there for half an hour. And yes, he's asleep."

"Oh," I said. "I guess I got a little lost in thought."

"Don't you think," Lansing asked, stepping closer to me and putting his hands on my shoulders, "that you've done enough thinking for one night?"

I fell right back into those eyes again, and as I let him pull me into his arms, my seldom-silent observer chimed in.

Oh Lansing, Lansing, my nemesis mocked. But I no longer was capable of a reply. My body and brain both were immediately and completely engrossed in kissing the man with the blue eyes.

21

SATURDAY

I won't go into prurient detail. We made love.

Well, okay, we made amazing love. So amazing that I lost all sense of where my body ended and his began. So amazing that he touched me in places I had just about forgotten I had but that came awake under his touch with sensations that were almost more than I could stand. So amazing that I couldn't remember ever having had an experience like it, and I hadn't been a virgin for a long time. So amazing that, some time in the middle of the night, we woke up and did it all again.

And so amazing that, when I found my way out of sleep into the growing sunlight of the next morning, I was truly terrified. Because there was no undoing what had happened between us, no forgetting it, no going back to the night before when I hadn't known what completely losing myself in another person was like, no pretending that there was any way I was getting out of this one with my defenses intact. I turned my head to look at Noah Lansing, in whose bed I had spent the night and who was awake, too, and smiling at me, and I pushed all my fears back down into their deep, dark holes, where I knew they would wait patiently to confuse me, but where I could keep them from escaping for a little while.

I rolled the rest of me over in the bed in Lansing's direction, and he reached up to brush a strand of hair out of my eyes.

"Stop worrying," he said, as if he had read my thoughts. "We're both where we're supposed to be."

"It's not that," I lied. "I have to go into the office and do some research."

You coward, my little voice piped up, apparently awake as well.

And it was right, of course, I thought to myself as Lansing kissed me on the forehead and let me up out of the bed. Probably his and Sarah's bed. In which David could very easily walk in and find me. That thought sent me fleeing the room. Oh, God, I groaned silently, now reminded of one more thing to worry about. How the hell could I possibly hope to compete with a dead woman who probably lived on in the memories of her husband and her son as the perfect woman?

I fled to the shower. And then to the office.

Halfway into the District, my cell phone rang. It was Cooper Diggs.

"I've got information for you," Cooper said when I answered. He sounded pleased with himself.

"Are you at the office? I'm on my way there now."

"No. At home. But I could stop by at lunchtime if you're still going to be there then."

"That would be great," I told him. "And yes, I'll be there most of the day." Even if I hadn't had things to work on, I wondered if I might not have manufactured some, anyway, just to give my head a chance to clear a little outside of Lansing's physical presence.

"Now, before you go through this stuff," Cooper was saying as he sat down in the chair he had pulled up next to my newsroom desk, "you have to appreciate that you gave me something of a challenge this time."

"Why is that?" I asked.

"Because I was going back to a time before most agencies and companies had the majority of their records on computers. You're talking about the midseventies here. The computerization was beginning, but it was by no means widespread. Especially in things like credit reports, legal records, etc. Although a lot of it has been computerized after the fact, particularly from the credit bureaus' records, not everyone has gone to the trouble or expense to put all their records from that time on computer. So what I'm giving you is everything that the computers can find on any of these guys, which is a lot, but I can't guarantee that other important stuff isn't gathering dust in a filing cabinet somewhere. Still, on the plus side, you also have some information you had no right to expect to get. The credit bureaus are supposed to remove stuff from their files after a certain number of years, but we all know how it is with computers. Even when something is moved from one file, it's almost never gone permanently. So I also found some things that really shouldn't have been there."

"I understand," I told him and took the sheaf of pages he had been holding. Cooper stood up.

"Since I'm here anyway, I'm going to run down to the library and take care of a couple of things," he said. "I'll be around for a little while, so if you have a question about anything, just call me in the library."

"Thanks Cooper," I said, my appreciation genuine. "I will."

It was a good forty-five minutes later that I noticed something that seemed out of whack. I had gone over each page in Cooper's printouts and newspaper articles carefully, looking at details but also trying to let my subconscious see the whole picture. There had been nothing that struck me as out of the ordinary in any of the information on Robert Coleman, Ford Truesdale, Lawson Thomas, or even on Arthur Williams until, of course, the time of his suicide and the financial disaster that followed it. It wasn't until I began looking through the pages on Henry Bryant, whom I had thrown into the mix almost as an afterthought, that my subconscious began to nag at me that something didn't fit. I picked up the phone and called the library.

"Can you come back up for a minute?" I asked Cooper when he answered. "I want to get your opinion on something."

"Be right there," he replied.

Sixty seconds later, he came into the newsroom through the stairwell door. When he got to my desk, he looked over my shoulder at the sheet of paper in my hand and at the pile through which I already had read.

"So you noticed it, too, huh?" he asked.

"Am I reading this correctly?" I asked him in reply.

"Tell me what you think you see."

"This is Henry Bryant's credit record. And according to this, he went through a really bad stretch in the midseventies, when his debts went through the roof. I'm assuming, based on the dates and some of the people he owed money to, that all this was during the time when his wife had cancer and then died." I looked back at the sheet of paper.

"There are all kinds of bad debts here," I went on, running an index finger down the list. "The hospital, doctors, department stores, credit cards, even the funeral home. And it looks as if, by that time, he also was about to lose his house. According to this, his mortgage was something like four months in arrears, and the bank was getting ready to foreclose on it."

"That's the way I read it, too," Cooper said.

"But here's what I don't understand," I told him. "Bryant owed a hell of a lot of money to a lot of people by the time he buried his wife. More than $200,000, which in the seventies was a lot more than it is now. Then, within a period of just a couple of weeks, he paid off every one of the bills, including the back payments on his house."

"Yeah? And?"

"If his financial situation was such that he couldn't avoid getting into such awful debt in the first place, where did he get the money to pay off all the bills at the same time?"

"Go right on thinking out loud," Cooper said, now smiling in obvious satisfaction that our minds had run along the same track in interpreting the information. "I'm listening."

"Well, first of all, I don't see any record here of him taking out any sort of loan to pay all the bills off, even if he could have found a bank that would have loaned him that much when he already was in such financial straits, and even if it wouldn't have taken him forever to repay it from his salary as an assistant state attorney."

"Neither did I," Cooper agreed, "and I looked for it. Again, it might be in a filing cabinet somewhere, but if he paid it off over several years, chances are there would be some mention of it somewhere in somebody's computerized records. Either the lending institution or the credit bureau or both. By the time he would have gotten it paid off and the time limits had expired for keeping it in his credit bureau file, all that stuff was on computers."

"So then, I'm thinking maybe he got it from an insurance policy that paid out when his wife died."

"Could be," Cooper said.

"But does it make sense that he would have risked losing the roof over the heads of his two little kids and his dying wife if he had a life insurance policy he could have cashed in sooner than that?"

"Not to me," Cooper said, shaking his head from side to side, which sent a clump of blond hair sliding down into his eyes. He reached up and brushed it back into place. "And none of the insurance databases I got into showed any such policy. So what else do you see?"

I studied the pages some more, once again trying to look at them as a whole picture and not just details. Something kept pulling my eyes back up to the photocopy of the newspaper article about Bryant's nomination to the Leon County Court seat. Eventually, I realized it was the date that was nagging at my subconscious brain, and when I focused on it, several things fell into place.

"Uh-oh," I said, realizing what I was seeing but still searching for its meaning.

"What did you pick up?" Cooper wanted to know. "The money was as far as I was able to go with it."

"Look at the date on this article," I said, pointing to it. "Bryant was nominated to his first court position only a week after he paid off all the money he owed. I've dealt with crooks and politicians far too long to think that's a complete coincidence. It has to mean something."

"How were county judges picked in Florida then?"

"Same as now. They run for election. Or, as in Henry Bryant's case, they're appointed to fill an unexpired term if a judge dies in office or steps down for some other reason."

"Appointed by whom?"

I looked at the article again to double-check my memory.

"By the governor."

"You think Bryant could have been involved in something shady with the governor?"

"Anything is possible, but I doubt it. For one thing, that was Governor James Baker. He's still considered to be probably the most honest governor Florida ever had. You know my take on an honest politician being an oxymoron, but from everything I've ever read or heard, in Baker's case, the reputation might have been genuine. Genuine enough that he left politics in disgust after his term was over and said he never wanted to touch it again with a ten-foot pole. They still talk about him down there, even though he's been dead for six or seven years now."

"So then what does all this mean?" Cooper wanted to know.

"Beats the hell out of me," I said, looking back at the newspaper article on Bryant's court appointment. "But I guess I'm just going to have to make some more phone calls and see if I can figure it out."

The first person I decided to call, once Cooper took his leave with a request to keep him posted on anything I found, was a man named

Steven Franks. He was quoted in the article on Bryant's appointment, in which Franks was identified as Governor Baker's chief of staff.

I called Tallahassee information and got a telephone listing for the man I hoped was the right Steven Franks, but when I called the number, I got an answering machine with a man's voice on the recording.

"This is Sutton McPhee," I told the machine, after it beeped at me. "I'm a reporter with the Washington *News*, and I'm working on a story that I'm hoping you might be able to help me with. It involves someone I think you knew a number of years ago in Tallahassee, when you worked for Governor Baker. If you could take a few minutes to call me, I'd really appreciate it."

I left my number and hung up, wondering if I had found Baker's former aide and whether I would hear from him.

In the meantime, however, I couldn't just sit around twiddling my thumbs, waiting for a phone that might or might not ring. Nor was I ready to head back out to Virginia and Noah Lansing. I decided the only thing left to do was to call Henry Bryant and ask him where he got the money.

22

Henry Bryant was, to put it mildly, quite offended by my question.

"My life is an open book," he shouted at me over the telephone when I reached him in his Mayflower Hotel room. "How many times do you think I've been investigated already for judgeships I've held? And don't you think the White House has gone through my background with a fine-tooth comb for this Supreme Court nomination? Who are you to question my affairs? No one else has ever even asked me about the loan."

"It wouldn't be the first time the White House has missed something in a background check, especially this White House," I pointed out in an extravagance of understatement.

"Well, they certainly didn't miss anything this time," Bryant said huffily.

"Look, Judge Bryant," I went on, "it's a simple question with a simple answer. But it was a lot of money, and your situation back then was very precarious. You were a hair's breadth from being thrown out of your house with your two children. I just want to know whether the money was a loan or a gift, and who it was from. I don't see why it requires secrecy."

"It was a private loan from someone who cared about me and my children," Bryant answered, sounding angrier by the minute. "It was repaid. I've kept the details to myself at the request of the person who helped me out, out of respect for them, and I'll thank you to show me the same respect as well. Not everything is fodder for the press, even now."

"Why does it matter after all this time who loaned you the money? Do you really think they care, after twenty years, that anyone knows?"

Bryant hung up on me.

Well, I thought, hanging up my own phone, so much for that bridge, which I suspected was smoking a lot, if not in flames. So now what?

The telephone rang.

"Sutton McPhee," I answered, my mind still on my conversation with Bryant.

"This is Steven Franks in Tallahassee. I'm calling in response to a message you left on my answering machine."

"Oh, Mr. Franks," I said, paying attention now. "Thanks for calling me back. Are you the Steven Franks who was the chief of staff for Governor Baker?"

"That's right," Franks said. "What is it you think I can do for you?"

"I'm sure you know about Judge Henry Bryant being nominated for the U.S. Supreme Court, and I'm hoping you can give me some information from when he was a county judge in Tallahassee."

"Oh?"

"In the research I've been doing, I saw that it was Governor Baker who nominated Judge Bryant to his first court position, back when the judge was an assistant state attorney."

"That was a long time and a lot of gubernatorial appointments ago," Franks said, "but yes, my memory is that the governor did make that appointment."

"What kind of process would Governor Baker have used to make an appointment like that?" I asked. "Where did he get the names of people who might be qualified when he needed to fill some position such as a county judgeship?"

Franks took a couple of seconds to answer. I assumed he was searching his memory from two decades before.

"From a number of places, actually," he said finally. "The people we consulted for possible nominees varied, depending on the position that was open, of course. But for a judge, we would have talked to people at the local and state bar associations, to other judges, perhaps even to the governor's long-time political and financial supporters, who frequently had all sorts of connections throughout the business and legal communities."

"By any chance, do you remember who suggested Judge Bryant's name? Was he someone the governor knew well?"

"Frankly," Franks answered, "I just don't remember. As I say, it's been a long time, and you have to understand that, in a four-year term, a governor could be required to make a lot of appointments to all kinds of judgeships, task forces, commissions. I just don't know, now, who recommended Henry Bryant. I'm sorry."

I could see there was no point in pushing further at the moment. Franks was trying to be helpful. I didn't want to piss him off in case he had a brainstorm later and remembered what I wanted to know.

"I understand," I told him, "and I know I'm asking a lot after all these years. I appreciate what you have been able to tell me. May I ask you to call me if you do remember at some point where his name came from?"

"Certainly," Franks said.

I let him go.

Damn it, I thought, hanging up. *Another dead end.* Clearly there was no point in calling Henry Bryant again and asking him who recommended him to Governor Baker. He would just hang up on me a second time. Who else could I call? I couldn't think of a soul who might be able to tell me anything helpful.

In frustration, I got up and paced around my desk, trying to think of what I could do now to find out what I needed to know, to find something that would begin to make sense of the bits and pieces I had. When I realized my pacing had reached the point that it was eliciting irritated looks from the two other reporters in the newsroom at the moment, I snatched the desk chair back out and sat down in it, sulkily. Then I picked up the pages Cooper had brought me and started reading back through all of them again, hoping for an epiphany. I just didn't know what else to do.

When enlightenment didn't strike, however, my frustration reached the point that even the coffee in the first-floor cafeteria sounded like an appealing distraction, so I went to get some. As I opened the stairwell door on my way back into the newsroom, coffee cup in hand, I heard a telephone ringing in the general vicinity of my desk, and I broke into a jog to answer it before the caller hung up. It was Steven Franks again.

"I find I'm able to answer your question after all," he explained when I expressed surprise at hearing from him again so soon.

"Did you remember something?" I asked, putting the cup of coffee down on my desk and sitting down.

"No, my memory hasn't improved that much since we spoke earlier," he replied, laughing. "But I have this stack of daily journals that I kept all through the governor's administration, thinking that one day I could use them to write a book of some kind. I'm ashamed to say I've never done anything with them, but they did tell me what you wanted to know."

"Yes?"

"According to my notes from that time, Judge Bryant was strongly recommended for the county court seat by Gerald Tharpe." The name sounded familiar to me, but at the moment, I couldn't place it.

"Gerry was an attorney in Tallahassee at the time," Franks went on, "although he left the area several years ago and went out to Oregon or Washington State or one of those places out west. He also was one of Governor Baker's strongest supporters. He was particularly good at bringing in influential people with money to give to the election effort, so later, we certainly would have looked closely at anyone he recommended for an appointive position."

"And you're certain that Judge Bryant's name came from him for consideration?"

"Pretty sure. I generally tried to make notes in my journals every night while things were still fresh in my memory, so I would say yes, it was Gerry who passed along Henry Bryant's name."

"And how much weight would the suggestion have carried coming from Gerald Tharpe?"

"If you're suggesting that anything underhanded would have gone on, I can assure you that wasn't the case," Franks said. "James Baker wouldn't have considered Judge Bryant unless Bryant was qualified for the position. But realistically, if he were qualified, the fact that Gerry suggested him certainly would have weighed in his favor in the governor's final selection."

"Well, that is the way the world works, isn't it?" I asked rhetorically. It certainly was the way the political world worked, even when the players had scruples.

"The world that I know does," Franks agreed.

I thanked him for going to the trouble of checking his journals and calling me with Tharpe's name, and we hung up.

So the impetus for Bryant's county judgeship had come not from Governor Baker but from a local attorney named Gerald Tharpe, I thought as I sat back in my chair. Which meant that Baker probably had no connection with Bryant's mysterious $200,000 loan, either. But who was Gerald Tharpe, and why did I know his name? I didn't think he was anyone I remembered from my years in Tallahassee, certainly not anyone I covered in connection with the education beat. Was it something more recent? I again picked up the stack of paper Cooper had given me. My memory was nagging at me that I had heard or read the name recently, but there was no mention of him in Cooper's material.

I put the stack back down and opened the file drawer on my desk, from which I pulled out the folder that held the newspaper articles I had copied in the library in Tallahassee. As I reached the article about Arthur Williams' suicide, Gerald Tharpe's name jumped out at me from the columns of newsprint.

I sat forward and read the paragraph in which his name appeared:

```
When contacted, Coleman's Washington office
staff referred a Democrat reporter to Talla-
hassee attorney Gerald Tharpe, who is acting
as Coleman's spokesman.
     "Mr. Coleman has no knowledge of any wrong-
doing at Three Rivers Development, which he
left more than a year ago," said Tharpe, "but
he considered Art Williams a friend as well
as a former business associate. Art's death
is a real tragedy for all his family and
friends."
```

"Holy shit!" I said, unable to take my eyes from the page on which Tharpe's name appeared.

"Holy shit what?"

I jumped a foot and a half, almost knocking over my cup of coffee.

"Damn it, Sy," I yelled, turning around to look at him where he had walked up behind me. "You scared the crap out me!"

"Only a small part of it, I'm sure," Sy replied snottily. "So what are you exclaiming over? Anything to do with *our* story about little Bobby Coleman?"

"As a matter of fact, yes. I think I may have just put a big part of the story together. And as much as it pains me to do it, you'd better sit down and let me tell you about it, so you can tell me if you come to the same conclusions I have."

Sy's glare looked a little less hateful and a little more interested. He took the chair Cooper had vacated earlier and looked at me expectantly.

"So shoot," he said.

Oh, I thought, *if only I could.*

23

"Okay, you're going to have to bear with me here for a little bit," I told Sy, "because the beginnings of this go back at least twenty years, and even though you already have heard some of it from Rob and me, it will make more sense if I tell it to you in chronological order. So just keep your mouth shut until I'm done, okay?"

"Would you just get on with it?" Sy asked sarcastically.

"Okay," I said, "back in the seventies, Robert Coleman was in Tallahassee, as the number-two guy in a land development company called Three Rivers Development. The owner was a man named Arthur Williams. Coleman left the company in 1977 to come to Washington; a year or so later, Williams committed suicide. His death was followed by the company's collapse and a huge scandal over how it had been run and how much money its investors lost."

"I already know all that, McPhee," Sy said, throwing his hands up in the air in a gesture of frustration. "When are you gonna get to something I don't know?"

"How about this? Not long before he left Tallahassee, Robert Coleman had been under investigation by the state attorney's office there, based on a complaint they had gotten from a former investor in Three Rivers. But the investigation was quashed, practically before it got started, and no charges were ever filed against Coleman."

"Oh yeah?" Sy asked. Apparently, I finally had said something he found interesting.

"Yeah. The assistant state attorney who was handling the investigation was a man named Henry Bryant."

"You mean the—"

"Sh-h-h!" I said forcefully. "Just listen. One day shortly into the investigation, Bryant got called into the office of Ford Truesdale, the state attorney for that part of Florida and Bryant's boss. When he came back out, he looked upset, and he told one of his colleagues that Truesdale had just ordered him to close the Coleman investigation for lack of evidence. So Bryant closed the case and got on with his other work, and a few weeks later, he left the state attorney's office when the governor named him to fill a vacancy on the Leon County Court bench.

"The colleague he told about Truesdale's orders to close the case was a man named Lawson Thomas, who also left the job not much later to get involved in politics and who now is a Florida state senator. Thomas told the story to me, and he also told me that when he tried to check on the information in the files from the Coleman investigation down there, it turns out the file has disappeared."

"Here we go," Sy said, rubbing his hands together in gleeful anticipation. "I love disappearing files!"

"Okay, at the same time all this was going on, Henry Bryant's wife was in the process of dying from cancer, leaving him with two little kids and $200,000 in debt. By the time she was buried, he owed everybody and his brother money and was about to lose his house. As far as I can tell, the only real asset he had was his salary from the state attorney, and you can imagine what that would have amounted to. But all of a sudden, the money appears from out of the blue, and Bryant pays everyone back, all within a few days. When I asked him about it directly, Bryant just about took my head off and told me the money was a private loan from someone trying to help him out. He said he eventually repaid it, but he refused to say who loaned it to him, and there's no record I can find of where the money came from. And just coincidentally, this loan' showed up right in the same time period as the Coleman investigation was being killed and Bryant was being given a judgeship."

The clownish grin Sy had been wearing dropped off his face.

"Goddamn!" he said. "You think the Florida governor gave him the money and a judge's seat? But for what? I thought it was Bryant's boss who stopped the. Coleman investigation."

"Yeah, but whose word do we have for that? Only Bryant's himself. No one else was in that meeting between him and Truesdale. It was Bryant who told Lawson Thomas that Truesdale ordered him to close the case. But just suppose it was the other way around. Suppose it was Bryant who convinced Truesdale that there wasn't enough evidence there to go after Coleman. If Truesdale trusted Bryant, he would have had no reason to believe otherwise, and as the lead investigator, Bryant could have manipulated the information he showed Truesdale. Now, I'm thinking maybe it was really Bryant who called the investigation of Coleman off. I think Robert Coleman bought him off for $200,000 and a judgeship, at a time when Bryant was under the ultimate stress. The quid pro quo was that Bryant saw to it that Coleman's case was closed and the file deep-sixed."

"So then you *do* think the governor was involved. He's the one who put Bryant on the bench, right?"

"Right, but I don't think he realized what was really going on. If Florida has ever had a more honest governor than Baker, I don't know who it was. And I talked to Governor Baker's former chief of staff, a man named Steven Franks. Franks told me that, according to notes he kept at the time, Bryant was suggested to them by a Tallahassee attorney named Gerald Tharpe, who had been influential in getting big donors to support Baker for governor. So Franks said they probably would have given Tharpe's candidate preference, all other things being equal."

"And who's this Tharpe guy?"

I picked up the article about Art Williams's suicide and handed it to Sy, my finger pointing out the important paragraph.

"Oh man!" Sy said, after reading the paragraph and then scanning the rest of the article. Finally, he looked back up at me, the question in his mind reflected on his face.

"But what does any of that have to do with Coleman being bumped off up here twenty years later? You don't think Bryant did it? Why would he kill Coleman? Coleman is the one who saved his nuts, even if it wasn't a kosher deal."

"I've been thinking about that while I talked through all this," I said, "and I think that's exactly why Bryant did do it. Something must have happened, now, to make Bryant see Coleman as a threat. Think about what Bryant has at stake here. Only everything he's worked for his whole life: his legal career, his reputation, a seat on the U.S. Supreme Court. By all accounts, he's been an excellent judge, all the way up the line. Everybody likes him, on both sides of the political aisle. I don't know, maybe being a good judge has been his way of making up for what he did back then to save his home and his kids. But he's lived with the knowledge of what he did and with his guilty conscience for twenty years. Something must have happened recently with Coleman to frighten Bryant into thinking that it all was about to come out. Maybe the risk of losing everything that he got at the cost of his self-respect, here at the end, was just too much."

Sy looked thoughtful, then excited.

"I'd be willing to bet a week's pay," he said, "that Coleman went to Bryant and wanted him to do the same thing he did before, to get this latest investigation killed. He probably figured that, as a federal judge, Bryant could pull enough strings here and there to do it, and maybe he threatened to take Bryant down with him if Bryant didn't agree."

"So," I said, finishing his thought, "Bryant couldn't handle the idea of having Coleman's threats hanging over him forever. He either killed Coleman or had him killed to shut him up. Although I think he must have gotten someone to do it for him. I couldn't see the man Magruder talked to in the park that day all that well, but I know it wasn't Coleman himself, and I don't think it was Bryant, either. I think he figured there was nothing that could surface in any investigation of what Coleman has been up to in Washington that could lead back to him. Ford Truesdale is dead. Art Williams is dead. The file in Tallahassee has disappeared. Killing Coleman would sever the last connection between Bryant and what went on down there twenty years ago."

Sy looked at his watch.

"We've got time to put this together before the first deadline," he said, looking back at me. "Along with the stuff on the same gun killing Coleman and Magruder, it's just too much to sit on. If you've got plans, cancel them, and let's get busy on this."

"There's nothing to get busy on," I argued. "We don't have the story yet."

"Are you dense? What do you mean, we don't have the story yet?" Now he was mad again.

"Where's our proof?" I asked hotly. Sy's I'm-in-charge attitude was pissing me off, and I saw a couple of the editors, who were starting to filter in to put the Sunday paper together, looking up at the sound of my raised voice.

"Right there in your hand," Sy said, his own voice going up a notch or two in volume.

"No, it isn't. All I've got here are some unexpected connections, some possible coincidences, and one great big chunk of money that Henry Bryant won't explain. Yes, the bullets match. Which doesn't tell us who pulled the trigger. I hate to break it to you, but no matter how we think those pieces fit together, we don't have enough proof to go with this in print."

"So what do you recommend we do with all this stuff then?"

That was what I had been wondering when Sy had turned up initially. Now, the answer popped into my head.

"I'm going to the cops with it."

"What?" he shouted, standing up so quickly that it slammed his chair into the desk behind him, causing every head in the newsroom to look in our direction. "Have you lost your fucking mind?"

"No, and stop screaming at me," I hissed back, standing up and moving in close so I could lower my own voice. "Peterson and Lansing are okay. If I take this to them, they might be able to use it to shake loose something that will put it all together. And they'll give us the story first. I've dealt with them both before, and if I help them, they won't screw me over."

So what was that Lansing was doing last night?

I can't fight with you right now, too, I thought. *I've got my hands full here.*

"And besides," I went on, "I'm the one who has somebody trying to kill me, somebody who thinks I know who they are. But I don't have any idea who it is, and I'll take help anywhere I can get it. It's my neck on the line here, Sy, not yours."

"This isn't just your story, McPhee. It's mine, too. The biggest story I've had since I got to this goddamn town. I'm not going to let you blow it for me, and I'm going upstairs right now to call Mark Lester and Mack Thompson. And by the way, it's not your neck you'd better be worried about. It's your knees, and I'm getting ready to cut you off at them."

He turned and started striding angrily away, only to stop again and look back at me.

"If I were you," he said loudly, glaring at me in full-blown hatred, "I'd wait right here and not go anywhere, 'cause I think Mack Thompson's going to have a few things to say to you real soon."

With that, he stomped over to the stairwell door, yanked it open hard, and went through it.

I looked at the faces staring at me from the copy desk and various corners of the newsroom, gave them a weak grin, and sat back down. I was furious with Sy, but nothing he had threatened to do had changed my mind about taking what I had to Lansing and Peterson.

There was someone out there who was far more of a threat to me than Sy was, and the police might be the only ones who could help me find out who it was. I had, I thought tiredly, run out of places to look. And that was when I remembered who it was I had forgotten, someone who could have been the man in the park. My hand shaking, I picked up the phone and called down to the library but got no answer. So I dialed Cooper's home phone number.

"Cooper," I said abruptly when he answered, "I need some more information, and I need it as quickly as you can get it for me. And I don't care how you get it, just get it now."

"What's the matter, Sutton?" he asked, apparently not liking the way I sounded.

"I don't have time to explain now," I told him. "Just track down everything you can in the next twenty minutes on this person and call me back with what you find. I'll fill you in later." I gave him a name, thanked him for his help, and hung up. And paged Noah Lansing.

By now, no doubt, Lansing recognized my office number when it appeared on his pager. He called me back within a few minutes.

"I don't want to hear anything about not coming back to the house tonight," he said lightly when I answered.

"That's not why I'm calling," I replied. "I need to talk to you and Peterson this afternoon. I've got some information I think you need to see. Can you get hold of him and meet me somewhere?"

Apparently the urgency in my voice communicated itself to him. He dropped the teasing tone with which he had greeted me.

"If it's important, I'll find him," he said, all business now. "Where do you want to meet us?"

"Name someplace that's near where you are now. I'll come out there."

"It's almost six o'clock, and David has gone to a friend's house to spend the night. Do you want to do this over something to eat?"

"Fine. Fine. Just tell me where to meet you. Someplace that isn't too busy and where I can just get a sandwich." Although I hadn't had lunch, the direction my thinking recently had taken also had dampened most of the appetite I normally would have had.

"How about Joe's Hole in the Wall Café;? You know it?"

"Where's that?"

"It's a little restaurant at Little River Turnpike and Pickett. It sounds like the right kind of place."

"Fine," I said. "I'm waiting for one phone call, and then I'll meet you out there."

"Okay, I'll track down Peterson in the meantime. And, Sutton?"

"What?"

"For God's sake, watch your back!"

Ordinarily, I probably could have come up with some double entendre for a response, but right now I was all out of humor.

"I will," I told him.

Barely within the twenty minutes I had specified, Cooper called me back.

"I don't have a lot, and I don't know for sure what it means, although I don't like the sounds of it," he said, sounding concerned, "but here's what I was able to find out in the little bit of time I had."

"That's okay, Cooper," I reassured him. "Just tell me what you have." He told me. Knowing my sudden inspiration had been right just made me feel worse, not better.

I thanked Cooper for his help, told him he might literally have saved my life, and hung up to call Sy's extension up in the national newsroom. I got his voice mail.

"It's Sutton," I told him. "I can't hang around here any longer. I'm on my way out to meet Peterson and Lansing. If you just can't wait to fight with me, we'll be at some little restaurant called Joe's Hole in the Wall Café; out in Fairfax. Otherwise, I'll get back to you later and we'll argue about all this then."

Actually, I thought as I cleared the line and then punched in Rob Perry's extension, *argue* was a gross understatement for the shit storm Sy probably was trying to bring down on my head. But if I were right with my latest idea about what had gone on, and if what I knew gave the detectives the push that they needed in the right direction, Sy Berkowitz could just kiss my ass. Not that he'd ever be lucky enough to get anywhere near it.

Rob didn't answer, either, so I briefly told his voice mail what I had learned, that I was going out to Fairfax to talk with Peterson and Lansing about it, and that I also had had to tell Sy and he was on his way to throw a fit with Mack Thompson.

"Be prepared," I said. Then I hung up, grabbed my purse, and left quickly before Sy could drag me into whatever mischief he was plotting.

24

Joe's Hole in the Wall was just about that, a tiny, nondescript café that one easily could overlook in the middle of the other storefronts that took up the two wings of the shopping center where Joe's was located. But I spotted it without any trouble as I drove slowly through the parking lot. I parked a couple of spaces away from what looked like Peterson's unmarked police car and Lansing's Explorer, which told me that they both had arrived at Joe's ahead of me.

Nothing inside the little restaurant belied its name, either. There were a handful of booths, upholstered in wine red vinyl, along the walls on either side of the door, and a small cluster of Formica-topped tables and simple wooden chairs in the center of the room. Across the back wall was the open kitchen area from which emanated a number of delicious smells and which was separated from the dining room by a waist-high countertop. Behind the counter was a somewhat beefy, dark-haired man of middle years and a nonspecific Mediterranean heritage. Behind him, a much younger man of similar coloring appeared to be cooking something on the grill.

Lansing saw me come in, from where he and Peterson sat in the third booth on the right, and he raised an arm to get my attention, as if I could have missed seeing him in such a small place. None of the other handful of diners scattered around the room paid me any attention whatsoever.

I walked over to join the detectives, sitting down beside Lansing when he slid over next to the wall to make room for me. By the partially eaten sub sandwiches and fries in front of him and Peterson, I judged that they already had ordered after tiring of waiting for me. At that moment, the young man from the grill appeared beside me to ask what I wanted to drink. I ordered a glass of iced tea and asked if I could get just a tossed salad. We discussed salad dressings, and after agreeing on the house vinaigrette, he returned to the kitchen.

"You don't look so great," Lansing said, eyeing me closely. "Did anything happen on your way out here?"

"No, nobody bothered me," I told him. "I just have a lot of information going around in my head, and it's coming together in a pretty ugly way."

"So what was it you got us out here on a Saturday to tell us?" Peterson asked, biting a fry in half.

The cook reappeared with my iced tea, salad, and dressing, and I thanked him. I took a couple of seconds to drizzle the dressing over the salad before answering Peterson.

"I've found something else that I'm sure has to do with Coleman and Magruder being shot," I said finally, spearing a tomato slice and then looking from Peterson to Lansing. "I'll tell you what I've got, but I have to have your agreement not to let it out to any of the rest of the press. And you have to promise me that, if it pans out, you'll make sure I know what you turn up before the rest of them do."

"If you have concrete information about either of those cases, you have a legal responsibility to turn it over to the police," Peterson said, predictably. I gave him a tired smile and an A for effort.

"Jim," I said, using his given name for the first time, hoping it would make him pay attention, "we have this same conversation every time I cover one of your big cases, and every time, it turns out the same way. If I had firm proof of what I think went on, you know full well I'd give it to you, but I also would be going ahead with a story at the same time. The bottom line right now, however, is that I can't prove it yet. But

I'm hoping that if I give you what I do know, and that you apparently don't, you *might* be able to prove it. I just want to make sure the competition isn't going to scoop me on my own story. So can't we just agree to a trade with first dibs on what the other one finds out?"

Peterson looked at Lansing.

"She's dealt with us straight so far," Lansing said neutrally.

Peterson looked at me and thought some more.

"All right," he said finally, "we'll keep what you tell us to ourselves and give you a heads-up about anything we find out as a result."

I took the two of them through the whole thing, laying out one by one the articles and reports that Cooper and I had collected, filling in the gaps with my guesses. They both listened thoughtfully, between bites of their food, while I gave them the outline, my salad forgotten now as I took them through the story of Henry Bryant's earlier investigation of Coleman, through Lawson Thomas's story of how it was halted and of the now-missing file, through Bryant's financial woes and the timely appearance of the "loan" that saved him, through Gerald Tharpe's recommendation of Bryant for the county court seat and Tharpe's connection to Coleman. I gave them my conclusion on what it all meant and on why I suspected that Coleman and ultimately Dan Magruder had been killed.

"Where did you get all this stuff?" Peterson wanted to know, pushing his empty platter aside and leafing through Bryant's financial records.

"Never mind that for now," I told him. "You guys can get it all again through kosher channels."

"I'm not so sure that all this fits together so neatly," Lansing said, frowning. "You think Bryant had Coleman killed, and you may be right. But you've got nothing concrete that really connects him, nothing that would give us enough for a search warrant to get into all his records. We have to have something more specific before we'll convince a judge."

From my purse, I took out the notebook onto which I had jotted down the last bit of information Cooper had given me just before I left the paper.

"Judge Bryant doesn't go anywhere these days," I told Lansing and Peterson as I opened the notebook, "without a man named Dell Curl. Bryant calls Curl his personal assistant, and while he may very well be that, I came away from meeting Curl with the distinct impression that he's there to protect Bryant as much as he is to assist him. He obviously keeps himself in good shape, and his appearance and the way he carries himself made me think he might be ex-military."

"So what does he have to do with anything?" Peterson asked.

"Just before I came out here, I got a call back from someone who checked Curl out for me." I looked down at my notes and back up at the two detectives.

"Dell Curl is a former Tallahassee police officer who was fired four years ago for pulling his gun when he found his wife in bed with a fellow officer and for holding the gun to the guy's head while threatening to kill him and the wife. Curl apparently went to work for Bryant not long after that."

"I think I see where you're going with this," Lansing said, "but none of that makes the guy a killer."

"No," I agreed, "but it does give him the body language of a cop and a uniform. Which might be what got Magruder to open his door. And while he isn't a dead ringer for the sketch that Magruder's neighbor helped you do, it certainly could be him."

"Is that it?" Lansing asked.

"No, there's still one other little thing."

"What?" Peterson wanted to know.

"According to Curl's records, he was an MP in the army before joining the Tallahassee Police Department. He got some training there in crime scene identification and the handling of explosives and who knows what else. When he joined the police, they sent him for still more training, and one of the things he did for them was to work with the Florida Department of Law Enforcement and the ATF on cases that involved explosives. You know, little stuff like car bombings."

"Jesus!" Lansing said, sitting back into the corner formed by the wall and the back of the booth. He looked at Peterson, who was looking back at him.

"So he would have had no trouble getting his hands on some dynamite and rigging your car to take you out so it wouldn't look connected to what happened to Coleman or Magruder," Peterson said, turning to me as he came to the same conclusion to which logic and intuition already had taken me. "He would know exactly how to do it."

"Call me crazy," I told them, "but my gut tells me Dell Curl has killed three people trying to protect Henry Bryant's nomination and that he still wants to kill me. Originally, it was because he thought I could identify him from the park. But now, I expect he's looking for me out there somewhere because I called Judge Bryant up and started asking about this so-called loan. Which tells them I've picked up the old trail that they almost had managed to wipe out."

I looked over at Lansing, who was giving me a measuring look in return.

"What?" I asked.

"Oh, I was just thinking that you probably were one of those kids who felt compelled to poke every hornet's nest you saw, just to see how much you could stir the hornets up."

I ate a few bites of my salad and then took a bathroom break. By the time I came back to the booth, Peterson and Lansing were in agreement on what they needed to do.

"Jim is going to call Detective Moore and fill the Alexandria P.D.

in on this," Lansing explained to me when I sat back down. "Moore says they haven't made much progress yet, and this might give them something that could break things open for them."

"And," Peterson added, "I think it's time for another powwow between them and us. If this Curl guy really is a suspect in all three cases, there's no point in us tripping over each other while we all look in the same places. I'll try to get us together with Moore and his people some time tomorrow or first thing Monday morning at the latest."

He slid out of the booth and reached into his jacket pocket for his wallet. I put my purse up on the table and began to get my own wallet out.

"This is on me," Peterson told me, waving at my purse in a gesture that said to put it away. "You didn't have that much, anyway."

"Then I'll have to leave the tip," I told him, standing up as well and moving to one side to let Lansing out of the booth. "We're not supposed to accept freebies from the people we cover. After all, I can't have you thinking you can buy me off, especially not for that little bit of money."

Why worry about that when certain people you cover can have you for free?

"Suit yourself," Peterson said, shaking his head and walking toward the cash register that sat on one end of the back counter. I ignored my interior critic, got out three one-dollar bills, and put them on the table.

"After this conversation, you're definitely coming back to the house tonight, aren't you?" Lansing asked as we walked over to the door and waited for Peterson.

"If I said no, it would just be another argument, wouldn't it?"

"Big time," Lansing agreed.

"All right, I'll come back," I said finally, "but I'm running out of clean clothes. I have to go back to the apartment and pick some stuff up."

"Then I'll ride over with you. I'll leave the Explorer here and we'll come back this way afterward and get it."

"Do you really think that's necessary?" I asked him, a little petulantly, no more fond now of the idea of needing to have my hand held all the time than I was before. "I've seen no signs of anybody following me at any point."

"That doesn't mean a thing," he said. "With your change of cars, your trip to Florida, and spending time at my place, whoever is after you may have had a hard time tracking you down. But he's going to catch up with you sooner or later, and your apartment is one logical place to do it. So just humor me and let me tag along."

"Fine," I said, "be my guest."

Peterson joined us at the door, and we went through it and out to the parking lot.

"I'll call you as soon as I'm able to reach Moore," Peterson said to Lansing, opening the door to his car and climbing in. "I'll let you know when we need to get together."

"I'll be there," Lansing told him. Peterson closed his door and started the car. As I walked over to my rental car, with Lansing right behind me, and unlocked the doors, Peterson drove past us in a U-turn that would take him out of the parking lot.

Lansing opened the passenger's side door and let himself in. I did the same on the driver's side.

"I'm surprised," I said to him sarcastically when I put the key into the ignition, "that you didn't insist on driving, too."

"I'm not saying the idea didn't occur to me," he responded, grinning, "but I wanted to live long enough to get you back to my place, and I figured if I broached that subject, you'd kill me."

I wouldn't know until later just how ironic that little exchange was about to become.

25

Although I had noticed Lansing readjusting the sideview mirror next to him as we pulled out of the parking lot onto eastbound Little River Turnpike, I hadn't said anything. But within a few blocks, it became clear that he was watching the traffic behind us. Even though I recently had developed a similar habit of my own, in hindsight, I suppose I felt free to tease him because his presence in the car made me feel safe. Of course, we all know what they say about hindsight. At any rate, after several minutes of watching him watching everyone else, I couldn't keep my mouth shut any longer.

"Seen any killers back there yet?" I asked as we approached the overpass that spans I-495, and he looked into the mirror for the umpteenth time.

"As a matter of fact," Lansing said, turning in my direction with a serious expression, "I am keeping my eyes on a couple of cars that have been back there since we left the shopping center. It doesn't hurt to be aware of what's going on around you, especially when somebody is trying to kill you."

"Well," I told him, "if you see anybody hanging out a window with a stick of dynamite in his hand, let me know."

Lansing looked back in the mirror again.

"Looks like at least one of them has decided you're going too slow," he said, giving me a play-by-play now. "It's a black Chevy Suburban, coming up on your left."

I glanced into my rearview mirror but only in time to catch the corner of some large dark vehicle disappearing into my blind spot. Looking ahead again, I took my foot off the accelerator in reaction to the slowing of cars in front of me that were taking the first ramp to the right onto southbound I-495. As the car immediately ahead cleared my lane, I accelerated slightly again and looked to my left as something hulking moved just into the edge of my peripheral vision. As I turned my head in its direction to eyeball the vehicle Lansing initially had thought might be suspicious, the Suburban veered suddenly and rammed my much smaller Pontiac on my front quarter-panel. That was all it took.

At the Suburban's unexpected movement in my direction, I instinctively had turned my wheel to the right, trying to get out of its path. But the impact of the much heavier vehicle against the car's side jerked the steering wheel in my hand even more to the right, adding to the momentum I already had given it toward the edge of the highway. It was more than I could correct for in the second in which it all happened. As Lansing shouted my name, we went off the road, taking out a section of the guardrail that extended up to the overpass.

In the expanded time that such moments bring, there was first what seemed like a long stretch of silence as the car hurtled out into groundless space above the steep, tree studded embankment that dropped down to the level of the interstate highway below. It was as awful as my worst dreams of falling, the kind where you know you're going to hit the ground hard, after a long, sickening drop. Then the car nosed down and began turning in a sideways roll until it struck the ground on Lansing's front corner with a loud *whump*. The force of the impact righted the car so that it didn't roll over after all. Instead, it dissipated the rest of its momentum with a furious sideways slide into a tree, against which it came to a halt with a second jarring crash to the passenger's side.

In the three or four seconds it must have taken from when the

Suburban hit us until we hit the tree, the observer part of my brain not only had time to watch us falling to what I thought had to be our deaths, but also to conclude that perhaps I should have let Lansing drive after all, that in my arrogance, I had managed to deprive David of the only parent he had left.

Once the car stopped moving, the instinct-driven part of my brain that was still in charge began yelling at me that we had to get out of the car quickly, in case it caught fire. I turned to Lansing to tell him that and saw that he was slumped over in his seat, held upright only by his shoulder strap, with blood pouring from some sort of ugly wound on the side of his forehead where it rested against the large, spiderweb pattern of cracks that now crazed the window next to him. It was obvious that Lansing wasn't going anywhere under his own power.

In a panic, I unfastened my own seatbelt and then reached over to unfasten his, which succeeded only in letting him slump completely down into the passenger's seat, still unconscious, and leaving an ugly smear of blood down the window. His door was pinned shut against the tree trunk. I tried to pull him toward me, but his dead weight, combined with the canted angle at which the car rested on the steep slope, defeated me. In frustration, I looked out the hole where my own window once had been, hoping that some of the drivers who had seen what had happened might have stopped to help.

What I saw, instead, was the Suburban backing into view up on the shoulder of the road above us and then stopping. In a second, the driver came around the back and began a sliding descent down the side of the embankment toward us. The driver, I saw, was Dell Curl, and as he came in our direction, he pulled out a gun. With which he obviously planned to finish the job on me, and with which he also probably would kill Lansing.

It wasn't my own life I saw flashing before my eyes, although I do remember being angry that I was going to die just as it looked like I might have found somebody to spend at least a large part of that life with. Instead, it was David's life I saw, and his future. A future without his mother or his father. I saw him and his father again in the kitchen, with David happily stirring the pot of spaghetti under Lansing's supervision, and I knew I couldn't let that be taken away from him.

There was only one thing to do. Expecting Curl to start firing at us at any moment, I reached over to get the gun Lansing wore. It took a second of struggling to pull it out of the holster since Lansing's weight was pressing against it, but I finally managed it. I said a prayer of thanks for the story I had done the year before on the firearms training that area police receive. My hours at the firing range with several Fairfax County Police officers meant that I now knew at least enough to find the safety and flip it off so the 9 mm pistol would fire. With the gun in my hand, I turned back toward my window while still trying to shield Lansing's body with my own.

Later, when I had time to run the movie through my head again, I decided that Curl's delay in shooting at us could have been due to one of several things. His footing coming down most of the steep embankment probably was too precarious for him to try to fire at us and keep his balance. Or, perhaps because Lansing and I both were slumped down in the front seats, Curl had to get much closer to us to see if we were still alive. Or he might not have trusted his aim from farther away. Whatever it was, when I turned back toward my window, Curl had made it within thirty feet of the car and was coming fast. Regardless of what had kept him from shooting at us until now, I thought, he certainly was about to see, if he hadn't already, that at least one of us was alive and conscious. And that would be it for me. I knew that that split second was the only chance I had.

I sat up abruptly, gripping the gun in both hands and holding it straight out in front of me. My movement apparently took Curl by surprise and he faltered for a second in his effort to stop his forward motion and raise his own gun. Aiming as best I could at Curl's middle, rather than going for anything fancy such as trying to shoot him in the head (another bit of advice for civilians that the police had given me), I pulled the trigger. And I kept pulling the trigger, shooting until the gun would no longer fire.

The observer part of my mind noticed the noise as one bullet after another exploded out of the gun's barrel, saw the blue flame, followed by the puffs of dust that shot up from the embankment behind Curl as most of the bullets went wide, and by the smell of cordite. That part noted the gun's kick in my hands and took note of the red splotches that blossomed on Curl's body, first on his left arm and then on his abdomen. It also registered the look of surprise in Curl's eyes when the first of the two bullets that I later was told had found their target, hit him. But the other part of my mind, the part that didn't want to die, the part that had decided I wasn't going to die or let Curl kill Lansing without putting up a fight, all that part knew was to hold onto Lansing's gun for all I was worth and to keep shooting until Curl either killed me or I shot him.

Even then, it wasn't over. Though Curl didn't seem to be moving, and though his gun was lying beside him on the ground where it had dropped from his hand at some point, I knew I couldn't take a chance that he would manage to retrieve his gun and get up from where he lay. I had to get the gun out of his reach.

I tried to open the car door, but it was jammed shut, apparently by the force of the accident. Holding Lansing's now-empty gun as nothing more than a visual threat, I crawled uphill out the empty window instead, still trying to keep my eyes on the unmoving Curl who lay in a rapidly spreading pool of blood on the grass and bush-covered embankment. Still in the grip of my adrenaline but made clumsy by my fear, I more or less fell out the window, dropping Lansing's gun in the process. I scooped it back up and in a thoroughly inelegant crawling and stumbling motion, crossed the few feet of ground to where Curl lay, and kicked his gun away from his hand. Then, scrambling to one side after it, I snatched it up and backed rapidly away in the same awkward manner until I bumped into the car behind me. From my half crouch, I reached up my right forearm and draped it over the windowsill, then levered myself into a standing position.

And then my legs turned to water and gave out from under me. I slid back down the side of the car to sit down hard on the ground. Above me, several people, who probably had stopped to help when they saw the accident, were standing in a row, apparently frozen in their tracks at the sight of the wrecked car against the tree and the clearly crazed woman who was sitting in the middle of all of it with a gun in each hand and a body at her feet.

I put the guns down on the ground, but not so far away that I couldn't retrieve Curl's gun if he showed any signs of reviving.

"Call 911," I shouted up to the people on the hill, though I wasn't certain just how loudly my voice carried. "Get us some help. And get the police."

One man broke away from the group and ran toward his car. No one else moved, probably reluctant to come down the hill for fear their own lives might be in danger, in their uncertainty over exactly what it was that had taken place below them. Curl lay unmoving as well, though his blood continued to pour out. Inside the car, I heard Lansing groan once and then go silent again. At least, I thought, he isn't dead, although God only knew what kind of shape he was in. I sat where I was, trying to look the car over and detect any sights, sounds, or smells of gasoline or fire. It would be the height of irony, I thought, if the car exploded and killed me, given that that was what Curl had intended for me from the first. But the car showed no signs of leaking fuel or of fire, and for that I was grateful, since I wasn't certain I could stand up again, even if I'd had to.

Don't you know you're supposed to avoid direct involvement in your stories? Obviously, my obnoxious little friend had survived the accident as well.

Don't you know, I asked in return as the last of the adrenaline began to drain away and my hands started to shake, *that I still have a loaded gun here?*

26
LATER

The only thing I wanted to know when the first cops showed up was whether Dell Curl was going to get up and try again to kill me.

"Is he dead? Is he dead?" I kept asking over the orders and questions the cops were shouting to me as they came down the embankment with their guns drawn. At Curl's body, one of them reached down long enough to check for a pulse and tell me that yes, Curl was dead.

The question I should have been asking—and eventually did, once Lansing and I made it to the trauma center at Fairfax Hospital and the doctors concluded from the CAT scan that he had a concussion rather than a fractured skull—was how Curl had managed to find me at Joe's Hole in the Wall Café.

I had watched my rearview mirror religiously all the way out to Fairfax from the District, and while I didn't claim to be as good at picking up a potential tail as Lansing, I was certain I would have noticed something as large and distinctive as the black Suburban if it had been behind me all the way out to the shopping center. But I didn't remember seeing it even once.

"So how," I asked Rob Perry on the phone as soon as I could get a moment alone on my emergency room stretcher to get my cell phone out of my purse and determine that it was still in working order, "did Curl know where I was going to be? We're not talking about one of the in places, you understand."

"Who besides me knew you were going out there?" Rob asked. He had been willing to change the subject from the question of my physical condition only after I had my nurse come in and confirm that I basically was uninjured, except for bruises and scrapes, from which, she said, I could expect to be sore as hell the next day.

"Just Peterson and Lansing," I told him. "Lansing suggested the place to me over the phone, and I left to go out there as soon as I hung up."

"And nobody overheard you, and you're absolutely sure Curl didn't follow you from the paper?"

"I'm sure. And I didn't tell—" But, I realized as a little more of my brain fog cleared, I had.

"Damn him all to hell," I said viciously. "If that son of a bitch—"

"Sutton, what are you talking about?" Rob interrupted.

"I just remembered who else I told," I answered heatedly. "I called Sy and left a message on his voice mail."

"Berkowitz?"

"Yeah. We had been arguing about my telling the police what I knew and whether we had enough for a story yet. He had stomped back up to his office to call Mark Lester and complain about me. So when I talked to Lansing and decided to leave, I called up there to let Sy know where I would be in case he managed to convince Mark. But why the hell would he have been talking to Dell Curl?"

"I don't know," Rob said, now sounding as angry as I was, "but I intend to find out. Check back in with me when you're done there."

"Oh, don't worry, I will," I answered and cut off the call just as the nurse peered again around the privacy curtains that were drawn around my stretcher.

"I have to ask you not to make any more calls on your cell phone from here," she said.

"But I'm fine," I protested. "I'm certainly up to talking on the phone."

"Yes, you're fine" she agreed, "but that's not the problem." She pointed to the phone she carried in her hip pocket. "Except for the ones we carry, which are made for use in a hospital, cell phones can interfere with some of the equipment we use. So if you are up to talking on the phone, we'll take you out to the pay phones. Now, are you also up to taking a short walk?" At her question, her expression changed from serious to a smile.

"This isn't going to hurt, is it?" I wanted to know. I had thought they were finished poking and prodding me.

"I don't think so," she replied, walking over to help me down from the stretcher. "Detective Lansing is a little more aware of what's going on now, and he's asking for you."

The trip from my side of the trauma area to the other side where Lansing was being treated was probably the longest fifty feet I had ever walked in my life.

It was Bill Russell who showed up at the hospital to make certain Noah and I both were okay and to tell us what was happening.

"The doctor tells me they're going to keep you overnight just for observation," Bill said to Noah when the nurse showed him into the treatment room where I sat beside Noah with a death grip on his left hand. He still seemed a little foggy at times, and I knew, from the size of the purpling lump beneath the bandage that covered the eight stitches he now had on his right temple, that his head must hurt something fierce where it had struck the window. But his doctor and nurse both had assured me, in separate conversations, that although they would admit him to the hospital overnight for observation, they expected he would be fine as well. Which I quickly pointed out to Bill, not wanting Noah to think he was getting any sort of run around about his true condition.

"Do I need to call the neighbors where David is spending the night and let them know what happened?" I asked Noah. The little boy had not been completely out of my mind since the moment when Curl had rammed the car and forced us off the road. I wasn't sure how much to tell him, but I knew he should be told something.

"It's John and Debbie Fitzgerald, same street as mine," Noah told me. "You can fill them in, but ask them for right now just to tell David that I got a cut on my head at work that took some stitches, and that I'm fine. And that I'll see him in the morning at home."

"I'll take care of it," I assured him.

"What's going on out there with all this?" Noah asked Bill, meaning with Curl and Henry Bryant. "Has anyone let Jim Peterson in on what's happened?"

"He's in D.C. right now hooking up with a couple of District detectives who are going with him to meet Judge Bryant," Bill said. "They've confirmed that the judge is at the hotel, and they've already put a uniformed officer up on the judge's floor to make sure he doesn't leave before they get there."

Noah and I both breathed sighs of relief.

"As soon as Jim heard the first call over his radio about a car being run off the road and someone being shot," Bill continued, "he thought the car description sounded like Sutton's rental car, and he said he just knew immediately exactly what had happened. He turned around and drove straight to where you were. You probably didn't see him there because he said they hadn't brought either one of you up the hill yet. But as soon as the folks on the scene told him you and Lansing were alive and Curl was dead, he ordered them not to release your names to anybody without his okay, and then he got on the phone to D.C. to let them know he was coming in after Bryant. Jim's supposed to call me as soon as they're with Bryant, so I can deal with the press developments."

At the news about Bryant, my overworked adrenal glands had started pumping again, but the last little tidbit threw me for a momentary loop. *Shit,* I thought, *if I let anybody else from the press hear about*

Bryant being questioned before Rob does, I might as well stay right here in the emergency room and save myself a trip.

"Bill, could you stay with Noah for a few minutes while I go call his neighbors?" I asked.

"Sure," Bill answered. "I'm not going anywhere until I hear from Jim."

Checking outside the door of Noah's treatment room to make certain I wasn't going to be stopped by anyone official, I stepped out into the corridor and wound my way around through a couple more short hallways, past the registration offices and the triage desk and out into the emergency department lobby, which already was packed with people in various stages of injury, impatience, or sleep. *Saturday night looks like a good time to avoid an emergency room visit,* I thought, as I walked past the automatic glass doors that led outside and turned into the small telephone room in the corner.

When I reached the Fitzgeralds, they put David on the phone and let me tell him about his father being injured.

"But he's okay?" David asked when I was done. His voice sounded very small and frightened. I could imagine what must be going through his mind.

"He's fine," I said, trying to sound as cheerful as possible. "When you both get home tomorrow, he can show you his lump and his stitches, and you can see for yourself."

I spent a few more minutes reassuring the little boy and then told him good night. And then I called Rob again to let him know Bryant was being visited by the police.

"I'll find James and have her get right on it," Rob said, when I told him what was going on, "and I'll get a photographer over to the Mayflower in case they arrest him."

"I don't think they'll do that yet, but I'm pretty sure they'll end up taking him out to Fairfax for questioning at some point. He's a judge, with a lot at stake, so he'll probably deny everything and refuse to answer any questions, especially without an attorney. Which means they'll have to get official. So you probably should send someone out there as well, although they may or may not get any shots of him, depending mostly on how pissed off Peterson is at him by the time they get there and whether he's ready to throw Bryant to the rabid dogs of the press."

"I'll do that," Rob agreed. "You keep me posted on anything new from your end, and we'll do the story under a joint byline for you and James."

"What about Sy?" I asked. "Won't he need to be in on it?"

"You called me just in time," Rob explained. "I was about to go upstairs to Mark Lester's office. He's supposed to have Sy there, cooling his heels until I get there, so we can discuss just how it was that Curl knew where you had gone. Since you called me the first time, I've done a little investigating of my own and found out from a couple of people who saw him that Sy was down here at your desk shortly after you left. I have an idea about what might have taken place. Let's just say that if I'm anywhere close to right, I don't think you need to worry about Sy on this anymore."

Next to hearing that Noah was going to be all right and that Dell Curl couldn't try to kill me again, that was the best news I had heard all day.

"I'll call you later for an update," I told Rob. "This is definitely one story I know I'll want to hear."

27
LATER STILL

Noah Lansing went home from the hospital on that Sunday and sat out Monday at home, under protest and only on the order of his doctors and his supervisor, and only after major browbeating by Bill Russell and myself. Even then, I think it was really the concern he saw in his son's eyes that finally convinced him to take a day off. On Tuesday, however, he told us all to shut the hell up, and he went back to work to make sure the case against Bryant was airtight.

Sy Berkowitz went back to New Jersey with his career and reputation destroyed and his tail between his legs. Rob Perry's idea about what had happened was right on the money. As soon as he had heard my voice mail, Sy had come tearing back down to the metro newsroom to tell me I couldn't leave, only to find me gone already and my telephone ringing. Which he apparently answered and found Dell Curl on the other end, saying he had a message for me from Judge Bryant and that he needed to talk to me in person.

Sy denied the whole thing, of course, so I can't imagine what he was thinking when he did it. I don't know whether he was so angry at me that he just blurted out to Curl where I was, or whether he was so calculating and completely without scruples that he told Curl deliberately, knowing full well what would happen. The reasons really didn't matter, because other people saw and heard him. The result was that he was fired on the spot by Mark Lester, his former mentor, given ten minutes to clean out his personal belongings from his desk, and escorted from the building by a security guard.

Henry Bryant went to jail, and Dell Curl went to the cemetery. It took a while to sort everything out, of course. Initially, Bryant denied knowing anything about what Curl had been up to. But Noah, Peterson, and Detective Moore used the information that Cooper and I had gathered, and which the cops were able to get legally and directly from the sources, to make a convincing enough body of circumstantial evidence that Bryant finally confessed to his role in what had happened. The immense international publicity surrounding the arrest of a federal judge and Supreme Court candidate as a suspect in a multiple-murder case also destroyed Bryant's nomination, his reputation, and his future on any kind of judicial bench.

So perhaps it was having to watch everything for which he had sold his soul being destroyed in spite of all his and Curl's efforts that finally took the fight out of Bryant. I don't know. Even when he admitted his involvement, he continued to insist that he had ordered only Coleman's murder, that it was Curl who had taken it upon himself to try to silence Magruder and myself. And in the end, that really didn't matter, either, as long as he paid for what he had done, whether it was done at his order or only with his acquiescence.

My hypothesis had turned out to be pretty accurate, according to what Bryant did tell the police. It was Coleman who had given him the money to pay off the debts under which he had been suffocating when his wife died, in exchange for Bryant's agreeing to see to it that the investigation of Coleman and Three Rivers also died an early death. They had had little contact since, Bryant said, and he had worked hard to be a good judge. But Coleman had returned to haunt him when Bryant's name was put forth for the Supreme Court, demanding that Bryant pull whatever strings he had access to in order to call off the federal investigators who were after Coleman.

Bryant said he refused, but Coleman said he would give Bryant up to the investigators if he had to, in order to make a deal for himself. It was then, Bryant said, that he knew he had to stop Coleman any way he could, and he turned to Dell Curl, whom Bryant had given a job when no one else would touch him.

So Curl had kidnapped Coleman from the parking garage underneath The Phoenix Group's offices and had driven him, in Coleman's own car, to Grist Mill Park, where he had shot Coleman in the chest and killed him. And then he walked back to Coleman's car, where he was intercepted by Officer Dan Magruder and his drunken prisoner, and things rapidly had gone downhill from there.

Eventually, the police pieced together the rest. They found the explosives company in Fredericksburg that Curl apparently burgled in order to steal several sticks of dynamite. They matched Curl's gun to the bullets that killed Coleman and Magruder. Magruder's neighbor identified Curl as the uniformed man he had seen in the apartment building. Not that any of it made any difference to Curl any longer. But it all helped build the case against Bryant.

I went back to see my shrink, once the Fairfax County Police Department finished its investigation of my having shot Curl with a police detective's gun and they and the commonwealth's attorney decided no charges should be filed against me. Still, I had killed a man. Granted, he was a murderer who had killed three people and already had tried once to kill me. And I had shot him to keep him from killing Noah as much as to defend myself. But I didn't want to find myself, weeks or months down the road, having recurring nightmares about what I had done or beating myself up with second-guessing whether I could have found some other way.

It was bad enough that I was dreaming regularly about the kid who was blown up with my car and who the police never could identify beyond his street name. So I spent several sessions with Elizabeth Parks, a therapist I had met when she was a high school guidance counselor and who once had helped me deal with the emotional aftermath when a U.S. senator had threatened to shoot me.

I also went back to my apartment in Landmark. Noah asked me to move in with him and David, and I turned him down. I told him that I wasn't quite ready yet to take that step, that I thought we should give that big a decision some more time.

"Are you backing away from what's going on between us?" he asked, as we sat in his living room on his one day of home recuperation.

"Not at all," I told him. "I'll admit I've resisted the way I feel about you, that it scared me because of my lousy track record when it comes to men. But when I saw Dell Curl coming toward us with his gun, when I knew he would kill you as well as me... well, let's just say I had a moment of clarity about what was important to me. So no, I'm not backing away."

"Not even if I tell you that I love you?"

I smiled. "Not even then. I love you, too. But I also want some time to get to know you and David, and for both of you to get to know me, before we take a step like living together. There's too much at stake here if it turns out to be the wrong decision, for either one of us."

He leaned toward me on the couch and put his arms around me.

"At least," Noah said, "I know it's not a permanent *no*.

"Oh really? And how do you know that?"

"Because now you're calling me Noah."

The next day, without my knowledge, he went to see the elderly woman who owns my building and convinced her that she shouldn't throw a heroine, who had saved a police officer's life and kept a little boy from becoming an orphan, out on the street. So I got to go home.

I also made a point of occasionally spending time with David, just the two of us. Although I knew that returning to my apartment was the right thing to do for now, it made me realize just how attached I already had become to Noah's son. As Noah and I spent time together, I began to really believe that this might be the one that worked, that it might be the relationship I had wanted but never had, and I understood that David would be a very important part of it. So I began asking David out to do something with me every couple of weeks: a trip to get ice cream, a visit to the Air and Space Museum to see the real versions of some of the toys in David's room, even a jaunt to an Orioles' game in Baltimore.

It was fun, and enlightening, because I had never spent much time with a young child before, and also frightening, because I soon came to love him as much as I did his father, and I couldn't bear the thought that one or the other of them might not always be there.

The final thing I did was to make a trip to the cemetery. Even after several sessions with Elizabeth, I still couldn't get the image of the teenager who had died instead of me out of my mind. Detective Moore told me at one point that, if the boy remained unidentified, he eventually would be buried in a pauper's grave at city expense. He had only been sixteen or seventeen, the medical examiner had said. And as part of their efforts to identify him, the Alexandria police had had a sketch of what he probably looked like before he was burned in the explosion produced for distribution around the country. Several street gang members in Alexandria had told the police that it definitely was the boy they called Espada. Once I saw that sketch, his face and his homeless, nameless status haunted my dreams night after night.

It didn't take many of those nights before I called Detective Moore and told him I wanted to pay to have the boy buried decently, in a way his mother would have buried him if she had known where he was. So at my expense, he was laid to rest in a plot in the Mount Comfort Cemetery, just off South Kings Highway in southern Fairfax County. I had asked Father Paul Wynants, the Catholic chaplain at Fairfax Hospital, who I had met once when visiting a friend there, to conduct a graveside service for the unknown Hispanic boy. Moore and Noah joined me for the few minutes the service took, and then they and Father Paul went back to work.

I stayed on for a little longer, looking at the simple plaque that said Espada. It was the name he had chosen for himself, after all, and much better than John Doe. I put the flowers that I had brought down on the grave, grateful to be alive and for the chance I knew I had been given to find some happiness with Noah and David, my men with the blue eyes. Then I turned and walked out of the cemetery to life.

ACKNOWLEDGMENTS

As usual, I must especially thank Officer Kevin Brown, formerly of the Fairfax County Police Department's Crime Prevention Section, for his invaluable help in making this manuscript as accurate as possible. But don't blame Kevin if I managed to screw it up, anyway.

I also must thank Amy Bertsch, public information specialist for the Alexandria Police Department; the folks at the Mount Vernon District police substation; Jeanie Hanna, former chief assistant county attorney for Hillsborough County, Florida; John O'Connor, my State Farm Insurance agent (Go Dawgs!); Peggy Meiklejohn and her vacation group; my next-door neighbors, Ron and Frances Deel; my agent and adviser, Joshua Bilmes, of JABberwocky Literary Agency; Gail Fortune, my editor at Berkley, an excellent editor and a pleasure to work with; Laura Ann Gilman, a Penguin Putnam editor, who first believed in Sutton's stories; and last, but never least, my husband Carey and my daughter Meagan, who love and support me, give me advice, and put up with my moods and silences when I can't drag my brain back out of a manuscript.

ABOUT THE AUTHOR

Brenda English has worked in news reporting, communications and publications management, book editing, and media relations. She lives in Florida with her family.

FOR NEWS ABOUT JABBERWOCKY BOOKS AND AUTHORS

Sign up for our newsletter*: http://eepurl.com/b84tDz
visit our website: awfulagent.com/ebooks
or follow us on twitter: @awfulagent

THANKS FOR READING!

*We will never sell or giveaway your email address, nor use
it for nefarious purposes. Newsletter sent out quarterly.

CPSIA information can be obtained
at www.ICGtesting.com
Printed in the USA
LVHW011634101218
599930LV00004B/864/P

9 781625 671721